A ROYAL ENGAGEMENT

The Young Royals Book 1

EMMA LEA

❀ Created with Vellum

OTHER BOOKS BY EMMA LEA

This is Emma Lea's complete book library at time of publication, but more books are coming out all the time. Find out every time Emma releases something by going to the website (www.emmaleaauthor.com) and signing up for her New Release Alerts.

SWEET ROMANCES

These are romantic tales without the bedroom scenes and the swearing, but that doesn't mean they're boring!

The Young Royals

A Royal Engagement

Lord Darkly

A Royal Entanglement

A Royal Entrapment

A Royal Expectation

A Royal Elopement

Bookish Book Club Novellas

Meeting Prince Charming

Broken Arrow Trilogy

Broken

Cursed

Eternal

SWEET & SEXY ROMANCES

In my Sweet & Sexy Romances I turn up the heat with a little bit of sexy. No swearing, or very minimal swearing, and brief, tasteful and not too graphic bedroom scenes.

Love, Money & Shoes Series
Walk of Shame

Strictly Business

Skin Deep

In The Money

All At Sea

Love, Money & Shoes Novellas
The Five Year Plan

Summer Fling

Standalone Novels
Amnesia

HOT & SEXY ROMANCES
Hot & Spicy Romances turn the heat way up. They contain swearing and sexy scenes and the characters get hot under the collar.

Recommended for 18+ readers

TGIF Series
Girl Friday

Black Friday

Good Friday

Twelve Days
Twelve Days of Christmas - Her Side of the Story

Twelve Days of Christmas - His Side of the Story

ABOUT THIS BOOK

A Royal Engagement
by Emma Lea

Despite being the second child of the king and queen of Merveille, Alyssabeth thought that if she kept a low profile she could stay out of the media's glaring spotlight and live a relatively normal life. That was until her father, the king, and her brother, the crown prince, were both killed in a hunting accident.

Her dream of joining the UN was no more and instead she needed to return to the small European country of her birth to pick up where her father and brother left off. Her Harvard degree in international relations was forfeit and in its place she must become queen, if the misogynistic Parliament can see past their prejudices.

Not much had changed in the small country in her four year absence, but there were two noticeable differences. Her brother's two best friends, Will Darkly and Jordan Wicks, had grown up into two very intriguing men. Jordan practically swept her off her feet from the moment she stepped off the plane but Will's more reserved, darkly intense interest in her gave her tingles.

Alyssa wasn't sure she was cut out to be queen, but she knew that she wanted to do her father and brother proud. She was willing to give it her best shot, even if it meant going toe-to-toe with Parliament. And then there was the small matter of her needing to be married in order to fulfil her birthright and take her place as the head of state.

This is a Sweet Romance - These are romantic tales without the bedroom scenes and the swearing, but that doesn't mean they're boring!

AUTHOR'S NOTE

A Royal Engagement takes place in a country that doesn't really exist. If it were to exist it would sit on the eastern edge of France bordered by Switzerland and Italy, quite close to Geneva. The country of Merveille (pronounced Mer-VAY) is a quiet, wealthy place ruled by a constitutional monarchy. Its capital city is Calanais which is situated on the shores of a beautiful lake called Lac Merveilleux and is where the palace, named Château de Conte de Fées, is situated.

This book is written using UK/Australian English.

This is for all the girls who dreamed of being a princess in a faraway land.

CHAPTER 1

"I disagree with Mr. Walsh's statements," I said, standing to my feet. I didn't yell, but I did raise my voice so that I could be heard across the lecture theatre. "The problem is too complex to just say, 'first in, first served'. These people are not lining up in the cafeteria, they are fleeing for their lives and they have taken extreme measures to get where they are..."

Meredith twitched beside me and grabbed my wrist. "Down Aurora," she said and it was the only warning I had before all hell broke loose. I obeyed immediately, the use of my code name causing me to react without thought as it was supposed to. It was a trigger, indicating that there was danger. I had been trained well and didn't question her as she dragged me to the ground away from my desk.

The door to the lecture room flung open and the rest of my security team filed in, guns drawn, but pointed down. I could hear the gasps of my fellow students and then the authoritative voice of my detail's team leader.

"Everybody stay seated," Benjamin said in a voice that brooked no argument.

Meredith had me secured on the ground and I was soon surrounded by the remaining four security guards. Benjamin stood close to the lecturer and his calm, yet in-charge, demeanour kept everyone where they were while Meredith, Scott, Jamie, Cody and Aiden began to hustle me out of the room.

Meredith kept a hand on my head, forcing me to keep it down, and the other hand on the waistband of my jeans as we moved out into the hall.

I couldn't see where I was going, I just followed them blindly. We had run the scenario a hundred times and I knew that their first priority was to get me out and into a waiting car. I wanted to ask questions, to find out what was going on, but I also knew that no one would answer me.

If proper protocol was being followed, the university would be in lock down until I was in the car and off the premises. By the eerie silence, only broken by the shuffling of our feet, I assumed that lock-down was indeed being enforced.

My heart thudded in my chest and it seemed like an age before I felt the kiss of the sun on my back. I was pushed into a car that had been parked on the footpath outside the building in a place where no car was ever allowed. The door slammed, enclosing me in darkness.

Meredith pushed me to the floor of the sedan as it roared away from university, her body covering mine.

"Aurora secure," she said into her mic, "En route to Phoenix Four."

Phoenix Four? They were putting me on the plane? I struggled to sit up, I needed to know what was going on.

"Stay down," Meredith hissed, "This is not a drill, Aurora."

"What's going on?" I asked, stilling my struggling and starting to panic as shock settled on me like a heavy, wet blanket.

"I don't know," she replied, "All I know is that you need to go home."

Home. I hadn't been home in four years, and the six years previous to that I had been in boarding school in France and only went home during the term breaks.

"Is it mother? Father? Jacob?"

Meredith sighed. "I don't know," she said with patience, "All I know is there was a security threat and that we needed to get you out."

"I don't believe you," I said, "Please, tell me the truth."

"I can't Lys," Meredith whispered, breaking protocol and calling me by my nickname. She was more than just part of my security detail, she was my friend. We had been playmates since I was a child and apart from the two years she had been gone to do her military training, she had been a constant fixture in my life. When I had decided to come to America to do my degree, it had been a no brainer that she would come with me and she'd enrolled in all the same classes, essentially studying the same degree as me.

"But it's serious?" I asked.

She gave me a quick hug, while maintaining her cover over me, "Yes," she said and the bleakness in her voice made my stomach drop.

The rest of the ride to the airstrip where the private plane was waiting was quiet. I could hear the wail of the sirens that escorted us through the busy traffic and the faint hum of chatter from Meredith's earwig, but I was too frightened to take any of it in.

The only reason I would be pulled out of class and hustled onto the plane to fly home would be if there had been a significant threat to me or one of my family members. And it must be something substantial to have included me at all. I was the spare and female. Despite my royal pedigree, I was pretty much forgotten in my home country, which suited me just fine. It was the reason I moved to the States, the reason I hadn't been home in four years. I didn't like the spotlight and I had done everything in my power to ensure that I stayed out of it.

I was studying international relations in the hopes of one day securing a position in the UN. My father had bemoaned my desire to get my degree, but eventually relented, although he took every opportunity to loudly argue against my choice. If he'd had his way, I would've stayed home and learned something more appropriate for someone of my station, like needlepoint. It was my brother, Jacob, who'd eventually gotten him to agree and I'd be forever grateful for his intervention.

The car pulled to a stop and the door opened. I was ushered out onto the windy tarmac and hustled up the stairs into the waiting Gulf Stream, my security detail in front of and behind me. Meredith pushed me down into a chair and secured my seatbelt before taking the one beside me. Benjamin was the last to board and then the door was closed and the plane began to taxi. Each member of my security team buckled in and no one spoke as the plane increased speed down the runway.

The force of the takeoff pushed me back into the soft leather of my seat and I closed my eyes. Normally I loved to fly, but not this time. This time there were too many unknowns and I was scared. Really scared.

"Aurora secure on Phoenix One," Benjamin said into his mic.

Phoenix One? What the hell? I turned to look at Meredith, but she refused to make eye contact. Her face was pale and her eyes sad and weary.

"Good Afternoon Princess Alyssabeth," a stewardess said with a short curtesy, "May I get you some refreshments?"

"Not until I get some answers," I said and her smile faltered, "Benjamin, I demand to know what the hell is going on."

Benjamin waved away the stewardess, waiting until the door to the galley was secure before speaking.

"Your father and brother were in a hunting...accident," he said, looking directly at me, his eyes compassionate, but hard.

"Accident?" I asked dumbly, "What kind of accident? Are they okay?"

I watched his jaw jump as he clenched his teeth and exhaled through his nose, "They're dead," he said softly.

"Lys." I woke to the soft whisper and gentle patting of Meredith.

After being told that the two most important men in my life were dead, I had escaped to the small private bedroom on the plane and cried until I'd fallen asleep. I hadn't even begun to process what it meant that the king and the heir apparent were gone, I was simply grieving for a beloved father and brother. All the rest would come later.

"Lys, we're about an hour from landing," Meredith went on, sitting on the bed beside me. "There is a change of clothes and a makeup bag in the ensuite."

I sighed, she was right. It would not do for the princess to arrive home wearing Levis and t-shirt. I'd probably never get to wear them again.

"Thanks," I said and as she began to move away I grabbed her hand. I looked up into her compassionate blue eyes and tried to smile, "I mean it Meredith," I said, "Thank you, for everything. Things are going to change now and I'm going to need you more than ever. I want you to know that even though it may seem like it at times, I've never taken you or our relationship for granted."

She smiled softly at me and wiped her eyes with the heels of her hands. "I know," she said, her voice rough with emotion. She bent down to hug me and I clung to her for a moment. "I've got your back, Lys," she whispered in my ear before pulling away and leaving me to change.

I swung my legs over the side of the bed and got to my feet. It was almost a nine and a half hour flight from Boston to Merveille, the small European country that was home to me, and I had spent about six of those in an exhausted, fitful sleep. I knew my eyes would be puffy and my waist length hair a tangle. I may be the grieving daughter and sister, but I was still a princess and when we arrived at St. Benét Airport in Calanais, the press would be waiting.

My days of messy buns, jeans and hoodies were done. I would no longer be the anonymous princess who stayed out of the limelight. I would be the crown princess of Merveille, soon to be queen. It was a situation that I had never entertained, a position I had never wanted. I was happy in my anonymity, in my relatively humble existence in Boston, in being just another Harvard student.

With a deep breath to fortify myself, I headed to the ensuite to brush my teeth, wash my face and try to tame my dark hair into some sort of smooth, sophisticated chignon. It had been a while since I'd had to put on the façade and I was out of practise. Once I got to the palace, I would be surrounded by lady's maids to help me with this, but until then I had to make the best of it on my own.

I stripped off my well-worn and loved Levis and looked at the sedate, black, knee length dress that had been provided for me. It was a Ralph Lauren sleeveless shift with a thin black belt and fitted blazer.

There were also flesh coloured silk stockings, complete with garter belt, fresh La Perl underwear and a pair of black leather Jimmy Choo pumps. So very far from the jeans and The Cure t-shirt I had been wearing.

It hit me then. I was no longer my own person. Everything I did from now on would have far reaching effects. Every step I made would be scrutinised by the press and judged on the altar of public opinion. The moment I stepped out of this plane and onto Merveille soil, I would be a servant of the people and my life would no longer be my own.

I didn't know if I was ready for that.

Sure, I'd been trained how to be a princess. I had impeccable manners, I knew every dance, greeting, and tradition of my people. I spoke four languages fluently, I could trace my family tree back to the dark ages and I could even needlepoint. But none of that really made any difference; none of it would help me rule my country.

No one had ever thought there would be reason for me to.

That was the reason I had been allowed to go off to the US and study, that was why I had been left relatively enough alone for the past ten years. I was just the baby, the sweet little princess who would marry and live out her days in obscurity. Jacob had been the apple of everyone's eye and he'd revelled in the attention. There was no way I could fill his shoes, or those of my father. They had both been born to rule, I had been merely an accessory.

I slumped onto the bed and dropped my head in my hands. What was I going to do? Merveille was not a country that was all that progressive when it came to women in authority. I didn't think there was even a female member of parliament. My mother couldn't rule because she had married into the family, and was not born into it, and I doubt that the very traditional members of court would welcome me into their midst.

Not only was I going to have to grieve publicly, but I was also going to have to fight for my birthright, one that I wasn't sure I even wanted. I knew that as we flew towards Calanais, the dukes and duchesses were dragging out the parchments and tracing their family trees to find out who the next in line should be. No one would expect me to succeed and I daresay most hoped I would abdicate in favour of a more suitable male heir.

But could I give up the legacy of several hundred years? Could I hand over rule of the country that I loved and essentially wipe away all my family had done?

There was a polite knock at the door and I heard Meredith's voice, "Do you need some help Lys?"

I looked down at myself wearing nothing but my cotton underwear and almost laughed. I was a mess. I was barely able to function on my own, how could I even contemplate ruling a country? I fiddled with the silver bangle on my wrist, turning it around my arm three times. It had been a gift from Meredith, she had a matching one on her wrist.

"Yes, please," I replied, feeling defeated.

Meredith slipped into the room and took one look at me and knew I was close to another melt down. She knew me almost better than I knew myself. With quick efficiency, she took charge and within record time I was dressed, my makeup was done and my hair was in perfect order. Just in time to take my seat for landing. She handed me a pair of dark glasses, buckled me into my seat and then sat beside me, taking my hand and squeezing encouragingly.

The plane touched down with barely a blip and then slowed to taxi to the terminal.

"Welcome home, Your Royal Highness," the plane's captain said over the intercom.

I STOOD ON THE PLATFORM AT THE TOP OF THE STAIRS LEADING down to the tarmac and took a deep breath of the cool, crisp April air. It was spring in Merveille, but with snow still covering the mountaintops in the distance, the air was cool and I was thankful for the blazer I wore. It was going to be a fine day, although the sun was barely showing its face above the snow caps across Lac Merveilleux.

At the bottom of the stairs was a motorcade, three dark BMW sedans with tinted windows and two police bikes. I would really have rather arrived incognito, but I suppose that was out of the question, what with the circumstances of my arrival and all.

There was a red carpet leading from the stairs to the middle car and it was lined with the Royal Guard in their dress blues complete with bearskin caps and rifles. At the end of the red carpet was the welcoming committee, including a man in an Army Lieutenant's uniform, a woman I knew to be my mother's personal secretary, the chief of police and the prime minister. My mother was absent, as was the custom for mourning. It was quite a turnout for seven in the morning.

Beyond the police barricade was the press and some die-hard royal fans - and possibly detractors, not that I wanted to think about that. The flash of cameras and the shouted questions from the press corps rolled over me without much impact, although I was glad of the dark glasses that shielded my weepy, red-rimmed eyes.

Cody and Aiden descended the stairs in front of me. After they had taken two steps, Meredith, keeping close to my side, prompted me to follow. Scott and Jamie followed closely behind and Benjamin brought up the rear.

I kept my head high, my shoulders back and refused to cower in front of the audience despite my overwhelming desire to crawl into a hole and curl up into a ball. I was the heir apparent and I needed to show the people of this country that their futures were secure with me.

The Royal Guard saluted as I moved through the guard of honour and I kept my eyes forward and focused on the door of the car. The quicker I could get out of the spotlight, the better.

When I reached the end of the carpet, the welcoming committee bowed and curtsied to me, which I acknowledged with a brief nod of my head. The prime minister took my hand and offered words of comfort and sympathy, although I'm not really clear on what he actually said. There was a low level buzzing in my ears which made it hard to hear and concentrate on what was happening. It took all of my self-control just to keep upright.

The chief of police also shook my hand and spoke solemnly to me. Beside him stood the man in military dress and as our eyes connected, I felt a rush of recognition. It had been at least ten years since I had seen Jordan Wicks and seeing him now brought home the very real fact that my brother was gone.

He took my hand, but didn't speak, he didn't need to. The depth of emotion in his eyes was enough to start mine watering again and I was twice thankful for the sunglasses. Jordan had been one of Jacob's closest friends and that he was there to meet me was testament to their relationship.

Lorraine, my mother's secretary, pulled me into a quick hug before ushering me into the waiting car. Meredith had gone in first and Jordan followed me in, securing me in the middle. He took my hand without speaking and I squeezed it gently in thanks. If nothing else, I had another friend on my side.

Lorraine took the front seat and the car moved away. I leant my head back against the seat and closed my eyes. I was jet lagged and grieving but there would be no respite for me in the near future. The matter of the crown's succession would need to be addressed as soon as possible and settled before the official mourning period had been completed to ensure a smooth transition.

"Your mother is waiting for you in the conservatory," Lorraine began, "Breakfast will be served as soon as you arrive."

"I need sleep, Lorraine," I said wearily.

"You will have some time this afternoon for a short nap, but there is much to do in the meantime."

I groaned, making a very unladylike and un-princess-like noise in my throat. How could I even face the business of the day when I felt like I had been dragged backwards through a bramble bush?

"Have some mercy, please," I said.

Lorraine sighed and turned to face me, her lips turned down in sadness, "I know how hard this must be for you," she said softly, "But there are some things you need to be made aware of. There are questions about the circumstances of your father and brother's deaths. The security team needs to brief you and apprise you of the changes going forward. There is also the matter of you appointing your own personal secretary and your choice of lady's maids and other personal staff. You will be installed in your old suite for now, until you have decided on how you want your father's suites redecorated. Your mother has requested to be moved into the chalet and will stay in her own suite until such time as the renovations on it are completed. There is also the reception to be organised and of course the funerals."

"Enough," I said, "I can't take anymore right now. If you are determined to torture me this way then I must be given coffee before I am required to make any decisions."

"Very well," Lorraine said, but I could hear the reprove in her voice.

"How is my mother?" I asked after a moment of blessed silence.

Lorraine's eyes misted for a moment before she took control of her emotions once again and cleared her throat delicately before speaking. "She is as well as could be expected," she said softly before turning around in her seat to face forward once again.

I sighed and turned to look out the window. The lush fields spotted with fat brown cows, the gently rolling hills and the blue expanse of the lake was postcard perfect. At long last, I was home.

CHAPTER 2

MY mother was indeed waiting in the conservatory for me when I arrived.

The motorcade had swung through the open wrought iron gates and moved smoothly down the long driveway that was lined with trees clipped into fanciful designs. My first look at the palace in four years caused my heart to burn. It may be a multi-storey stone fairytale castle to some people, but to me it was home and I'd missed it. It sat on the banks of Lac Merveilleux and the sun sparkled on the water, shining highlights on the centuries old building making it look magical. With the still snow-capped mountains in the distance, it was picture perfect.

The palace staff had lined the stairs to welcome me home and Lorraine led me through the lower level to my mother's sanctuary. It had always been her favourite place in the whole of the palace and she said being surrounded by the exotic plants she bred gave her serenity.

There was a breakfast table set and my mother sat in a chair with a cup of tea in her hand. She looked thinner and dark circles marred her still beautiful face. Queen Margot had been a French actress when she had captured my father's heart. She had given up her life to marry him and I had never questioned just what that had cost her until now.

She stood as I walked close and gathered me into her arms. I felt the tears well in my eyes again as the warmth of her body enveloped me. It was just us two against the world now. Two women in a world of men. I clung to my mother, wanting to break down, to fall apart and let her take charge, but I wasn't a child anymore. I needed to be strong for her and for my country.

A small cough reminded me that we weren't alone and I gently pulled away from her, but kept hold of her hand as I sat at the table. One of the attendants poured coffee into the fine china mug that sat waiting and I didn't even bother to doctor it with cream or sugar before gulping down a large, hot swallow. I was going to need the caffeine in my system to keep me on my game today.

Jordan sat opposite me and Meredith sat on the other side of me. Lorraine took her place beside my mother, making for a very odd seating arrangement. Jordan sat by himself on one side of the table facing off against the four of us women.

"Thank you for coming Jordan," my mother said as she resumed sipping from her tea, "I'm sure Alyssabeth was glad to see a friendly face."

"It was my pleasure, Your Grace," Jordan replied, "I'm glad to be of service at this particularly difficult time."

"So what have you been up to since I saw you last?" I asked as I spread some thick raspberry jam over my toast.

"I've been at the Embassy in France for the last few years, but I recently moved back to Merveille. I'll be serving here, in fact."

"Here in Calanais?" I asked.

"Here in the palace," he corrected, "Military Attache and Liaison to the foreign dignitaries."

I nodded as I ate, chewing thoughtfully, "That was your father's position here as well wasn't it?"

He looked down and smiled, his cheeks colouring slightly, "It was," he replied, "He's retired now, of course."

My father and Jordan's father had been friends. Jordan and Jacob had been practically inseparable as kids and I had fond memories of time spent together in the carefree days of childhood. He had grown into a good looking man with strong jaw, blonde hair and greyish/green eyes. His military training had endowed him with an erect posture and was no doubt also responsible for the way his uniform strained over his wide shoulders.

My observation and subsequent attraction to Jordan was inappropriate, but my skittish brain was bound and determined to latch onto something other than the reason I was home. Was it really such a bad thing to ogle the pretty soldier?

"Your father was with the hunting party," my mother said and my head snapped to the side to look at her.

"He was," Jordan replied softly, "He suffered a deep wound to his leg in the attack."

I gasped and covered my mouth with my hand as I looked at him, "Is he okay?"

"He is," he replied, "Still in hospital and with a long angry wound and many stitches. Of course he wishes that it had been himself and not your father who had borne the brunt of the boar."

"They were hunting boar?" I asked, confused.

He shook his head, "No, deer."

Lorraine cleared her throat, "I think it would be best to change the subject. Princess Alyssabeth will receive a full briefing from the security team in an hour."

He nodded respectfully and then stood. He bowed to me and then my mother, "Thank you for your hospitality," he said, "And welcome home Princess Alyssa, although I wish that it were under better circumstances. If it is alright with you, I shall take my leave. There are many Heads of State due to arrive soon and I must be about my duties."

"Thank you Jordan," I said standing and going around the table to take his hands in mine. They were warm and large and engulfed mine completely. "Thank you for meeting my plane, I appreciate you being available to us at this time."

He lowered his head in a small bow of acknowledgment, "I am at your service," he said softly and his smooth voice was like a balm to my frayed nerves. With one last squeeze of my hands, he turned and left, striding with purpose out of the room. I watched him go, admiring the way he filled out his uniform.

"Oh, do sit down Alyssa," my mother said with a smirk.

I resumed my place and held up my cup for a refill. Having Jordan in the palace could be just the distraction I needed to get through the next few months.

"After the security briefing, I have a few people for you to interview for the position of personal secretary," Lorraine said, breaking into my musings, "And this afternoon there is a small reception."

At my surprised and, dare I say, angry glare, she continued.

"It's not anything big and it's not formal. It is just a gathering of close friends of both your brother and your father. They wish to pay their respects and this is the most efficient way to do it." She flipped a page in her folder and read a few lines before speaking again. "Until you have decided on lady's maids, I have assigned Bridgette and Annette. They come highly recommended from Lady Caroline. I have a selection of outfits laid out for you and they will be able to help with your hair and makeup as needed."

"Thank you Lorraine," my mother said wearily before standing, "I will leave you to your security briefing, *ma chérie*," she said kissing the top of my head, "Come and find me when you have a spare moment."

Why did I suddenly feel like I had been thrown to the wolves?

"So what you are telling me is that my father's and brother's deaths may not have been accidental."

"That is correct Your Majesty," Von Bartham, the head of royal security said with a nod, "But at this stage it is just supposition."

I crossed my arms and leaned back in my chair, not quite knowing what to say. Meredith sat beside me, the rest of my security team spread around the large conference table. The room was not unlike the American president's briefing room as depicted in Hollywood movies. It was the first time I had ever stepped foot in the place and I'd had to stop myself gawking like a common tourist.

Apart from my own personal security, there were also some other members of the royal security in attendance, notably my father's and brother's men and the chief of police. I looked into the faces of the two men that had been with my father and brother when they had lost their lives and felt pity for them. Outwardly they appeared professional, but their eyes gave them away; these men were distraught by the loss of their assets. I didn't doubt that they would each try to resign because of their presumed dishonour.

"Okay," I said taking a breath, "Tell me again what happened."

"We were trekking through the woods," Daniel, my father's head of security said, "When a herd of boars charged us. There was a lot of commotion and the king was separated from us. The prince followed him and found him to be under attack by one of the animals. The boar had speared him with a tusk and he was bleeding heavily. Several shots rang out from the hunting party and one of the stray bullets hit and killed the prince. Several of the other guests were wounded in the attack and we lost two of our security team to gunshot wounds also."

I exhaled loudly, trying to keep my stomach from emptying its contents all over the large mahogany table. "So why don't you think it was an accident?"

Von Bartham took up the narrative, "Both the hunt master and the gamekeeper assured us that there were no boars in the forest. This hunt had been planned for months and the king specifically wanted to hunt deer. The gamekeeper had been ridding the forest of any unwanted game in preparation."

"And the gunshot that killed my brother?"

"We have been as yet unable to determine whose gun it came from," Von Bartham replied, "Although our investigation is continuing. But we believe it to be intentional, the fatal wounds of the security team as well."

"Has there been any significant threats against the royal family?" Benjamin asked.

Von Bartham shook his head, "No credible threats, just the usual oddball stuff."

"So what does this mean for me?" I asked, "I assume there will be changes to my security in light of these events?"

"Yes, Your Highness," Von Bartham went on, "You will need to have at least two members of your security team with you at all times. While you are inside the palace, two will suffice, outside in the palace grounds we will require you to have four and if you leave the grounds, there will be eight."

"Are you kidding me?" I said, stunned, "I need *two* guards inside the palace?"

"Until we know for sure about the hunting incident, we think it would be best, yes."

"No," I said, "Absolutely not."

"I'm sorry, Your Highness, but this is not up for negotiation."

"Von Bartham," Benjamin said, standing to his feet, "May I have a moment with the princess and my team?"

With a sharp nod, Von Bartham and his team exited the room leaving me with Benjamin, Meredith and the rest of my detail.

"Your Highness," Benjamin began.

"Oh cut the crap Benjamin," I said, "Don't stop calling me Alyssa now for God's sake."

He smiled a quick smile at me and nodded in acquiesce, "Alyssa," he began again, "I know it seems extreme, but there are just too many questions about your father and brother's deaths. I understand that you are used to living in relative freedom, but that is no longer an option. Over the next few weeks there is going to be practically a highway through the palace gates as every dignitary from here to eternity comes to pay respects to your father and brother. This is big news and not just Merveille big, world big. To have the reigning king and his heir killed in the same accident is unprecedented. Regardless of your personal feelings, you need to let us do this. You are the last remaining St. Benét alive and we can't afford to lose you."

Meredith grabbed my hand and squeezed, "And we love you," she said, "Did you see Carlos and Daniel? Carlos was your brother's closest confidant and Daniel had been working your father's detail for twenty years. They are completely gutted by their deaths and I can assure you that if they could've died in the king's and the prince's places, they would have. We feel the same for you, every one of us." She shared a look with each member seated around the table. "You are going to be queen and we are prepared to do whatever it takes to keep you safe."

I sighed and dropped my eyes to the table, "How long?"

"Until we know definitively what happened in the forest."

"Okay," I said on an exhale, "Who are the two extras going to be?"

Benjamin sighed, "Carlos and Daniel have requested it," he said, "But I'll only agree if you're comfortable with it."

I nodded once. I knew both men well and had no qualms about them joining my detail. I looked up to catch Benjamin's eye, "The two men who were also killed," I said, "Did they have families?"

He shook his head, "Both were unmarried," he said and I felt some measure of relief. "So I can tell Von Bartham that you're agreed?"

"Yes," I said standing, "Now apparently I need to interview for a personal secretary. Who's with me for that exciting task?"

There was a round of chuckles before Meredith and Jamie stood up to accompany me out.

My feet were killing me. It had been a blissful four years since I'd had to stand in a receiving line wearing high heels and I was woefully out of practise. Lorraine had assured me that it was a small reception, but I was pretty sure I had been standing there for at least three hours greeting people who'd come to pay their respects to my family and me. Okay, so it probably wasn't three hours, but it felt like it.

While we waited for the next person to enter, I looked over my shoulder to see Meredith stifling a yawn and smirked at her.

"How many more?" I whisper-yelled to her and she just shrugged.

I turned back to greet the next person and my mouth went dry. Standing in front of me was a vision. Tall, dark and handsome didn't even begin to describe the adonis that was waiting to greet me. I had thought Jordan had aged well, but he had nothing on Will Darkly.

Will bowed to me before taking my hand and raising it to his lips. His clear blue eyes arrested me in their gaze as he touched his lips to the back of my hand. The contact sent a jolt through me and my voice was breathy when I spoke.

"Will."

"Your Highness," he said softly, "I am so terribly sorry for your loss."

And then he moved on without a backward glance. Will had been the third musketeer in Jacob and Jordan's trio. The three boys had barely been separated in their younger years. Will had teased me mercilessly and I had vowed never to speak to him again. Little did I know then under what tragic circumstances we would be reunited. One thing was for sure, his touch had never done that to me before.

The next few guests passed in a daze as I automatically went through the motions of welcoming them to the palace. And then a welcome voice broke through my fugue.

"I believe I am the last," Jordan said after he had bowed and greeted me, "May I escort you in?"

Since I had no consort and Jordan had been a close friend of the family for many years, it would not be deemed inappropriate for him to walk with me into the reception, and truthfully, I was grateful for the company. I was functioning on caffeine alone at that point, having been denied my promised nap in lieu of getting ready for tonight.

"I must say, princess," Jordan said as we walked arm in arm along the marble floored hall towards the reception room, "You look absolutely stunning tonight."

I blushed and smiled shyly, "Thank you," I replied.

"This morning when I saw you deplaning, you reminded me of a young Audrey Hepburn and I'm pleased to say that tonight is no different." He stopped and turned to me. "Alyssa, you are breathtaking."

I felt my cheeks burn with embarrassment. I did not take compliments well. I always thought they were a very insincere form of flattery, but Jordan made me think that he was truthful in his assessment of me.

"Thank you, Lieutenant," I said as we resumed walking, "That is very kind of you to say."

The double doors to the reception room opened and the noise inside died down as I entered. There was a shushing of fabric as the men bowed and the women curtsied. I nodded to the people and allowed myself to be steered through the masses. Most, if not all, of these people held titles or rank of their own and those who didn't were landed gentry or by special invitation. I was essentially among my peers, but I had never felt more alone.

"May I get you something to drink, Your Highness?" Jordan asked.

"Yes, please," I replied, "I don't suppose I could have a beer?"

He laughed heartily and I felt the stress in my shoulders loosen just a bit.

"I'm afraid not," he said, "Will wine do?"

I nodded, "Yes, thank you," I said and he turned away. I grabbed Meredith's hand and pulled her close. "I need to sit down before I fall down," I whispered harshly in her ear.

She led me through the crowd to a circle of arm chairs and I sank down into one gratefully. I looked up to see Will staring intently at me, an expression of contempt on his face. I wondered why he would feel that way toward me and I felt a bit miffed by his seeming instant dislike of me.

Jordan returned momentarily and I sipped from the crystal glass he handed me. The wine was delicious; a crisp white that was produced in Merveille. A passing waiter offered me a tray of canapés and I took one thankfully. There had been no time for dinner before the reception and me and wine on an empty stomach did not mix well.

I bit into the wafer thin cracker topped with brie and caramelised onion and moaned with pleasure.

"This cheese is amazing," I said around my mouthful, "Where did it come from?"

"That would be from me," Will said as he appeared beside me.

Jordan clapped him on the back, "Ah, yes. Our very own cheese baron. How's it going my old friend?"

The waves of dislike rolled off Will palpably as he turned to address Jordan, "I am well, and yourself? I see you are back in Merveille."

"Yes," Jordan said, a devious smile on his face, "I have just recently taken up a position here in the palace." He sipped his drink. "How is your sister?"

The muscle in Will's jaw bulged as he ground his teeth, "Georgina is well," he said through gritted teeth.

"Is she here tonight?" I asked, uncomfortable with the undercurrent of hostility between the two men despite their polite words.

"No," Will replied, turning back to me, "She is away at school for another week. She sends her regards and her deepest sympathies."

"Tell her thank you from me," I said, "And please let me know when she returns, I would love to catch up with her."

"Of course," Will said, snapping a bow, "Now, I must be off, if you will excuse me."

He turned and left without waiting for a goodbye.

"He must have to go and check on those blasted cows of his," Jordan said with a sneer.

CHAPTER 3

I bent at the waist and sucked in lungfuls of air. Meredith was doing the same and I had to smile, knowing that she wasn't any fitter than me. I looked up and caught Jamie's smirk as he looked on from the side of the room and growled.

"Do you want to replace Meredith for the next match Jamie?" I called to him and his grin widened.

Meredith and I sparred regularly. It had started out as self defence training but had morphed into a quasi-fitness/mixed martial arts thing. We were pretty evenly matched, although she had the benefit of being able to train with the men and had an edge on me. So far none of my other security detail and taken me up on my offer to spar and I didn't know whether it was out of some misguided loyalty or whether they didn't think I would be much of a challenge for them.

"Maybe another time," Jamie replied.

"I'll hold you to that," I said, pointing a finger at him, but he just nodded and smiled.

Meredith straightened and looked at the big clock on the wall, "We need to get moving, Lys," she said, "You have an appointment in an hour."

I sighed, "Right," I said. The appointment was with my new secretary to go over her duties. We had met briefly yesterday when I had interviewed her, along with the other candidates. I had known them all, cousins once or twice removed, the offspring of my father's relatives, although we had never really spent much time together.

My father had been the only male offspring of my grandparents, with three younger sisters. My grandmother, God rest her soul, made sure that each one of the sisters made good marriages into royal families from other countries. Each of the sisters, along with the other royal cousins, had produced an heir and a spare (sometimes more than one spare), as was the way of the families of peerage, and those female spares had been brought to me for consideration as my secretary. There had been five interviews in all, the rest having been weeded out by Lorraine beforehand, and I had chosen Alexandra because she seemed the most competent and accomplished amongst them, also closest in age to myself.

The women not chosen would form my court of ladies in waiting - an outdated but necessary tradition. These women were to become my confidantes and close friends as well as support me through the transition from heir presumptive to heir apparent and finally queen. Each one of them also had a claim on my throne were anything to happen to me and I had to wonder at the wisdom of those long ago bastions of propriety who decided that friends must be kept close and enemies closer.

Not that I was worried that one of them had an eye my crown. After speaking briefly with each of them I was convinced they had loftier goals, that of marrying wealthy, good-looking men and never having to work a day in their lives. Alexandra had been different and I actually looked forward to getting to know her better.

I sighed, not looking forward to the coming appointment, or the one after it to meet with the bishop and finalise the funeral arrangements for my father and brother.

I followed Meredith out of the gymnasium to the lifts. The palace was centuries old and the elevators had been installed not long after they were invented. The king at the time was intrigued by evolving technology and had made it a priority to have every last gadget that he could. It had sparked a tradition amongst the St. Benét monarchs which resulted in the Château de Conte de Fées being the most technologically progressive palace in Europe. My brother had even studied computer sciences as part of his degree to ensure the tradition continued.

The thought robbed me of my previously light mood. It would be up to me now to ensure the tradition continued; not that I was a technophobe, on the contrary I had a fascination with it. But I knew my brother had had big plans and now none of them would come to pass. It was a sad thought.

The elevator that took us to my suite had recently been updated and was a long way from the original one installed in the palace in the late-1800s. It glided silently and quickly to my floor and opened directly outside my suite of rooms.

That was another thing that would change. The rooms I had grown up in would no longer be my private sanctuary. My mother's plans for the modest chalet on the palace grounds would not take long to finalise and she would be moving into it within the month. Then I would need to begin work on the king's quarters and remake them into my own. I understood why I needed to move; they were bigger and could accommodate my growing entourage and they were more centrally located with predesigned escape routes to ensure the ruling monarch could be secreted away if necessary. But it didn't make it any easier.

I had yet to have a moment to myself in which to mourn properly, and it would probably be several more days until I would get the chance. The funerals were to be held within the week, two of them, one for each and a wake after each one. Then there was the business of my accession, which had to be ruled on by Parliament. I was the first female in the long line of St. Benét's to be the heir apparent and with a Parliament that had a very patriarchal view of authority, I had no doubt that they would not be happy.

Well, good for them. I was the rightful heir and I intended to do my father and brother proud. I refused to tarnish their memories by being anything less than they themselves had been. Now I just had to find a way to make it so.

I SAT WITH ONE LEG CROSSED OVER THE OTHER, LEANING BACK IN MY chair and idly playing with my silver bangle as Lorraine went over the duties expected of my new personal secretary, Lady Alexandra Fornette. The poor woman was looking very much like she had the desire to ram something down Lorraine's throat as the other woman went on in a particularly condescending tone.

"Excuse me Lorraine," I said politely, "If I may?" Lorraine nodded, but I could tell she was not happy at the interruption. "Lady Alexandra, were you employed before being summoned to Merveille?"

Alexandra nodded, "Yes, Your Highness," she replied.

"And what was it that you did in your previous employ?"

"I was the personal assistant to the CEO of a multimillion dollar investment firm."

I smiled at her and then turned to Lorraine, "I think that Lady Alexandra has a firm enough grip on the tasks that I will require of her, don't you agree?"

Lorraine flushed and her lips thinned in disapproval, "Of course, Your Highness," she replied, "However I do think that her role as the queen's personal secretary has a little more import than that of being an assistant to a banker." She said the word banker as if it tasted sour on her tongue.

"Actually," I said, "I disagree. Lady Alexandra grew up in a royal household and knows the protocols that need to be heeded. On top of that she has worked for, what I daresay, was a particularly difficult man, and excelled. I would not have chosen her if I did not think that she was up to the task."

Lorraine knew when she was beaten, although she was not gracious in defeat. "Very well," she said, standing, "Then if you have no further use of me, I shall return to the queen...I mean the queen mother." She curtsied briefly and left the room.

I sighed and looked back at Alexandra who had a small smile on her face and a mischievous glint in her eye. Meredith, who was seated beside me, had her hand covering her mouth and was attempting to disguise a giggle.

Alexandra was gorgeous and I felt rather plain beside her. Her smooth blonde hair was twisted into a perfect French knot without a stray piece out of place. Her blue eyes were large and clear, framed by incredibly long lashes and her red lips were full. She was dressed in an impeccable dove grey, tailored skirt suit with a purple silk blouse underneath. The woman had class and she seemed to be sweet as well.

"I'm sorry, Lady Alexandra," I said and Alexandra's face broke into a full-fledged smile, "She was incredibly rude to you."

"It's fine, Your Highness," she replied, "It is not the first time I have been found wanting."

"Please, call me Alyssa," I said, "We're going to be working closely with one another and I don't like the fussiness of titles."

"Of course," she said, "And I prefer Alex. My name is such a mouthful without adding the *Lady* part to it."

"Have you officially met Lady Meredith Bingham?" I asked smirking at my best friend.

Meredith rolled her eyes at me before smiling at Alex, "We have met, but don't you dare call me Lady Meredith. I have a hard enough time with the rest of my team without them latching on to that little nugget."

I raised my eyebrows, "Benjamin doesn't know you're titled?"

"Of course *he* knows, but none of the others do. I made him promise me on pain of death that he wouldn't tell them."

"Your father is the Duke of Monterey?" Alex asked.

Meredith nodded, "Yes," she said with a sigh, "He will be arriving today with my mother." She grimaced. Meredith's mother was not at all fond of the fact that she had decided to train to become my personal body guard, although her father had been delighted.

"Is Frédéric coming as well?" I asked.

She huffed out a laugh, "Of course he is," she replied, "He asked about you."

Now I rolled my eyes. I loved Frédéric, but he was a well-known playboy and I had no desire to become another one of his many conquests.

Meredith laughed and Alex looked between us, puzzled.

"My brother, Earl of Avonlea, is an incurable flirt," Meredith said, "And it doesn't help that he is as handsome as sin. Fortunately though,

Lys here has been able to resist his charms and he cannot for the life of him understand why."

I chuckled, "You know I love him dearly," I said, "And he is quite pretty to look at. Unfortunately he is all too aware of how he looks and I know that no sooner would I say yes to him than he would be scouting for his next conquest."

"It is the truth," Meredith said with a sigh, "And one of these days his roving eye is going to get him into trouble."

Alex checked her watch, "As much as I am enjoying hearing about your charming, but devilish brother, I'm afraid we need to go. The bishop will be waiting for us."

I stood wearily to my feet and smoothed my skirt. I was dreading this meeting and not just because I had a peculiar dislike for the bishop. Having to make funeral arrangements was just one more thing that brought home the fact that my brother and father were gone.

When I had woken in my childhood bedroom that morning after a night where I slept like a log, I had a moment where I forgot that they were gone. In my newly woken state, I had recognised my room and had immediately thought of walking down the stairs into the dining room to hear my father's deep voice and booming laugh. And then I remembered that I would never hear those two things again.

I was going to miss him and Jacob terribly and I knew that right now I hadn't even begun to grieve properly. I was holding it together to get through the next few weeks of royal engagements and then I would finally be able to let myself fall apart. But it would only be a short reprieve. I didn't have the luxury of mourning that common people had. I needed to start to govern, although in what capacity that might be, I was still unsure. Merveille had a constitutional monarchy, which meant the Parliament pretty much handled the everyday running of the country. I had no idea what my duties were to be or even if I would be allowed to do them.

THE BRISK, SPRING AIR STREAMED THROUGH MY HAIR, TUGGING AT my braid and freeing wayward strands from its tight confines as I rode hard through the green field. It felt good to have the raw power of horse flesh under me and the freedom to ride far and fast. Meredith, Jamie and Alex trailed me on their own mounts, and Carlos and Aiden followed on ATVs, but I had pulled ahead of them all with my need for a small slice of solitude.

Meeting with the bishop had been harder than I thought and I had almost snapped at the disagreeable man, nearly allowing my grief to overrule my years of etiquette training. I hardly thought it was my job to decide on who sat where or what refreshments would be served. There was a whole staff of people to look after those minor details. Both my father and my brother had had staff better suited to such tasks.

And what would happen to those staff now?

It was yet another question to which I didn't have the answer.

When we had arrived back at the palace, the walls felt like they were closing in on me and I needed to get out. I needed fresh air and a semblance of escaping, just for a while. The pain of realising that I would be burying my father the next day and my brother the day after was almost too much to bear. I'd made a beeline for the stables and now here I was, riding hell for leather across the lush, rolling hills of the palace grounds.

I pulled my horse to a stop as I reached the top of a hill and looked down towards a boundary fence. On the other side of the fence there was a paddock filled with unfamiliar looking cows. I thought I knew all breeds of cows in, if not Merveille, then at least Calanais. It was what our small country was famous for and what ensured our coffers stayed full.

Our fortune was made on the back of a cow, well a cow's milk more precisely. The Merveille Guernsey produced a milk that was highly prized by both the chocolatiers of Switzerland and the cheesemakers of France and Italy. But the cows in the field over the boundary fence were not Merveille Guernseys, although they were similar.

I heard the others approach and stayed where I was until they pulled up beside me. Jamie and Meredith had both been away from Merveille for the last four years with me and Alex had grown up in another country altogether, so I didn't think that any of them would have the answers to my questions, but I asked them anyway.

"Whose property is that?" I asked, pointing to the paddock beyond the boundary.

"I believe that belongs to Maison de Pemberton," Jamie replied.

"Will Darkly's estate?" I asked, surprised.

Jamie nodded.

"And those would be his cows?" I asked, dumbly.

"I assume so," Jamie replied, "They look like his breed."

"His breed?"

Jamie nodded again, "The Pemberton Jersey, I believe," he said, "The Lord of Pemberton developed the breed and his cheese is made entirely from the milk they produce."

"So that's what Jordan meant when he called him the cheese baron," I mused, "Did the elder Lord of Pemberton instigate the breeding program?"

Jamie shook his head, "I don't know, but I don't think so. The elder Lord of Pemberton passed away a few years ago."

"Oh," I said softly. I had no idea that Will's father was dead, "And the Lady of Pemberton?"

"I believe she died a few years before her husband," Jamie replied.

Will and Georgina were alone, not that they were children, but still. Losing my own father, despite being an adult, had left a hole in my life. I couldn't imagine being without my mother as well.

I turned my mount and started back towards the stables. It was easy to believe that I was the only one going through a hard time, but the fact was that I had it better than most. Yes, I had lost two significant people in my life, but I was healthy, I had a roof over my head, more money than I could spend and I wasn't alone. How many people in the world were worse off than me? Most of them, more than likely.

I had never thought of myself as selfish and had believed that I had grown up without being too affected by my title. While in the States I had learned to cook and clean and do my own laundry. I didn't rely on Meredith to serve as a maid, even though I knew it was what my mother and father had expected. But despite my desire to be independent, I had never really had to struggle. I had a safety net and no one would have thought twice if I had come home because it had all been too hard for me. Was it still considered being brave if there was no real way you could fail?

I would never know what it was really like to be an independent student striking out on my own. I didn't have to hold down a job to pay my way through university, I didn't have the threat of student loans hanging over my head and I hadn't had to exist on Ramen noodles and tinned soup like many other students did.

Yes, I had lost my father and I had lost my brother, but so many people had lost so much more. That's why I had wanted to work for the UN in the first place; to ease the suffering of those less fortunate than myself. I knew I needed to grieve and that I would more than likely have a fight in front of me to claim the throne, but in the grand scheme of things, I was still better off than so many other people and it was time I remembered that.

CHAPTER 4

"M Y dearest Princess Alyssabeth."

I barely controlled my lips from turning up in a smirk as Frédéric, Meredith's brother, Earl of Avonlea, bowed deeply before me. I was standing in the library, perusing the extensive collection of leather bound books, when the footman had announced him. I had already received the Duke and Duchess of Monterey, who were now settled in one of the guest suites in the palace, and they had informed me that Frédéric would not be far behind them.

Where Meredith had vibrant red hair and grey/blue eyes, her brother was dark and his eyes were a striking blue, being darker around the edges and lighter towards the centre. He was tall and strongly built and he wore a suit better than any man I had ever seen. He really was pretty to look at.

"Get up," I said with a grin, shoving him.

He stood and matched my grin with one of his own before leaning in to kiss me affectionately on the cheek, his Armani fragrance swirling delicately about me.

"How are you Lys?" he asked, seriously and I had to blink several times to keep the tears at bay. My ride through the paddocks had not done much to lighten my mood.

I sighed, "I'm okay," I said as I sat down in one of the overstuffed chintz arm chairs.

Frédéric sat opposite me, his hands steepled and his chin resting on their tips, a look of concern on his face.

"Please," he said softly, "If there is anything I can do..."

"Thank you Freddie," I said with a sad smile, "I really appreciate it."

The door opened once again and admitted Alex who was ushering in the maids with a tea service and a tiered tray of cakes.

"Your Highness," she said, curtseying, "I thought you might like some tea."

I smiled at her and Frédéric stood.

"Thank you Lady Alexandra," I said, "Have you met Lord Frédéric?"

I saw Frédéric's eyes light up as he ran his gaze over her. "I don't think I've had the pleasure," he said taking her hand and kissing it.

Alex blushed prettily and I had to hold back my grin. It was always a delight to see how other women reacted to Freddie's charms.

"Why don't you join us for tea," I said to Alex who looked askance at me but didn't refuse.

The maids set the tea table between us as Alex took a seat next to me and opposite Freddie. He waited for her to be seated before taking his own seat.

"Shall I be mother?" Alex asked, leaning forward to pour the tea and dismissing the maids.

"Lady Alexandra is my one of my many cousins," I informed Freddie, "And is to be my personal secretary."

Freddie leaned back in his chair after she handed him a dainty cup and saucer of hot tea and smiled indulgently.

"Really?" he said, "So I dare say we will be seeing a lot of you then."

"Oh?" I asked, "You're staying in Merveille?"

He nodded, "Yes. Father has determined that I have spent enough time scouring the earth and sowing my wild oats and he has requested that I return home and learn the family business."

"And have you?" Alex asked, and then blushed.

"Have I...?"

"Spent enough time scouring the earth and sowing your wild oats?" she finished.

He laughed heartily, "I don't think I will ever tire of it," he said, "But I have a duty to my family and our shareholders, so, for now anyway, I will be curbing my wild impulses and will become a monk of Calanais."

The library doors sprung open forcefully and Meredith ran into the room.

"Freddie!" she yelled as she threw herself into her brother's arms, who had risen just in time to catch her.

"Steady on there Mer," he said with a gleeful laugh, "I'm an old man now."

Meredith, who had wrapped her legs around her brother's waist and her arms around his neck, gave him loud smacking kiss on the cheek before lowering her legs to the floor and releasing him from her strangle hold.

"You've always been an old man," she said as he straightened his navy blue suit. He wasn't wearing a tie and his white shirt was open at the throat displaying a triangle of tanned skin and a hint of dark hair.

"Are you free to join us Meredith?" I asked indicating the tea.

She plopped down on the armchair beside her brother with a sigh, "I have a few minutes free," she said, "But then I am under strict instructions to bring the Earl of Avonlea here to meet with the duke and duchess."

Freddie rolled his eyes, "I've only just arrived," he said, "And I only saw them not an hour ago."

"I believe the duchess said that the duke had monopolised you from the moment you arrived and had not left sufficient time for her to greet you properly."

Freddie grimaced, "God," he said, "You know what that means, don't you? She has a list of prospective wives for me."

"You're getting married?" Alex asked.

"Not if I can help it," he replied, "But that doesn't stop the duchess from throwing every eligible daughter of a noble birth in front of me whenever I come home."

"Oh," Alex said and looked down at her cup.

"Since you're staying in Calanais for a while, you will be able to work yourself down the list," I said, "There will be enough receptions and dinners and the like over the summer for you to become quite intimately acquainted with each of them."

He dropped down to his knees in front of me and clasped his hands in supplication, "Oh, please, Lys. Won't you marry me and save me from this torture?"

The three of us giggled and I patted him on the shoulder, "Oh dearest Freddie, I would that I could."

He stood to his feet, "Ah, well, the offer is there if you change your mind," he said, "I suppose I should go and get this over with."

Meredith stood to accompany him but he shook his head.

"It's alright, sister dear," he said, "You stay here and keep the princess and her delightful secretary company. I am not too cowardly to face the music on my own."

He turned to me and bowed again and then took Alex's hand once again and kissed it.

"I very much enjoyed meeting you," he said softly before standing and leaving.

MY LADIES IN WAITING, SAVANNAH, MARGARET, PRISCILLA AND Jeanette, along with Alex and Meredith were gathered around the table as I dealt the next hand of poker. These women were all related to me, even Meredith, but apart from Meredith, I didn't know them very well at all. We had all grown up apart and had very rarely the occasion to mix. But they were here now and they were to be my support team, so a night of poker and alcohol had been scheduled to 'get to know' one another.

The current topic of conversation were the eligible men who were currently staying in or near the palace. Each of my ladies in waiting were on the lookout for a good marriage, preferably a titled or landed gentleman with money. Oh, and he needed to be gorgeous.

"What about Freddie?" I asked as I picked up my hand and fanned the cards.

"Ooh, he is delicious," Savannah agreed.

"And so charming," Margaret added, to which Meredith rolled her eyes.

"And a player," she said, frowning at her cards.

"I thought he was sweet," Alex said quietly.

"He seemed quite taken with you," I added and she blushed.

"I'd prefer a blonde," Jeanette said, "Lieutenant Wicks is quite nice to look at."

"He is," Meredith agreed, "But I think he has his eyes set on someone else." She looked directly at me and I ducked behind my cards.

"The Lord of Pemberton does it for me," Priscilla said, "He's so dark and brooding."

"Ooh yes," Savannah squealed.

I blushed. Thinking of Will made my stomach flop and my skin heat.

"He is rather rude, though," I said.

"Hmm," Jeanette agreed, "And I think the family must have fallen on hard times. The suit he wore last night was a bit threadbare."

I stared at her in shock. "Threadbare?" I asked, incredulous. There had been absolutely nothing wrong with his suit.

"Well maybe not threadbare, but definitely a couple of seasons old," she amended.

"It was Armani," Savannah added, "But the colour was definitely from two seasons ago at least. And he needs a haircut."

"And he works with all those cows," Margaret said while crinkling her nose.

"Yes, but haven't you ever had a cowboy fantasy?" Meredith asked, flipping a couple of chips onto the table. "A sweaty, virile man, his tanned skin glistening in the sun as he hauls bales of hay, his jeans sitting low on his hips and his shirt off to show well defined pecs, washboard abs and that wonderful vee of his obliques."

"Yummy," Savannah sighed.

There was a general murmuring of agreement around the table and small sighs of contentment as we each visualised Meredith's cowboy.

"But I'd still want him to have money," Margaret said, snapping everyone out of their reverie.

"Money or looks?" Jeanette asked, tossing a couple of cards down and taking a drink.

"Looks don't last forever," Priscilla said, "But money can. If invested well."

"But what about personality? You have to live with the guy after all." This from Alex who looked perplexed at the discussion.

"True," Jeanette shrugged, "He'd need to be able to hold a conversation, at least, and not embarrass me in front of people."

"Okay, so money and looks but no personality or looks and personality but no money?" Savannah ventured.

"Money and looks," the three other ladies in waiting agreed as I dealt their replacement cards.

"What about personality and money but no looks?" Alex asked.

"I'd probably prefer looks and personality without money," Priscilla replied, "I'm sure daddy would pony up with an allowance."

I shook my head subtly and Meredith barely contained her laughter. Alex just looked shocked. She was a lot more buttoned up than I had imagined.

"What was the CEO like that you worked for?" I asked, "Was he looks and money but no personality? Or personality and money without the looks?"

"He had it all," she said dreamily and then shook herself out of it, "But he was married."

"Happily?" asked Margaret.

"Oh, yes," Alex replied, fussing with her cards, "She was his previous PA."

"Dipping the wick in the company inkwell," Meredith said and I snorted in laughter.

Alex blushed, "Oh, I don't..."

"It's okay Alex," I said, "Meredith is just being cynical. She doesn't give much credence to romance."

Meredith shrugged, "I'm yet to be convinced that love is real and not just some made up sentiment designed to sell diamonds and chocolates."

"Someone broke your heart," Savannah said, patting Meredith's hand.

"What? No," she said shaking her head forcefully.

"What about you, princess?" Jeanette asked, "Ever been in love?"

I shook my head and sighed, "No. I was too focused on my studies when I was at university to have time for men and before that I was in an all-girls boarding school."

"What about now?" Margaret asked.

I shrugged, "I wouldn't say I'm in love," I said, "But there are one or two gentlemen who've caught my eye."

Meredith smirked but thankfully didn't say anything.

"God," Priscilla shook her head, "Can you imagine the media frenzy when you announce your engagement? The country will go insane."

That was the last thing I'd been thinking about. But I suppose it would eventually be expected of me to get married and produce an heir. What chance did I have of falling in love with someone when my every move was being watched and documented? And why hadn't I spent some of my university years gaining some experience with the opposite sex? At this point in my life, I should've at least been kissed.

But I never expected to become queen and I never expected that I would have to navigate a romance with the whole country watching. My mood soured and I sipped my drink morosely.

"Cheer up, Princess," Meredith said, "It could be worse."

"Oh really?" I said, "And how could it be worse?"

"You could've been forced into an arranged marriage."

THE PALACE WAS DARK AND QUIET AND I TRIED TO WALK WITHOUT making too much noise. Not that I was sneaking, I just didn't want to wake anyone. Scott and Daniel followed me and were much better at keeping quiet than I was. Their night vision was probably better than mine too.

I finally made it to the kitchen and switched on the overhead lights, blinking rapidly as my eyes adjusted to the brightness.

"You know you could have called someone to get you a midnight snack Your Highness," Scott said, amused with my final destination.

"It's not quite the same as searching through the fridge myself," I replied turning back to the kitchen.

"It's not really a fridge though, is it?" Daniel said, looking around the space.

He was right, it wasn't a fridge, it was a cold room. The kitchen in the palace was probably better equipped than most five star restaurants and had every gadget known to man in it. Chef would be livid if he found me in here, but I didn't care. I couldn't sleep and I was hungry.

Scott was also correct in saying that I could call someone to fix me a snack. There were kitchen staff on call for just that eventuality, but I refused to rouse someone from sleep when I could do it myself. And I knew exactly what I wanted.

I pulled the heavy door of the cold room open and stepped into its frigid interior. It was about four metres wide by four metres deep and was lined with shelves that were stocked with food. I ran my gaze over the stock until I found what I wanted. Cheese.

I pulled out a selection and stepped back into the kitchen, closing the cold room door behind me. Putting the cheese on the stainless steel bench, I then went in search of crackers. The walk-in pantry was at least twice the size of the cold room, most likely more and resembled a small grocery store. I browsed the aisles until I found a packet of thin wafers and returned to the bench with my bounty.

I didn't bother with a plate, but I did look for a cheese knife. I cracked open the packet of wafers and offered them to my two body guards. Daniel declined, but Scott was familiar enough with me to be comfortable eating with me. Daniel was still trying to work me out.

I picked up a small, round wooden box that contained brie. The label had the Pemberton Crest on it and I traced my finger over the familiar insignia. This was Will's cheese made with the milk from Will's cows.

Now, there was a man I couldn't work out.

I couldn't deny the attraction I felt towards him, but he seemed to be giving off mixed signals. He was so cold and standoffish most of the time, but then there was that rare occasion when the spark between us could set us both on fire. I didn't know what the hell was going on.

"Are you going to eat that or just admire it?" Scott asked, nodding towards the cheese I still held in my hand.

I poked my tongue out at him and then cracked the seal. I sliced off a generous portion and smooshed it onto a cracker before popping it in my mouth. I moaned as the creamy *fromage* melted on my tongue.

"This has got to be the best cheese I have ever tasted," I mumbled with my mouth full as I reached for another cracker.

Scott had his eyes closed as he chewed on his mouthful. He swallowed and savoured the taste for a moment before opening his eyes. "You're not wrong," he said.

"Daniel," I said, "You have to taste this."

"Thank you, Your Majesty, but I am quite well acquainted with Lord Darkly's cheese."

"That's right," I said, "You haven't been living in cheese exile like I have. Seriously, who thought cheese in a can was a good thing?"

Scott chuckled as he stuffed another cracker into his mouth, "It's not that bad," he said and I raised my eyebrows at him, "Well, it's not *cheese*, but as a totally unrelated product, it's not bad."

"I'm going to try and forget that you said that," I remark haughtily. There was no way I was going to rank *cheese in a can* anywhere on the same scale as what I was currently eating.

Okay, admittedly, I was a cheese snob. It's hard not to be when you were raised in a country that produces the perfect milk for making cheese. I was also a chocolate snob and I was proud of it. You couldn't tell me that your garden variety chocolate block can compare to Swiss or Belgian chocolate. Even better than those two chocolates was the one that was made here in Merveille, Ashby Chocolates. I tried not to eat too much of either chocolate or cheese, so when I did indulge, I wanted only the best.

And this Pemberton Brie was definitely the best I had ever had.

"Daniel," I said, "What do you know about Pemberton Cheese?"

Daniel crossed his massive arms over his chest and stood with his legs shoulder width apart, staring me down.

"Carlos could probably tell you more," he said, "He and Prince Jacob spent a lot of time with Lord Darkly."

It was an uncomfortable reminder that Jacob was gone and I hadn't even gotten a chance to say goodbye. Maybe Will's coldness had more to do with his grief than with me.

I swallowed the rest of the food in my mouth and then packed away the detritus. I scrawled a note to Chef so that he wouldn't kill one of his staff when he discovered the remains of my midnight snack. Scott and Daniel waited out in the dark hall so that they could let their eyes adjust while I wiped down the bench.

I would be burying my father tomorrow and here I was snacking in the middle of the night like everything was normal. I felt guilty, like I was doing something wrong by enjoying an indulgence when my father and my brother would never be able to do the same again.

Would it always be like this? Would I always feel this guilt for living when their lives had been cut so drastically short?

CHAPTER 5

THE wind whipped at my wool coat and pulled at the umbrella Benjamin held over my head as we stood in the cemetery and watched my father's body be entombed in the family crypt. Scores of St. Benét monarchs were interred here and the next day they would get another one.

I gripped Jordan's hand and felt the warmth of it through my glove. He had stood by me during the funeral and had spoken eloquent and beautiful words about my father and now he was again by my side lending me his strength to get through this awful day.

And it was a truly awful day. The sky was heavy with the steel wool clouds of a thunder storm and the wind was icy cold as it blew down from the Alps. The temperature had dipped low and I was freezing through my many layers. They were predicting a fall of snow, not unheard of for April but definitely not a regular occurrence.

The ceremony in the cathedral had been long and solemn, as it should be when a king has passed, and the weather had certainly added to the depressing atmosphere. The wake that would be held in a few hours was supposed to be a celebration of my father's life, but at this moment I couldn't imagine ever smiling again.

The mausoleum closed with an ominous boom and I held back a

sob. I stood for a moment, staring up at the imposing grey stone building and thought about my own mortality. This, too, would be my final resting place and I wondered what my legacy would be. My father was a beloved king who had been known for his compassion and benevolence. My brother had been known for his loyalty and friendliness. He would've made an exemplary king. But what would I be known for? The fact was, the people of Merveille knew very little about me and that was the way I liked it. Except now everything had changed and I was going to have to let go of my privacy in order to step into my father's shoes.

Jordan turned and began to walk back towards the car, his fingers letting go of mine as I remained where I was. Benjamin turned also and in doing so removed the protection of the umbrella. A gust of wind buffeted me, swirling around me and getting under the brim of my hat, forcing it from my head and blowing it away. I reached for it, but was too late, so I turned to follow it and came face-to-face with Will who had plucked my hat out of the air.

His face was etched in grief as he handed it to me and I had the disturbing desire to burrow into his chest and have his arms wrap around me. I may have even leaned toward him before I came to my senses. I took the hat from his outstretched hand, my hair tossed medusa-like around my head as the wind tore it from its pins.

"Thank you," I said, looking up into his blue eyes.

He nodded to me, his mouth turned down and his brow furrowed. We looked at each other for a moment that stretched into two and then three before the spell was broken by Jordan taking my hand.

"Come along Alyssa," he said, "You must be freezing."

Will turned without speaking to me and stalked away, leaving me to look at his retreating back and wonder what I had done to injure him so.

"Don't worry about him," Jordan remarked as he looked to where I was gazing, "He has always been a surly kind of fellow and it has only gotten worse since his father drank the family fortune."

I let Jordan usher me to the car, grateful for its enveloping warmth. All I wanted was to go home, have a hot bath and crawl into bed, but I still had a wake to host. I dropped my head back against the seat and closed my eyes as the limousine glided through the cemetery and back out into the streets of Calanais. I was thankful for Jordan's silence and his comforting hand holding mine.

I don't know what I would've done without his presence. Normally it would've been Meredith propping me up, but due to the increased security risk she had been tasked somewhere else. Jordan's military background had meant that he could step in and be extra protection if need be.

He gently squeezed my hand, alerting me to our arrival at the palace. I lifted my head, opened my eyes and gave him a small smile of appreciation. The car came to a stop under the portico and my door was opened. I was helped out by the doorman and Jordan joined me, taking my elbow to escort me inside.

The large front doors stood open and were flanked by both security and footman. One of my lady's maids stood by to take my coat and gloves, while another one fussed with my unruly, windswept hair. With another coat of lipstick and a dusting of powder on my nose, I was released to face my waiting guests. My steps echoed on the marble tiles as we walked toward the room where the wake would be held. I took a deep breath, sliding my public façade into place as the doors opened and my arrival was announced.

Walking into the room was eerily similar to the previous night's reception, except everyone wore black and the mood was quite a bit more sombre. I just wanted it to be over, I just wanted a minute to myself. But instead I greeted and glad-handed the titled and the landed and the close personal friends of my father's. I looked up at Jordan and pleaded with my eyes.

"Drink?" he asked in a whisper, to which I nodded.

"Something stronger than wine," I whispered back.

Aiden stepped up to take Jordan's place at my side as I continued into the room. The sentiments and sympathies offered to me were a blur and just when I thought I could not stand another moment a cool glass was pressed into my hands.

I sipped it gratefully tasting a very good craft ale. I looked up to thank Jordan, but it was Will standing in front of me. He also held a small plate of canapés, an assortment of crackers and different cheeses.

"You seemed to enjoy the one you tried last night," he said haltingly, "I thought you might like to try the rest of our range."

"You produce all these?" I asked as I selected a creamy blue vein.

"Yes," he replied.

"I saw your cows," I said before biting into the cracker. "Oh my, this is divine," I mumbled.

One side of his mouth quirked up quickly before returning to its previous downward position.

"Darkly," Jordan said as he arrived with a glass of what looked like scotch. He smiled, but it didn't reach his eyes. "I see you found a drink in my absence," he said nodding at my glass.

"Yes," I replied swallowing the canapé and reaching for another, "Will brought it to me."

Jordan's lips thinned as he pressed them together. Will handed the plate of canapés to Aiden and bowed to me before walking away, once again leaving me to watch his retreating back.

"JACOB WAS LIKE A BROTHER TO ME," WILL'S DEEP VOICE FILLED THE cathedral as he stood at the podium to deliver his speech. "We grew up together, spending many hours exploring the wonders of our beautiful countryside. He loved Merveille and everything it had to offer. He would have been a wonderful king had he been given the chance." I watched his Adam's apple bob as he swallowed harshly and felt my eyes fill with unshed tears. "Jacob stood by me when I lost my mother and then again when I lost my father. He was there through all the many trials that I fought in the aftermath. His loyalty was unsurpassed and I treasured his friendship above all others. I will miss him greatly, as I'm sure we all will. Today we bury a man who could very well have been the best king this country has ever seen and we are poorer for the fact."

I could tell how much it cost him to speak without breaking down and my eyes tracked him as he stood down from the podium and returned to his seat. A pretty blonde woman embraced him fiercely and he wrapped his arms around her in return. The sight irritated me and I tore my eyes away and turned back to the front.

I tuned out the rest of the service, knowing that the words spoken now would not bring my brother back to me or bring the crown prince back to Merveille. My spirit was low and I did not know how it would be possible for me to go on beyond this day.

There were so many expectations on me that had never been there before. How on earth did Jacob stand it? I'd had my future pretty much mapped out and now it was all gone. I hadn't asked to be born into a royal family and I hadn't asked to be thrust into this position of heir apparent, queen in waiting. Nobody had asked my opinion on any of this, but I was expected to walk away from what I had dreamed of for my life to live the dreams of someone else.

I grit my teeth as I listened to the empty platitudes of nobles who could care less about my grief and suffering. All any of these people cared about was how it affected them and their future; nobody spared a thought for the reluctant princess.

Intellectually I knew the angry thoughts that circulated my brain were part of the grieving process, but that didn't help to dampen the ire. I was angry. I was angry because just about every other person in this chapel, in this town and in this country got to choose their own destiny. But not me. I had no say in the matter. With the careless decision of someone to wipe out half of my immediate family they had taken away my choice.

My fists clenched into hard balls at my side and my posture was rigid as I sat surrounded by selfish, entitled morons. I knew that as soon as the official mourning period was over, their sickeningly sweet smiles and empty platitudes would turn to snide remarks and back stabbing. I may be inexperienced in court machinations, but I wasn't blind to them.

The problem with the way our government was run was that every member was there with their own agenda. The four year term of office meant that government only planned for things they could get done within the timeframe. It was shortsighted and did our country no favours.

In the same vein the nobility of our country, for the most part, were only in it for what they could get out of it. I'm sure there were peers that did seek to do some good with the privilege they had been afforded, but there were far too few of them. Money had become synonymous with power and the nobles fought over it just as mightily as starving beggars in the streets. The nobility were only dressed better.

The congregation stood to sing a final hymn and it broke me out of my fast spiralling hate-fest, not exactly the most appropriate thing to be ruminating over at my own brother's funeral. I unclenched my hands and let the tension fall from my shoulders as I stood with everyone else and sang of the amazing grace of our Lord.

If my brother could read my thoughts from his throne in heaven, I have no doubt that he was laughing his backside off. He loved the intrigue of the court, thrived on the political manoeuvrings of Parliament and adored the showmanship of his title. He had often riled me up about the politics of our country just for sport and I was sure he would have found my ugly thoughts entertaining. It made me smile, in a way, and was probably a fitting tribute to him.

Jordan moved away from my side to take his place as pallbearer, as did Will, Carlos and several other of Jacob's friends. I held my mother's hand as we followed the casket down the long aisle of the grand the Cathédrale Saint-Etienne de Calanais as the organ played and the choir sang. I had done this walk twice in two days and I would be glad to never grace the footsteps of this place again.

As the casket was loaded into the hearse for its scenic trip through the city, past all of the grieving subjects and on to the mausoleum where we so recently laid my father to rest, I made a promise to Jacob. I would rule where he could not. I would take up his mantel and his birthright and step into his shoes to fulfil the promise he could not. And I would leave a legacy that not only would he and father be proud of, but so too the many St. Benét's to come after me.

I STARED AT THE CEILING OF MY BEDROOM AND WONDERED WHY IT was that on the first day that I'd had that I could actually sleep in, I was awake before the sun was even up. Today was the official start of the palace's mourning period. It would last three months for me, six months for my mother. I would be required to wear black and to stay within the confines of the palace as much as possible. There would be no outside visitors, no visiting heads of state and no engagements, royal or other. I was pretty much grounded.

That didn't mean I got to be a lady of leisure though, despite what the public might think. This was a time of metamorphosis for me as I changed from the child princess into the queen. The coronation would be held at the end of my mother's mourning period and I had a lot to do if I wanted to ensure my crown and my throne were secure.

But today was a rare day off. I could stay abed if I so desired and order food to be brought to my room like I was ensconced in a fancy hotel. But instead, I was restless and I couldn't sleep. I threw the heavy covers back and switched on my bedside lamp. The door opened and Scott stuck his head inside to see what was happening.

"I'm going for a run," I said to his unasked question, "Can you see if Meredith's awake?"

He nodded and pulled the door closed. I knew that they would wake her if she wasn't already awake and I wasn't the least bit perturbed by it. I needed to run and think and talk and she was my preferred partner in all of those activities. Besides, I'm pretty sure she wouldn't mind.

The door opened again as I was lacing up my runners and she stuck her head in.

"Ready?" she asked and I nodded.

As per Von Bartham's instructions, since I was going running in the palace grounds, I had four guards accompanying me. Luckily they knew me well enough to stay back and let me have some quiet time with Meredith.

We didn't speak at first as we ran. The monotonous sound of our pounding steps in the foggy, barely light morning had a calming effect on me and almost lulled me into a sense of being alone. I know my security detail did their best to stay unobtrusive, but I always knew they were there. It was an odd feeling to be watched constantly and I didn't really know what it would feel like to be completely on my own.

I've heard it said that the English Queen Victoria's first request as queen was to have an hour of absolute solitude. Up until that point in her life, she had been watched constantly. I understood her desire and had begun to think I might make the exact same request myself.

There was something to be said of those English queens and I could probably learn a lot from them. Unlike my own ancestors, Elizabeth I, Victoria and Elizabeth II had all become queens in their own right and not through marriage. The first Elizabeth had to fight for hers and Victoria had a remarkable influence over the government of her time. Elizabeth II stood the test of time and survived scandals, caused by her offspring, to remain a well-loved queen who showed the utmost dignity in all she did. Yes, I could definitely learn something from them.

The promise I made to my brother weighed heavy on me. I was determined to step into his shoes, but I really had no idea where to start. He was naturally charismatic and charming and I had spent the better part of my life hiding from the public. I knew I could hold my own in conversation and could probably fumble my way through a sitting of Parliament without embarrassing myself, but I had no idea how to charm the snakes that waited for me in the grass.

I was not exactly subtle... more like a bull in a china shop. My brother, on the other hand, seemed to have a delicate touch. I had strong opinions and when challenged I was not too shy to stand on my soapbox and proclaim them to anyone and everyone. Not exactly the best way to win over a politician who excelled at double-speak and plausible deniability. I was honest to a fault and had a habit of speaking my mind without thinking first.

Thus far my breeding and extensive training in etiquette had saved me from putting my foot in it, but I knew that wouldn't last for long. For the moment I was off kilter and not thinking clearly, but as soon as I found my feet, I would have to work extra hard to keep my mouth shut. I needed to find allies, not alienate people.

We rounded the palace and I noticed a white van parked in the loading dock. A familiar figure helped to unload boxes from the back of the van and I saw one of the chefs shake his hand as he took the last box and turned to go inside.

Will turned to get back into his truck and our eyes met. I lifted my chin in greeting, but he didn't return the gesture. In fact, he didn't move at all. He just stood there and watched us run past with an unreadable expression on his face. I didn't know what to make of the man who was once such a close friend of my brother's. He looked at me like I was beneath him and yet he had shown me kindness in the most unexpected ways. His gaze did things to me and his touch ignited my veins, but then his cool manner and standoffish demeanour sent back off signals to me. He had me completely flummoxed and more than anything, that irritated me.

CHAPTER 6

"**E**XCUSE me Alyssa," Alex said as she came into my office.

I looked up from my laptop, "What's up?"

"You have a visitor."

I sat back in my chair and stretched. It had been a week since the official mourning period began and my days had consisted of little else except running, sparring with Meredith and reading though all of the dry-as-dirt constitutional folderol that I would need to know to dazzle Parliament.

So far I hadn't found anything that forbid me from becoming queen, but I couldn't help but think that the old-boys-club that was our current sitting Parliament had something up their sleeve.

"I'm not allowed visitors," I replied when it finally registered what she had said to me.

She smiled, "Oh, I think this one will be allowed." She stepped to the side and I noticed Jordan standing behind her.

He walked into the room and his tall, well-built frame draped in his military uniform looked out of place in the soft, feminine space that was my office.

"Good morning Your Grace," he said formally and bowed, "I'm here to steal you away for lunch."

I grinned up at him as he stood once again, "As much as that sounds like a wonderful idea," I said, "I don't think I'm allowed to go to lunch with you."

"Ah," he said, holding up a finger, "I think I have found a loop-hole in the requirements for your mourning period."

"Do tell."

"Well, the rules state that you aren't to have any 'outside' visitors. I am not an outside visitor. I live on the grounds and I work in the palace. Second, you're not allowed to leave the palace grounds, but that doesn't mean I can't take you for a picnic within the boundaries. So what do you say?"

He was technically correct. Having lunch with him would be no different to having lunch with my ladies in waiting or Alex or Meredith. But I knew that there were detractors in Parliament who would look for any opportunity to oppose my accession. Having a picnic lunch with Jordan could come across as ignoring the protocols of mourning.

"I don't know..." I said.

"Come on," he cajoled, "If you're worried, I can grab some folders from my office to make it look like a business lunch."

I bit the corner of my mouth in indecision. I wanted to go. I really liked Jordan and liked spending time with him, but I really couldn't afford anything that could be misconstrued. Ah, what the hell? Why not?

"No, don't bother," I said standing and shutting the lid on my laptop, "Let's go. I desperately need a change of scenery."

He offered me his elbow as he escorted me out of my office and into Alex's. There, he picked up a large wicker basket with a tartan blanket sitting on top and we headed out to the elevator, my security detail of two following discreetly.

"You were pretty sure of yourself," I said, indicating the basket.

He shrugged, "If I couldn't entice you outside then I would've set it up in your office."

"What if I'd said no to lunch altogether?" I asked.

He just grinned at me and was saved from answering by the elevator doors opening.

He led me through the hallways until we reached the back door, which led out onto a large stone patio. I stopped and took a deep breath of the clean, crisp air. The sun was shining and the sky was blue; it was the perfect day for a picnic.

There were two golf carts waiting for us as well as two more body guards, as per Von Bartham's request that I have four whenever I stepped outside. Jordan led me to the first and secured the picnic basket on the rear seat while I climbed in the front. The four security team members climbed into the second cart and we set off across the lawn in a weird looking motorcade. I had to restrain myself from laughing at the four bulky men squeezed into the one golf cart. It looked like a clown car, only the clowns were wearing Armani suits and were packing heat.

Jordan drove us to a reasonably secluded spot that overlooked Lac Merveilleux. The large expanse of water was still, reflecting the mountains that sat on the other side of it like a mirror. I took a moment to stand and just look, appreciating the natural beauty of the place I had, at some point, begun to take for granted. Did everyone become so blind to the amazing and beautiful things if they were surrounded by them all the time? Being in the States for so long, I had forgotten what was essentially right on my doorstep for most of my life. As I stood there now and took it all in, I promised myself that I would never forget again.

Jordan spread the blanket out and began removing the food. He must have planned this with Chef in advance because I saw all of my favourite things on the menu. Including Will's incredible cheeses.

I sat beside Jordan and sighed, feeling my muscles relax and the tension in my neck and shoulders ease as I leant back on my elbows.

"Now," he said, holding up an empty plate, "What can I get for you?"

"A bit of everything," I said with a laugh realising just how hungry I was.

Jordan started piling the plate with generous servings. By the time he handed it to me, it was covered by a small mound and, as hungry as I was, I didn't know if I could actually eat it all. I sat up and took the plate from him with the proffered fork while he began to fill his own plate.

I snagged a piece of cheese off the top and put it in my mouth, savouring the creamy taste on my tongue. I moaned appreciatively.

"God, I love this cheese," I mumbled.

"Meh," Jordan said with a shrug, "It's okay, I guess."

"Okay?" I said, surprised by his lack of enthusiasm for this ambrosia, "How can you be so dismissive of it?"

He chewed thoughtfully for a bit before swallowing to answer me.

"I suppose I am a little prejudiced," he said, "Will and I, well, we had a falling out."

"Really?" I said, completely surprised by his admission, although the animosity between them now made sense. "What happened?"

"I don't want to speak ill of him," Jordan said, "But since he lost the family's fortune, he hasn't been the same."

"I don't understand," I said. When had Will lost his family's money and how? "How did that happen?"

Jordan sighed and I could tell he was reluctant to tell me the story.

"After Will's mother died, his dad kind of spiralled. He started drinking heavily and the business suffered. Will was away at university, so I helped where I could, but they were haemorrhaging money and there was nothing I could do to stop it."

I covered my mouth with my hand as I gasped, "Oh my God. I had no idea."

"By the time Will returned, his father was too sick to work and there wasn't much left of the business. I was dating Georgina at the time and I tried to explain to Will that we had done what we could, but he completely lost it. He ran me off and forbid me to see Georgina again and accused me of all sorts of horrible things. His father died a few months later and Will took over the farm and the business."

"Oh Jordan," I said, laying my hand over his, "I'm so sorry. Were you...were you in love with her?"

He smiled sadly, "Georgie will always be special to me, but it was three years ago and I've moved on. I'm sure she has too."

"Will must be doing well now, though," I said, "His cheese business must be booming."

"Maybe," Jordan said, "But his father had accumulated a lot of debts. I wouldn't be surprised if Will was barely making ends meet."

JORDAN TOOK ME BACK TO THE PALACE AFTER LUNCH, BUT WENT TO his own office rather than riding the elevator back with me. Lunch had been nice and it was great to have a break from the monotony that'd become my life.

Carlos and Aiden rode the elevator with me, being my two inside-the-palace security detail today. I hadn't spent much time with Carlos and from what Von Bartham had told me, he was one of Jacob's most dedicated men. He frightened me a bit and seemed to look at me with contempt and I had no idea why.

As we walked back into the office, they both stopped outside the door between mine and Alex's rooms to give me some semblance of privacy. But I needed to get to the bottom of whatever it was that had Carlos so upset. I couldn't have him on my team if I didn't feel comfortable around him.

"Carlos," I said before stepping over the threshold into my office, "Can I have a minute?"

He clenched his jaw and nodded, following me in.

When the door had closed, I indicated for him to take a seat on the sofa set beside the window. He perched on the very edge like the floral fabric might somehow drain the masculinity out of his body. I settled myself opposite him and took in his tight shoulders and erect posture.

"You don't seem to like me very much," I said and he blanched.

"No, that's not true at all," he said. His voice was deep, almost baritone, and it suited his dark chocolate complexion and very large body.

"Then what is it?" I asked, "Do you disapprove of me becoming queen?"

"Not at all, Your Highness," he said, "I think you will be a wonderful queen."

"Are you unhappy being assigned to me for some reason?" I asked feeling like I was interrogating him.

He shook his head, "I requested this assignment," he replied.

"So what is it then?" I asked, feeling frustrated with his tightlipped answers.

He clenched his jaw again and looked over my shoulder. I waited him out. I needed to know what was going on with him.

"May I speak frankly, Your Highness?" he asked, resigned.

"Please."

He exhaled harshly, "I don't like some of the company you keep," he finally said.

"Oh?" I raised my eyebrow in question.

"I don't mean to offend you," he said, "But I don't trust Lieutenant Wicks, Your Grace."

"Jordan?" I was shocked. "I have known him practically my whole life. He was one of Jacob's closest friends."

He swallowed hard at the mention of Jacob, but then his expression turned to stone.

"Maybe he was once," Carlos said, "But they hadn't been on speaking terms for a while."

I sat back in the armchair and looked at him with surprise.

"Really? I had no idea. Jordan hasn't said anything."

"Maybe not, Your Highness, but I know that Jac...His Royal Highness hadn't seen Lieutenant Wicks for three years or more."

"He was out of the country," I said, making an excuse for Jordan, but not knowing why I felt the need to.

"Yes, Your Grace, he was, but he was home plenty of times too."

It didn't make any sense.

"They hadn't even been in the same proximity for months until the hunt."

"Jordan was on the hunt?" I asked, breathless.

"Yes, Your Highness. Jacob, I mean, Prince Jacob wasn't very happy to see him either."

"But why? Do you know what happened between them?"

"No, Your Highness, I don't. I just know that Lieutenant Wicks was *persona non grata* around the prince."

I sucked my bottom lip into my mouth and tried to sort out the mess in my head. What could have possibly happened between the two friends? I'd thought it strange when Jordan had told me that he and

Will had had a falling out, but to find out that he and Jacob had as well was doing my head in.

"What about Lord Darkly?" I asked, "Was Jacob still speaking to him?"

"Yes, Your Highness," Carlos replied, "They had a standing appointment every week and Prince Jacob never missed it."

So maybe Jacob had taken Will's side in the argument he'd had with Jordan, but that didn't make sense. Why would Jacob do that? It had nothing to do with him, and if anything, Will had been in the wrong. So why remain Will's friend but not Jordan's?

"Thank you Carlos," I said, standing.

"Yes Your Highness," he replied, standing also.

"Is it going to be a problem for you to be on my team if I continue to socialise with Lieutenant Wicks?" I asked.

His jaw worked and his eyes hardened, but he shook his head, "No, Your Highness," he replied.

I reached out and laid a hand on his forearm. "I know you and Jacob were close," I said, "And I know how hard this must be for you at this time. If you need some time off..."

He shook his head, "No Your Highness, I don't. The prince and I were close and I am devastated that he is gone, but I want to be here. I don't want to frighten you, but I don't believe that what happened to the prince was an accident and it would be remiss of me to think that there is no longer a threat to the crown. Until we know what really happened on the hunt, I need to be here, close to you. I think you're in danger and I want to do for you what I couldn't do for your brother."

He bowed and then turned and left the room leaving me feeling off-kilter. On top of everything else, was my life in danger too?

I COULDN'T CONCENTRATE ON THE CONSTITUTIONAL READING I'D been doing and instead found myself staring out the window. I just couldn't reconcile Carlos' story with what I knew of Jacob and Jordan. Will had always been a bit of a hot head, so I could understand that, under the influence of grief, he might have said some things to Jordan that he shouldn't've, but that didn't explain why Jacob had cut Jordan off too.

But maybe Carlos had it wrong. Maybe it was simply friends growing apart or the fact that Jordan had been gone for so long and with Jacob's increased responsibilities the time needed to maintain the friendship was not there.

Whatever it was, it wasn't helping me learn the ins and outs of the constitution.

I stood from my chair and walked into the outer office where Alex was hard at work.

"I'm going for a ride," I said to her.

"Okay," she replied. "Is everything okay?" she asked looking up at me.

I shrugged, "Yeah, I just can't stand to read that crap anymore. I'm brain fried."

I gave her a wave and headed for my bedroom so that I could change. I really wanted to pull on my Levi's, but they weren't black, so instead I pulled on a pair of black jodhpurs and a black t-shirt followed by my riding boots. I beelined for the stables and wasn't surprised to find Monty saddled and waiting for me. The big bay gelding had been Jacob's and the moment I had laid eyes on him the other day I'd fallen in love. He was a gentle giant with a smooth gait and lots of power in his hindquarters.

I nodded to Cliff, the Master of Horse. "Did Alex call down to let you know I was coming?" I asked.

"She sure did, princess," he replied, "And I know how much you enjoyed riding Monty t'other day. He's been a bit off his feed, probably missin' the prince like the rest of us. A run'll do 'im good."

"Thanks Cliff," I said and boosted myself up into the saddle, not waiting for anyone to give me a hand up. I turned to my body guards, "Are you guys coming?"

"Benjamin's bringing the ATVs," Aiden replied, "We'll follow behind with him and Jamie."

I gave them a nod and then nudged Monty into a trot out of the stable yard. Once we were past the buildings and out into the paddocks proper, I gave Monty his head, not really caring where we ended up. I could hear the ATVs in the distance behind me and was glad that they weren't riding alongside of me, at least this way, I was kind of alone.

The clear, crisp air filled my lungs and tugged at my clothes and hair as we galloped through the lush green grass. Here and there I spotted some early wildflowers blooming amongst the long blades. The sight of the unfamiliar cows on another rise caught my attention and I headed in their direction.

I halted near the small herd and dismounted, tying Monty's reins around his neck so he wouldn't tread on them. I gingerly approached one of the cows and it lifted its head to look at me with large brown eyes. They were quite cute, these Pemberton Jerseys with their pale caramel coat and soft faces. They were small, though, smaller than the Merveille Guernsey. What I had taken for calves, were in fact adult cows, with very full udders.

"Moo," the cow mewled at me and ambled closer.

I heard the ATVs approach and then the engine cut. "Are you okay Aurora?" asked Benjamin.

"I'm fine," I yelled back, "But are these our cows? I didn't know we owned any of Will's breed."

Benjamin was beside me when he answered, "No, we don't. They must have escaped their paddock."

Benjamin cocked his head and before I could make sense of what he heard, I was surrounded by four very large, very hostile men, their backs towards me as the circled me for protection. That's when I heard the approaching ATV.

"Lord Darkly, is that you?" Benjamin called when the ATV had cut its motor.

"It is," I heard Will reply.

"Please stay where you are," Benjamin continued, "And state your business."

"I was doing a fence inspection and found a hole. I came to get my cows."

"Did you notify the palace that you would be crossing the boundary?" Benjamin asked.

"I did," Will replied, "They gave me authorisation number F7982J."

"Thank you Lord Darkly," Benjamin replied, "Would you mind waiting there while we remove the princess."

"Stop it Benjamin," I said, fed up with this overly formal crap. "I'd like to say hello to Lord Darkly. I have some questions about his cows."

"Your Highness, it is highly irregular for you to..."

"Oh, quit it," I huffed, "Just let me talk to Will." I didn't wait for them to move and just started pushing my way through their shoulders, but they were like brick walls and refused to budge.

"If you are not going to let me out, then I'd still like to ask Will some questions," I groused.

"I can hear you just fine from there," Will called to me, "What would you like to know?"

"Your cows are a bit on the small side," I said, "Any reason for that?"

"Yeah, I bred them that way. They eat less and need less space, but they still yield a good amount of milk."

"So lower overhead costs?"

"Definitely. And they're a good size for a small hobby farmer."

I tried to get a peek of Will from between Aiden and Carlos' shoulders. He was wearing dirty jeans that sat low on his hips and a dirty white t-shirt that fit him snugly, revealing muscles that I didn't know he had. Over the t-shirt was an open plaid shirt, the sleeves of which were rolled up to the elbows, leaving his well-defined forearms bare. He also had a hat on his head, like a real American cowboy, and I felt my face flush as I was assaulted by Meredith's cowboy fantasies.

"Are they descended from our Merveille Guernsey?" I asked, wanting to prolong the conversation. My voice sounded strange to my ears, breathy and low.

"Not exactly," he replied, and I caught the brief flash of white teeth as he smiled. "But I can't go giving away all my secrets." His voice was also low and I closed my eyes as it washed over me, imagining him whispering all his secrets in my ear as he kissed me. I shuddered with anticipation, my entire body breaking out in goosebumps.

These were the most words I'd heard Will say in over ten years and he actually sounded relaxed, playful even. The few times we'd met over the last couple of weeks he had been stiff and cold, but this Will sounded like the guy I had known all those years ago and I didn't want this moment to end.

"If that's all the questions for now, princess, I really need to get these ladies back to the milking shed."

"Of course," I said, disappointed, "Thanks for the talk."

"My pleasure," he said softly and it sent an irrational thrill through me. I tapped Benjamin on the shoulder, "Can I get back on my horse now?"

"Lord Darkly would you mind terribly turning your back so the princess can mount her horse?"

"Are you kidding me Benjamin?" I hissed.

"You are in an official mourning period and no one outside the palace is to lay eyes on you," Benjamin hissed back.

"It's okay, princess," Will called, "I don't mind."

My face flamed with embarrassment, anyone would think I was naked or something! As soon as I was able, I ran for Monty and swung up onto his back, kicking him into a gallop to get as far away from there as possible.

CHAPTER 7

OVER the next ten weeks, my life fell into a predictable rhythm. I woke early for a run, and I'd be lying if I said my motives were pure. I was hoping to get another glimpse of Will delivering the palace's order of cheeses, but no such luck. Because of the mourning period that was enforced on the castle, no more deliveries were made. Instead, the kitchen staff took a van into the city to pick up what they needed.

After my run, I sparred with Meredith. I hadn't yet tempted any of the other guards to spar with me, but I thought I'd begun to wear Jamie down. Each time I challenged him, I could tell he was a little closer to giving in. Carlos remained standoffish, but he no longer looked at me like something he'd have to scrape off his shoe. I hoped that seeing me hold my own against Meredith lifted his opinion of me. I wasn't, and never had been, a pampered princess and I didn't intend to be a pampered queen.

Alex was a dream assistant. The woman was so organised I suspected she colour coded her underwear drawer. She was also a whiz at research and had been helping me learn the finer points of the constitution as I armed myself against the fight with Parliament that I knew was coming.

Savannah, meanwhile, had appointed herself my personal stylist. Because I was neither allowed to leave the palace nor have any one come to see me, she had begun taking trips, with Margaret in tow, to meet with designers and order a new wardrobe for me. She had also decided to clean out my current wardrobe and I'd had to hide my favourite Levi's to ensure they didn't get thrown out. I actually had to snatch them from the pile she had declared unsuitable for a future queen.

Once a week I had a fitting with her and she had turned it into a girls' night where I would model all my new outfits for her and the rest of my ladies in waiting and then we would drink cocktails and eat nibbles (of which Will's cheeses played a large part) and watch chick flicks. Even my two lady's maids had become part of the group. Bridgette was a gifted hairstylist and Annette a magician with makeup.

Jordan had continued to visit me and we had a standing lunch date every Wednesday. Each time he took me to a different part of the palace or the grounds to enjoy a wonderful meal prepared by Chef. We had become close friends and Carlos' warning about him faded from my mind as I became very comfortable around Jordan. Our relationship was easy; we didn't argue and seemed to have similar views on politics and international events. He was knowledgeable and a great conversationalist and I treasured the time we had together. I began to think of what it would be like to have him as my consort when I became queen and it wasn't awful. There wasn't the strange electricity between us like I felt when I was near Will, but I was attracted to him and looked forward to feeling his hand in mine or his fingers pressed into the small of my back as he guided me to our latest lunch venue.

It had become such that each Wednesday I took more care with my appearance. It was the one day when I asked Bridgette to do my hair and Annette to do my makeup. Jordan noticed and complimented me, which caused me to blush, but I was secretly thrilled each time. Both Alex and Meredith had noticed. I could tell by their shared looks, but neither commented, for which I was glad. I didn't know what was happening between us, but I wanted to keep it protected for the time being.

But it wasn't all fun and games. I had regular security updates to be advised on the progress of the investigation into my father's and brother's deaths. I also sat in on reports of national security and any relevant international situations that could have an effect on us. And then there was my royal apprenticeship. This was usually a two-year program to acquaint the incoming king of his duties. My brother had been eighteen months into his when he died. I had six months to complete it.

The Lord Chancellor, Dominique Furore, had been appointed to my brother to advise him through the transition from prince to king, and was now my almost-constant companion. He was younger than I had expected, being only three years older than me and the same age as my brother. But he knew everything there was to know about ruling our country and had been training for his position for seven years before he had been assigned to Jacob.

And he didn't like me.

I don't know what I had done to put him offside, but from the moment he came into my life, he had made it his job to make mine miserable. I could not do anything to please the guy. He was churlish and bossy and I was yet to make him smile. I was beginning to hate him.

Luckily, I had Priscilla with me whenever he was around. Priscilla was my advisor on issues of protocol and Dominique seemed to like her, although it was hard to tell when the man never smiled. At least he approved of her and her impeccable manners. Her job was to refine me and teach me the minute details of interacting with other royals and dignitaries. I found it all rather boring and outdated, but on this point both Dominique and Priscilla were in agreement; it was essential for me to observe the traditions of the court in order to secure my crown. When I was queen, I could chose to change those traditions which I disliked.

I really didn't see the point of people having to walk backwards out of my presence or them having to stop eating their meal just because I was finished mine. It all seemed kind of ridiculous. And would I really cause an international incident if I seated the wrong people together? Or spoke to the person on my left first instead of the person on my right? It was all these little unspoken rules that had made me want to flee the court in the first place. But now I was knee deep in it and I had no choice but to learn all I could.

THE DAY THAT SIGNIFIED THE END OF MY OFFICIAL MOURNING period dawned like any other day. I ran with my security detail, sparred with Meredith, showered and dressed as usual. In fact by the time I stepped into my office, I had forgotten that it was actually my first day of freedom in three months.

By nine a.m. however, I was more than aware that things had changed. It started by a visit from the prime minister's aide with a summons to attend the sitting of Parliament in a week. Whether it was proper protocol for Parliament to summon me thus, I left to Dominique and Priscilla to fight over. I was rather offended by the coldness of it though. It almost felt like a subpoena rather than an invitation to the future head of state and I had to wonder what political manoeuvring had been done in the time I had been sequestered in the palace. Being out of the public eye for three months had definitely put me at a disadvantage.

After the arrival of Parliament's gilt edged invitation, a flurry of others also arrived. It seemed every man, woman and child wanted an audience with the queen in waiting. Alex was in her element as she sorted through the mountain of engraved mail, no doubt she would have a detailed spreadsheet to me by the end of the day with every request she received. They would no doubt be ranked by importance and probably even colour-coded.

I couldn't help feeling like a prized pig to be trotted out for inspection by the masses. I had never been interested in celebrity gossip and couldn't understand why the people of my country would care what I wore or what I ate for breakfast. But, according to my social media guru, Jeanette, those were the two most asked questions on Twitter.

Before becoming queen in waiting, I hadn't even had a Twitter account. My personal Facebook page had been taken down and would be relaunched along with my new Twitter account @HRHAlyssabeth. I, of course, had no access to these and they would remain the purview of Jeanette. I had a mind to set up my own account, without their knowledge, and spoof the official one with inappropriate comments and retweets. My lack of access to a mobile phone, however, foiled my plan. I knew I could do it on my laptop, but that was monitored and I would be found out before I could have any real fun.

I don't know why I had suddenly become so outwardly rebellious, as it wasn't my normal MO. I was the type of person who liked to keep the status quo and not rock the boat. Sure, I'd stood up to my father and insisted I be allowed to study in the States; however, if he had really opposed it, I wouldn't have gone. I avoided confrontation whenever I could. Okay, so that wasn't *exactly* true. I quite enjoyed a spirited debate, especially when the subject was one I was passionate about. When it came to *actual* conflict, though, I was a big sissy.

Something about being forced to jump through all these hoops was igniting a resentment in me. I had no problem taking up the mantel of queen, if that was what was required of me. What really got to me was all the crap that went along with it. I hated all the pomp and circumstance that was synonymous with the role I was supposed to fulfil and it was why I had wanted to live my life in obscurity.

But obscurity was the furthest thing from my life now, starting with tonight. Tonight there was to be a ball that would act as the official commencement of my coronation. The next three months would be a montage of royal engagements, hosting foreign dignitaries, meeting with other heads of state and generally *being seen* by the people. I had been incognito for nearly ten years and now all that was about to change. I couldn't lead the people if they didn't know who I was.

A knock on my door interrupted my thoughts. I looked up and smiled at Jordan as he stood leaning casually against the door jam. Protocol regarding his visits had been relaxed due to the frequency of them and he no longer had to be announced before he came into my office.

"Jordan," I greeted him with a smile.

"Hello, princess," he replied, "How's your first day of freedom?"

I frowned, "It feels more like my first day of purgatory," I replied.

"Do you feel like getting out of here for a bit?" he asked, a mischievous glint in his eye.

I stood and walked toward him, "And by 'out of here' you mean?"

"Out of this office, out of the palace..." He smiled a charming smile as he let the words fade away and my stomach flopped over.

"You mean, leave the grounds?" I whispered.

He nodded and held out his hand to me. I looked down at my simple black pencil skirt and black shirt and knew I would have to change. I had put on my mourning clothes without even realising, but a trip to town would mean I would need to dress to impress. My first outing after mourning would be a press worthy event.

I took his hand in mine and let him draw me close to him. I inhaled the familiar spicy scent of his aftershave and felt the warmth of his body, even though only our hands touched.

"Give me an hour," I said.

My first call was to Savannah and then she gathered the others. We met in my room and she had already pulled out a selection of outfits for me to wear.

"You need to make a statement with this outing," she said, "What you wear today will be talked about for weeks and will set a precedent. All your other outfits will be judged by this one."

"It's only lunch," I replied, despondently. My enthusiasm for this lunch date was waning. If it had just been Jordan and I then I would be perfectly happy, but that's not what this was going to be.

"You can't really believe that this is a spontaneous date," Priscilla said, "Jordan and I have been in negotiations about this for weeks."

"And you didn't think to inform me?" I asked, cranky at the subterfuge. I'd thought Jordan had asked me to lunch because he liked me, not because it had been negotiated.

"Oh stop pouting," Meredith said as she slumped into a chair, "Did you really think Jordan could just waltz into your office and ask you out for lunch without having it approved by three different committees and your security detail?"

"So you knew too?" I turned on her accusingly, "Thanks Mer, I thought we were friends."

"Jordan asked us to keep it quiet. He wanted to surprise you." This from Margaret.

"Seriously? A little heads up would've been nice." I crossed my arms and sulked. These were supposed to be my girlfriends and I thought that they would be loyal to me.

"Focus, Lys," Savannah said, "What's done is done. Jordan wanted to surprise you and be the one to re-introduce you to the world. It's a major step in your relationship. Him being the first one to accompany you is like him staking his claim on you."

That didn't make me feel much better. I liked Jordan and I did want our relationship to progress, but I wanted it to be on my terms. I didn't want him making grand gestures that would be interpreted by the press as a relationship status update without discussing it with me first. Didn't I have a say in what I wanted to project to the media?

"Maybe I shouldn't go," I said, "Maybe it's too early to have my name linked with his."

"Too late," Jeanette said, "He mentioned your date in a tweet and it's gone viral. You have so many new followers, Twitter is practically blowing up."

"What?" I jumped to my feet in indignation, "What if I'd said no?"

She shrugged, "You didn't so it doesn't matter."

"Please Your Grace," Bridgette said, "Please sit so I can do your hair."

I sat with a huff and let Bridgette do her job, but I wasn't happy. What I thought was a date with the man I liked was turning into a three ring circus. Was this what my life was to be like from now on? Every step orchestrated and programmed for maximum effect?

The most disappointing thing of all was that I didn't think Jordan was into all that. I thought he was in agreement with me on flying under the radar. I did not think he would be the type to turn our simple, intimate lunch date into a media frenzy.

"Since you refuse to decide," Savannah said, "I choose this."

It was navy dress with a small white polka dot. Loose, flowing skirt with a pleated halter neck and pussy cat bow. It was chic and elegant and conservative. It was perfect. She paired it with strappy white sandals and a gorgeous wide brimmed hat. But the excitement had gone out of the day and I couldn't appreciate any of it.

Jordan met me on the front steps of the palace. A small motorcade was assembled and he helped me into the back seat of the waiting BMW. I was quiet as we drove out of the palace grounds and along the country roads that would take us to the city of Calanais.

"Is everything okay, Alyssa?" he asked, concern furrowing his brow.

I shrugged, "Not really," I replied.

"Have I done something to upset you?"

I turned to him and sort out his eyes, "Why did you ask me to lunch?" I asked.

"Because I wanted to celebrate your first day of freedom," he replied, puzzled.

"And was this a spontaneous decision?" I asked, my voice firm.

"No," he said shaking his head, "I've been planning it for weeks. I had to run my proposal through Benjamin first and then schedule it with Alex. I had to negotiate the protocols of it with Priscilla and finally talk to Jeanette about how we were going to let it be portrayed in the media. Why?"

My anger deflated. When he explained it like that, it made sense. I was the heir apparent and everything I did as going to be news worthy. If he hadn't planned how our date would come across in the media, it would have been hijacked and turned into something else. I felt naive and a little foolish for doubting him.

I reached out and took his hand, "Forgive me Jordan," I said, "I don't mean to sound so ungrateful." I sighed, "It takes a bit of getting used to all this..." I made a motion with my hand indicating the motor-cade and police escort and bodyguards.

He smiled and lifted my hand to his lips, pressing a soft kiss in the centre of my palm.

"I understand Lys," he said softly, "And I'm here for you. I want to do what I can to help you navigate this. I hope you know I only have your best interests at heart."

I nodded, "I know, I do. I just hate being the centre of attention."

He chuckled, "Unfortunately I can't do anything about that, Your Highness. You are a princess, the heir apparent, queen in waiting and you are now the sun in our country's universe. There is no more hiding for you."

"I know," I said, "And that's what I'm afraid of."

LUNCH WAS AWFUL.

Because Jordan had tweeted where we were going, by the time we got there the streets were lined with people and paparazzi hoping for the first glimpse of the queen in waiting.

It was horrifying.

When our car pulled up to the restaurant, Jordan got out and walked around to open my door. As soon as I stepped out into the August heat, cameras started flashing and people started yelling questions and commands at me.

"Look here, Princess Alyssabeth!"

"What does it feel like to be queen?"

"Who designed your dress?"

"Over here, princess!"

Benjamin and Jordan flanked me with Meredith walking in front of me and Carlos bringing up the rear with Scott and Cody. Aiden and Jamie were waiting for me at the door of the restaurant and I spotted Daniel inside near one of the windows.

The noise from the gathered crowd dimmed as we made it inside and were seated by the owner. I looked around, expecting the other patrons to be glaring at us for the interruption, or at least staring at us to see what all the fuss was about, but the restaurant was empty. It was just Jordan and I, my eight body guards and the restaurant staff. I think that was actually worse than having an entire restaurant full of people staring at me.

I leant across the table and spoke to Jordan in a low voice, "Please tell me that this restaurant is not losing money by turning away all its other customers so we could have lunch here."

Jordan smiled, "The owner has been well compensated and besides, it's quite a big deal for him to host you. People will be lining up for months to dine here. This is the best form of advertising for his business that he'll ever get."

I was not mollified by his words. What type of person demands that the owner of a restaurant refuse other paying customers just for them? Me, apparently, and I didn't like it.

A waiter approached timidly, obviously unsure how to address his royal guest. I smiled encouragingly at him, but I think it just made him more nervous. He cleared his throat and adjusted his collar before bowing awkwardly.

"Are you ready to order?" he asked, a nervous tremble in his voice.

Jordan ordered for both of us and I was a little miffed, I didn't even get to see the menu. This was definitely not high up on my list of favourite dates, or even favourite times spent with Jordan.

Jordan beamed at me as the waiter scurried away, but I didn't return his smile.

"So, you're ordering for me now?" I asked. I knew it sounded bratty, but I didn't really care.

He shrugged, "I think I've gotten to know your likes and dislikes over the past few months," he said calmly, confidently, "Was there ever a lunch you didn't enjoy?"

He wasn't wrong. Every lunch we had together, he had chosen the food and there hadn't been one I didn't like. He was either very perceptive or he had an in with the chef. Probably the latter.

"It's just nice to order for myself once in a while," I said, my tone softening.

He was prevented from answering when the waiter returned with the wine. Our glasses were filled and I took a sip. It was good and that made me a little mad. I would've been happier if I didn't like it and then I could have an excuse for being so upset that he'd ordered for me without even consulting me.

He grinned like he knew what I was thinking, like he knew he'd won.

"Relax, Lys," he said as he returned his glass to the table, "This place is amazing. Everything on their menu is delicious. Trust me."

What was it about those words that rubbed me the wrong way? I was sure there was a saying about never trusting someone who said 'trust me' and it'd been a rule I'd stuck by. Hearing Jordan say it made me uncomfortable.

And the rest of the meal didn't get any better.

Our conversation was stilted and nothing like the intimate lunches we'd shared during my mourning period. It all felt fake and I hated that there were still people outside, trying to get photos of us eating or holding hands or something else to put on their front pages to sell papers.

And Jordan seemed off too. He was too charming, too friendly, too sweet. It came across as forced and sleazy and I rushed through my meal wanting it to be over as soon as possible. I felt like I was in the twilight zone and nothing was as it seemed.

Had Jordan always been this cheesy or was he hamming it up for the cameras? And if that's what he was doing, how did I feel about that? He knew I hated being the centre of attention, but this date had been nothing if not all about the attention.

All I wanted to do was go home and shower. Sitting in this restaurant with no other patrons felt a lot like sitting in a goldfish bowl and it made me question Jordan's motives for bringing me here.

The food was good though, what I ate of it anyway, but that didn't mean I was enjoying myself or that I would be in a hurry to repeat the experience. It felt tawdry, orchestrated, and flew in the face of everything I stood for.

I was glad when the whole thing came to an end and I didn't speak to Jordan at all on the way home. As soon as the car came to a stop, I was out of there and up the palace steps without looking back.

CHAPTER 8

O UT of the frying pan and into the fire.

Lunch was over, but I still had the ball to get through. Luckily Frédéric would be my escort. I was so annoyed at Jordan that I needed a few days to cool off before talking to him again.

From the moment I stepped back into the palace after that train wreck of a lunch date, it was all battle stations go to get me ready for the ball. I was primped, prodded, brushed, waxed, polished and dusted to within an inch of my life. And this wasn't even a gathering of foreign heads of state, this was for local nobility only.

I did not get an opinion about any of it. Between Savannah, Margaret, Bridgette and Annette all my choices were made for me. My floor length gown was a white satin sheath covered by a sheer, intricately beaded, organza layer. It had an empire waist and small capped sleeves. Long white gloves covered my forearms finishing above my elbows. I was wearing sheer white La Perla underwear and Louboutin Cinderella shoes.

My long dark hair had been twisted and pinned up in an elaborate up style that set off the princess tiara that I wore on my head. The royal treasury had also been raided for a stunning diamond necklace - but it was more than a necklace, being part choker as well. The weight of it was substantial as it sat around my neck, wound up my throat and lay across my décolletage. There were matching earrings and a matching bracelet and to top it all off, my pale blue sash of the Order of St. Benét and its diamond star and broach.

After hours of me feeling like a dress-up doll, I was finally declared ready. Alex came to get me and led me to a room that was set up as a photography studio. I was photographed sitting, standing and every which way before Frédéric joined me in all his Earl of Avonlea regalia. His black tails, starched white shirt and white bow tie were complimented by his red sash of the Order of St. Catherine and his medals of service.

He bowed formally to me and then took my arm and placed a kiss on my cheek. Having him close helped me to relax.

"You look breathtaking," he whispered in my ear before walking with me to the big double doors that led onto the mezzanine level of the ballroom.

"Thanks Freddie," I whispered back and smiled at him.

The doors opened and the crier tapped his staff three times to get everybody's attention. He then announced us in his loud, baritone voice. The room bowed and curtsied as one and Frédéric escorted me down the stairs. I prayed that I wouldn't trip and fall and was thankful for his hand at my elbow.

As the crowd rose, my eyes connected with Will's and my heart skipped a beat. He wore a dark tux, crisp white shirt with white bow tie. His deep purple sash of the Order of the Griffon gave him an air of regency that had been lacking in our other *tête-à-têtes*. He inclined his head in acknowledgement of me and the edge of his lip quirked up in what I could only imagine was the beginning of a smile. I ran my eyes down over his wide shoulders, chest and arms and realised he was not alone. The stunning blonde woman I had seen him with at Jacob's funeral was on his arm. My lips thinned and I felt a spike of...something, annoyance maybe? I dragged my eyes away and scanned the rest of the crowd, a hollow feeling in the pit of my stomach.

Frédéric led me to a seat, well a throne, really, on a raised dais. It was where I would receive everybody, seated thankfully. Frédéric helped me to sit and then Dominique was beside me, along with

Priscilla. They would handle the introductions (and there would probably be a quiz after). I knew most of the people here, but this was all part of the formalities. Each person would be presented to me so I could be made aware of the rank in the hierarchy of the court. I settled in for a long wait.

They began at the bottom and worked their way up the ranks. Jordan and his parents were there and I greeted him coolly. Meredith's parents were further up the chain, as was Will.

"Your Royal Highness, may I present The Duke of Camphrey, Lord of Pemberton, Will Darkly and his sister Lady Georgina."

He bowed low and his sister (the gorgeous blonde I had been jealous of) curtsied prettily.

"Welcome My Lord and Lady," I said, finding my voice. I had forgotten how high in the peerage Will's family were; in fact, I think they even had a claim on the throne.

They moved on, but I couldn't get past the look in his eyes when they rested on me. They had darkened and his nose had flared and I'd felt my pulse quicken in response. There was some sort of chemistry between us and I didn't rightly know if it was a good thing or a bad thing.

I smiled politely and nodded my head as I welcomed each person, but my thoughts were on Will and the strange way my body reacted to him whenever he was near. Part of me wanted to explore it, but another part of me was scared as hell about what I might discover if I did.

And then there was Jordan to consider. Yes, I was mad at him at the moment, but he had been a good friend to me and a comfortable companion throughout my months of mourning. Him taking me out was a declaration of a sort, although he had yet to actually speak to me about what exactly it was that he was declaring.

I didn't even know if Will liked me. So far we had only had one civil conversation that didn't end in him stalking off. All of this chemistry could just be one-sided. At least with Jordan, I knew he had feelings for me.

With the introductions complete, Frédéric materialised at my side once again in order to escort me to dinner. We were the last to enter the dining room and everyone stood behind their chairs waiting for me. Again, with the traditions. No one could sit until I did, no one could eat until I ate and once I was finished, everyone's plates were removed, whether they were finished or not.

I sighed inwardly as I took my place at the head table and sat. The room was large and ornately decorated. The head table sat across the end of the room with three long tables running perpendicular to it and down the length of the room. The tables were dressed with crisp white linens and set with gold plated cutlery, gold edged china and luscious floral centrepieces. Portraits of centuries of ruling monarchs graced the walls and my breath caught when I spied the recent portrait of my father.

In the corner a string quartet played and the lighting was soft, but not dark. The soft hum of conversation swelled as drinks were poured into crystal flutes. I had the prime minister seated on my right, his wife on my left, Frédéric on her left and the chief of police on the prime minister's right. I barely knew these people and yet I was to make conversation with them.

I scanned the tables looking for familiar faces. My ladies in waiting were seated at about the middle of the first table. Jordan was seated with his parents towards the front of the second table. Will and his sister were at the head of the first table, which took me by surprise. His estate may be broke, but his influence in the court was still high. It was the strange thing of peerage that I never really understood. In most of the western world money equalled power, but in the royal court, it was rank.

The first course was served, a creamy white soup, and I sipped it slowly aware that if I ate too fast some people may not even get a bite of theirs.

"Are you enjoying being home, Your Highness?" the prime minister asked me between slurps of soup. The man was a noisy eater.

"Very much so," I replied, "I just wish it were under better circumstances."

"Of course," he said with an inclination of his head. "Such a tragedy."

"Indeed," I replied.

"Your gown is lovely," the prime minister's wife commented into the lull.

"Thank you," I replied, "How are your children?"

The conversation was stilted and uncomfortable, small talk not being one of my strengths. Course after course was placed before me and I ate slowly and sparingly. I sipped more water than wine and just wanted the dinner to end. Finally, with the completion of dessert, I was escorted back into the ballroom.

Frédéric led me out onto the dance floor to get the dancing started and I relaxed in his arms. He was a wonderful dancer and his witty repartee loosened the tension that had been building up in my shoulders throughout the night. When the song ended, I was handed off to another man. The instant his hands touched me I was lost. It was Will and his blue eyes stared down at me intently.

"Your Royal Highness," he said as we began to dance.

"Lord Darkly," I replied, my voice breathy.

"You look...wonderful," he finally said and my cheeks warmed with the compliment.

"Thank you," I replied, my eyes downcast.

He cleared his throat and I looked back up at him, "How," he paused and tried again, "How are you?"

I know that he wasn't asking after my health, but rather how I was dealing with the loss of my father and brother. Tears pricked my eyes unexpectedly and his gaze softened.

"I'm sorry," he whispered, "I didn't mean to upset you."

I smiled sadly at him, "It's okay," I replied, "The strangest things set me off. I suppose it is all part of the grieving process."

The truth was, no one had actually asked me how I was coping, they just expected me to cope. His kindness, the compassion in his voice, was what made me tear up.

He nodded in agreement, "Yes, that's true," he said and I saw a sadness in his eyes. He knew loss too and it gave us a kind of kinship.

"How're your cows?" I asked, trying for levity, "Are they recovered from their misadventure?"

He smiled, disarming me with the way it lit up his face, "Oh yes, they are quite recovered. I fear they had a little moment of 'the grass is greener.'"

I chuckled at his joke, "You know it really is wonderful what you have done," I said seriously, "And your cheese is absolutely incredible. I can't get enough of it."

He blushed slightly before he replied, "I noticed the palace's order had increased," he said with a wink.

My body flushed with heat and my stomach flipped over at his playfulness. The man was an enigma.

The song wound down and Will was tapped on the shoulder as someone attempted to cut in. Jordan. Will's eyes darkened and his jaw clenched as he laid eyes on the other man. Jordan looked good in his formal military dress, but I didn't like the cocky grin he had on his face.

Will bowed to me and then moved off, without saying goodbye.

"That was rude," I said to Jordan as he took Will's place.

"Yes," he agreed, "The man is intolerable."

"Not him," I said, "You."

He looked at me with mock horror, "What did I do?"

I shook my head, "We were in the middle of a conversation, Jordan," I said.

His eyes softened and he looked at me adoringly, "Yes, but I couldn't stand to see you in his arms for another minute."

I huffed my annoyance, but I was secretly pleased with his response.

"Let's get out of here," he whispered before leading me off the dance floor and out one of the side doors.

THE CLEAR, DARK SKY WAS STUDDED WITH THE SPARKLE OF STARS and I took a deep breath of the cleansing, cool air. The sweet scent of roses was heavy as we walked arm in arm through the garden. It was a nice evening for a stroll and I realised that I was happy. I even forgot about the body guards, who kept their distance but were still shadowing us.

"Are you having fun tonight?" he asked me.

I smiled, "I am now," I replied.

"Oh," he said, stopping and turning towards me, "And why is that?"

His voice was a soft caress and his eyes lingered on mine before dropping to my lips. He was standing close to me, his hands gently gripping the tops of my arms above my elbows, flesh on flesh.

"Because I'm here with you," I whispered.

"Lys," he said my name like a prayer before he dropped his head and brushed my lips with his.

It was my first real kiss and it was perfect.

He lifted his head and his eyes searched mine for permission before he captured my lips again, longer this time. I felt myself melt and I opened to him, allowing him to deepen the kiss, to make it something more. His arms encircled me and pulled me closer so that our bodies touched. It felt wonderful, amazing, and I lifted my arms and wound them around his neck.

When he lifted his head again, I was dazed and felt a little out of breath. Slowly he pulled back, releasing his arms from around me and the cool air of the night rushed in and prickled my skin with goosebumps as I missed the heat of his body.

"Alyssa," he said, gently cupping my face, "You have completely astonished me. I didn't know who you were going to be when I went to meet your plane, but I didn't expect this. I didn't expect to feel this way about you."

What could I say to that? I hadn't expected this either, I hadn't expected to be swept off my feet by a man who I hadn't seen in ten years. A man who had been one of my brother's closest friends.

"I know you have a lot on your plate and that you are still finding your feet as the queen in waiting, but I really want to pursue this, see where this is going."

He kissed me again, just a tender brushing of lips, but it was full of anticipation, full of what could be between us.

"Jordan, I…"

"Shh," he said, placing a fingertip on my lips, "I know it's a lot to ask, but I feel something between us, something special. You don't have to answer now, I want you to think about it. The next three months are going to be tough, but I want to be by your side, if you'll let me."

"Oh, Jordan, you have made these last three months bearable. I would have been lost without you. I want you by my side, I feel it too, but..."

I looked down, not sure how to phrase what I was going to say or if he would be offended by it.

"But?" he asked, lifting my chin to search my eyes.

"I'm not ready to make this, what's between us, public. Not yet, not until everything is sorted out with Parliament. I don't want the public and the media fixating on our relationship when there are matters of state at hand. Also...I don't want what we have to be sullied by the press. Can you understand that?"

He smiled and nodded before kissing me again. I could let him kiss me all night, I wanted to. I didn't think a single kiss could have such a big effect on me, but it did. It ignited something inside me. There was a warmth in my belly and an ache in my chest. My heart rate increased and my pulse fluttered at my throat.

A soft clearing of the throat from one of my security team brought me back to earth and we stepped away from each other as someone came along the path behind us.

"I should go," he said, "It probably wouldn't be wise for us to be seen together un-chaperoned."

I smiled at him as he placed a kiss on the back of my hand and then turned it over to kiss my palm and then my wrist.

"We'll have lunch again this week," he said as he walked away, back to the party.

I walked in the opposite direction, towards a hidden grotto in the garden. I liked to come here as a child during my parents' functions, just to get away from all the adults and the formality of the evening. I slipped into the small alcove and sat down on the stone bench. My security team melted into the shadows and for all intents and purposes, I was alone.

I lifted my hand and touched my lips where only moments before

Jordan had kissed me. I don't think I could have wanted anything better for my first kiss. His lips had been firm but gentle, his arms warm and secure as he held me close. It had been divine.

I heard the approaching footsteps and leaned back into the darkness of the alcove, not ready to face anyone just yet.

"She's beautiful, don't you think?" a woman's voice said, "I think she's beautiful."

"She's...okay," a male voice replied. A male voice that I would know anywhere. Will.

"How can you say that?" the woman scolded him, "She is absolutely gorgeous. And that dress! Stunning."

"A bit overdone, don't you think?" he replied.

"Overdone? Don't be ridiculous. She is practically our queen, if anything I thought it was understated."

Oh my God, they were talking about me. I blushed with embarrassment. Will thought my dress was overdone and that I was only okay looking? That hurt.

"Will you dance with her again?" the woman asked.

"I don't think so Georgie," he replied gruffly.

"Why ever not?" she asked and I leant forward to hear his answer. I, too, wanted to know why he wouldn't dance with me again. "She looks like she's a good dancer and you seemed to be having a pleasant conversation. I don't understand why you won't ask her again."

"Leave it Georgina," he replied, his voice a low growl.

"Not until you tell me why," she replied.

"Because once was more than enough, okay? Satisfied? I did my duty, we represented our family and I danced with her. Now can we please go home?"

Georgina sighed, "You are such a spoilsport Will," she said, "But yes, I suppose we can go home if you wish."

Their voices faded away and I was left sitting there feeling like I had just been kicked in the guts. Will only danced with me out of obligation and duty. And I had thought it so much more.

The euphoric feeling of being kissed for the first time was now overshadowed by Will's cruel words. I got to my feet and slowly made my way back to the ballroom. I was hurt and confused, but I was also a queen in the making. All my life, I had been schooled in not letting my real emotions show, although I had been sorely lacking in practise. I drew on my inner strength and pasted a polite, aloof smile on my face as I reentered the room.

Meredith was by my side in an instant and she seemed to know that something was wrong. I don't know whether she had heard what Will said through her earpiece or whether she could just read it on my face, but for whatever reason I was grateful for her support.

She steered me through the crowd towards Frédéric and handed me off to him instructing him to dance with me and cheer me up. I rested my head on his shoulder as he waltzed me around the dance floor and listened to his witty commentary on each of the guests that came near us. By the time the song had finished, I was laughing with him and my smile was genuine. I reached up and kissed him on the cheek.

"Thanks," I whispered in his ear.

"Anytime," he whispered back.

CHAPTER 9

I was so done. My feet ached, my body was sore and even my hair hurt. I wanted this night to be over in the worst way. I searched through the crowd looking for Priscilla, needing to know if it was appropriate for me to leave or if I needed to stay and be the last person standing.

"What do you need, Your Highness?" Carlos bent down to speak to me as I sat on my 'throne.'

"I really want to go to bed," I said to him, "But I need to find Lady Priscilla to make sure it's okay."

He smirked and little smile, "I'm pretty sure you are allowed to leave whenever you want," he said, "You are the boss."

"You'd think that, wouldn't you," I said, "But if I leave before Priscilla and Dominique deem it appropriate, I will be in big trouble."

He chuckled, "I'll find them for you," he said, straightening up and speaking softly into his wrist.

Jordan had danced with me after Freddie had rescued me from my meltdown and it had felt nice to be in his arms. It felt safe. I knew I could be myself around him and that helped to soothe my frayed nerves. I refused to think about what I overheard Will saying, it just wasn't worth the heartache.

"Priscilla is on her way," Carlos informed me and I huffed out a breath in relief. I really wanted to get out of here and away from all the prying eyes.

I saw Priscilla walking towards me and she had the rest of my entourage with her. I couldn't help but smile at the picture they made. Six beautiful women dressed to the nines headed towards me with purpose. It was like the glory shot of the tough guys walking away from the scene of an explosion.

"Your Highness," Priscilla said as she curtsied to me, the others following suit (Meredith with a sardonic smile).

"Lady Priscilla, may I please go to bed now?" I asked, well (whined was probably more like it).

Her lips thinned, but not in disapproval, she was trying not to smile. "I think that would be okay," she replied and then turned looking for someone.

It wasn't as easy as just leaving, there were protocols for that too. I had to be escorted out by my date (Freddie) and my ladies in waiting had to follow me. I had to do a round of farewells and there was the national anthem to be played and by the time I finally got to my suite, I'm pretty sure an hour had passed.

I dismissed everyone except Meredith and my lady's maids. When I was changed and ready for bed, I let Bridgette and Annette go too so it was just me and Meredith. I needed to debrief and I needed my girl-friend with me to do it.

"So Jordan kissed me," I blurted out as soon as the maids had left the room.

She rolled her eyes, "I know," she said, "Carlos wanted to punch his lights out."

"Seriously?" my eyes widened.

"You know he doesn't like Jordan," she said, "None of them do."

This was news to me.

"So, your first kiss. How was it?" she asked mischievously.

"Perfect," I whispered.

"Everything you had hoped for?" she asked.

"Yes," I replied.

It might seem odd to outsiders that a twenty-four year old woman was only now getting her first kiss, but those people didn't have around-the-clock security. Not to mention that I had no desire to have my private life splashed all over the covers of the latest trashy magazines. I had avoided media attention by staying under the radar and that meant no dating...ever.

"So, does this mean you and he are going steady now?" she asked.

I rolled over to look at her. She was smiling and there was no mockery in her eyes.

"No," I replied, "I told him I want to take things slow. I don't want it getting out to the press before I'm ready to announce it."

I thought back to what she said earlier, about the guys not liking him.

"So none of my detail like him, huh? What about you?" I asked, "Do you like him?"

She sighed, "He's cute and he looks real good in a uniform," she raised her eyebrows lasciviously, "And I know you like him, so yeah, I suppose I do."

"But?"

"What but? There was no but." She smiled at me.

"Come on Mer, I know you. You like him because I like him, but there's something you're not telling me."

She blew a breath out and flopped back on the bed.

"We've been looking into him and his family."

"What? Why?"

"Because both he and his father were on the hunt and we are investigating everybody who was there," she said patiently.

"And what have you found?" I asked, not really sure if I want to know the answer.

"Nothing," she said.

"So, isn't that a good thing?" I asked, confused.

"When I say nothing," she replied, "I mean absolutely nothing. No one is that squeaky clean. There's not a speeding ticket or a report of youthful misbehaviour or even a lost library book. It's like he and his father have been scrubbed clean and Benjamin doesn't like it, especially since he has such unhindered access to you."

"But he's not dangerous or anything is he?" I ask.

"Nah," she said, "I just think he's a little too smooth, too charming, you know?"

I laid back on the bed and stared at the ceiling, "Yeah. I wasn't real happy with him after lunch today."

"That's an understatement. What did he do?"

"Nothing really," I said, "I just didn't like the set up with the media and everything. It felt too rehearsed and he even seemed to play up to the press, which you know I hate."

We were quiet for a while, lost in our own thoughts.

"So you want to talk about what happened with Will?" she asked.

I covered my face with my hands, "You heard it?"

"We all heard it," she said, "Carlos wasn't the only one who wanted to hit *him*."

I rolled over and buried my face in my hands, "God, I'm so embarrassed."

"What do you have to be embarrassed about?" she asked.

"Why do you think he hates me?" I asked rolling back onto my side towards her. I was about to be crowned queen of a small European country, but that didn't mean I was immune to the effects of a good looking guy rejecting me.

Meredith rolled over on her side so that she was looking at me, "I don't think he hates you," she said softly, "But why does it matter? You like Jordan."

I sighed, "Yeah I do," I replied, "It's just, I don't know, there's something about him. I thought we could be friends, at least. He was close to Jacob and I'd like him to be..."

"You'd like to be close to him too, so that you have a piece of Jacob."

"Is that silly? I know Jacob was helping him, with his business, and I'd like to think I could help him too."

"Have you...have you been through your father's or Jacob's offices yet?" she asked gently.

"No," I replied, "I don't know if I can."

She reached out to tuck a stray piece of hair behind my ear, "I think you need to. I know their secretaries can bring you up to date on what they were working on, but I think you'll get a better feel for what they wanted to achieve if you took a look at their notes."

She was right, I knew she was right, but the thought of walking into their private spaces, smelling their aftershave, touching things that they'd touched, it all seemed like too much. But I was going to have to do it soon. The Lord High Chamberlain was clamouring for me to decide on the designs for my father's rooms so they could get started on redecorating. I needed to move into them soon, now that my mother had transitioned to the chalet.

"Tomorrow," I said, closing my eyes and letting myself drift off, "I'll do it tomorrow."

BUT TOMORROW WAS TOO FULL OF ITS OWN CRAP FOR ME TO ADD another thing to it. It was Saturday, but that didn't matter. Alex was in my room early, luckily bringing coffee and breakfast with her.

I dragged myself out of bed and pulled on a robe, plopping down in a chair and snagging a cup of coffee to sip on while she ran through the day's itinerary. I had morning meetings with my decorator, the Lord High Chamberlain, and the chef. The latter two would be regular occurrences going forward, although I didn't know why that would be in my purview. I don't think my father met with the chef and the head of the household on a weekly basis, although I knew my mother did. I had an awful feeling that I was about to be lumped with both the king's and queen's jobs, much like a single parent had to fill both roles, and I wondered if anyone had thought about the implications.

Intuitively I knew that Parliament had and it would no doubt be a reason why I would not be fit to rule. But there had to be a way around it. Why couldn't the queen mother continue in her role while I took over the role of the king? I was, technically, the head of state and that's where my focus should be.

But we were a nation that had never found itself in this particular predicament. As far back as the St. Benéts had been ruling Merveille, all the heirs had been male. There was no precedent for a female heir, but there was also nothing stopping us from having one. Unfortunately, I didn't think Parliament would see it that way. They were stuck on the labels of king and queen. There were 'king' duties and there were 'queen' duties and now I would be responsible for both.

"Are you listening to me Alyssa?" Alex gently chided me.

"Sorry," I said, "I was just thinking. I'm about to become a single parent."

"What!" she stood suddenly and I realised what I'd just said.

I laughed, "Sit down," I said, "I meant metaphorically, not literally."

She sat down gingerly, looking at me strangely, "What do you mean?" she finally asked.

I sighed and picked up a piece of bacon to chew on while I enlightened her, "I'm to be queen," I began, "But we've never had a queen as head of state, it's only ever been a king."

"Yes," she said, "We know this already."

"No, I know," I said, "What I mean is, it's like I'm expected to hold both offices. I need to run the country but I also need to fulfil all the duties that the queen would normally fulfil. And what if I get married? Would my husband then become responsible for the running of the household? Would he attend the garden parties and mix with the wives of the other heads of state?"

"I've never thought of it like that," she said, "We should get Priscilla to work on this. There are other countries that do it, so there must be some sort of protocol."

I nodded my head thoughtfully, "Yes," I said, "I need a report on how other female rulers manage the flipped roles. And something before the Parliamentary meeting would be good."

Alex made a note on her tablet and then moved on.

"This afternoon there is a garden party to meet with the wives and daughters of the local nobility," she said, "And then you have a security briefing this afternoon. Tonight there is an intimate dinner with some of your father's closest allies."

I groaned and leant my head back against the chair, closing my eyes. This was exactly what I was talking about.

"I'm going to need coffee and lots of it, all day," I moaned.

"You have a day off tomorrow," she said kindly.

"Thank God," I replied.

"Yes, after church, you have the day off."

I groaned again. I had avoided church since the funeral due to my period of mourning. It's not that I had a conscientious objection to religion. I believed in God myself, I just had an objection to having to conform to what society determined was religion. To me, it was a private thing, something to be worked out between me and God, but if I skipped the service it would be yet another black mark against my name.

"Well, if I have to go, everyone does," I said, "That means you and Meredith and all the others."

She grimaced slightly but nodded.

"I also want to make some time to go through my father's and brother's offices," my voice was soft and hesitant. I didn't really want to do it, but I knew I had to.

"Do you want me to help you?" she asked.

I nodded, "And Meredith," I said, "But no one else."

I knew that I needed to do it at my own pace. Having Alex there would help to keep me on track and stop me getting side tracked and Meredith would be my emotional support.

"We could probably organise something for tomorrow afternoon," she said, tapping on her tablet, "How much time do you think you need?"

"Probably a couple of hours," I said with an exhale, "We'll start with my father's office this week and maybe do Jacob's next Sunday."

She tapped and swiped and typed and then nodded, "Okay, done. Now you need to get dressed and head into your office."

She stood to her feet and smoothed down her skirt. I reached out and grabbed her hand.

"Thanks Alex," I said sincerely, "I'm glad you're here."

She smiled shyly at me and dropped a small curtsey before leaving and ushering Bridgette and Annette in to get me ready for the day.

THIS WAS THE THIRD CHANGE OF CLOTHES FOR THE DAY, AND I STILL had one more to go. I was so glad I had Savannah to organise my wardrobe, as I would've been happy to just wear the one dress all day. That was until I had been looked down upon by all those women at the garden party. It wasn't hard to see that the local nobility did not approve of me becoming their ruler.

Thank God that was over. The only bright spark had been when I'd had a chance to sit and chat with Lady Georgina, Will's sister. She was delightful and I could see us becoming friends. I had already made mention to Alex that I would like to have tea with her during the week so that we could really get to know one another.

Now I entered the briefing room for my security briefing. Von Bartham was there, as was Benjamin and the rest of my detail. The chief of police was also in attendance, which I thought odd.

The men stood as I strode into the room and waited for me to sit before they resumed their seats.

"What have you got for me?" I asked determining that I needed to take control of these meetings from this time out. The Lord High Chamberlain and the chef had practically steamrolled me this morning and I wasn't in any mood for it to be repeated here. If I was going to be the absolute ruler, then I needed to rule absolutely.

"Things seem to be going smoothly so far," Von Bartham reported, "There has been no change to the threat assessment and no increase in threats or hate mail."

"God," I gasped, "I get hate mail?"

"It's not personal," Benjamin assured me, "We always receive some measure of hate mail and death threats. They're usually from crack pots and anti-monarchists."

I knew this, *abstractly*, but being confronted with it so blandly was hard to take.

"If anything," Von Bartham resumed, "The fan mail has increased. I think they like you."

That was nice to hear, but there were still people who hated me. I wasn't really used to that. I had always kept my head down and tried to walk the middle road so as not to upset anybody.

"Don't let it upset you, Your Highness," the chief of police remarked, "The people who pen these letters are not entirely sane."

"I don't think that makes it any better," I said, "They're even more of a threat if they're unstable."

"True," he acknowledged, "But it also means they are unorganised and sloppy. We usually have them picked up before you even know about it."

I really didn't like his arrogant tone.

"Except that something happened to my father and brother," I retorted.

"Yes," Von Bartham stepped in, "But we are not convinced that that was the result of an outside threat."

"You're saying that my father and brother were killed by someone in the palace?" I asked, my voice bordering on hysterical.

"Or at least someone close, with open access to them."

"Who?" I asked.

"That we don't know," Von Bartham said with a sigh, "It was a large hunting party and we are still trying to lock in where everyone was when it happened."

"If this was CSI they would have wrapped it up by now," I said petulantly.

"We have our best investigators working on it," the chief assured me, somewhat offended.

"So am I in danger?" I asked.

Benjamin sighed and shared a look with Meredith, "Possibly," he finally said, "It depends on what their endgame was. If it was just to cause instability in the country, then they have achieved their goal, but if it was to actually take over control, then you may still be in danger."

"Who has the most to gain from my death?" I asked, looking around the room. Meredith wouldn't meet my eyes.

"Frédéric," she said, "Or more accurately, my father."

"And were either of them on the hunt?" I asked, chilled.

She shook her head, "No," she replied, "And I don't believe for one minute that they would ever even think of such a thing."

I reached over and laid my hand on hers, "I don't either," I assured her.

"We have run a full investigation into the Duke of Monterey and the Earl of Avonlea and have cleared them of any involvement."

I turned to Meredith, "Did they investigate you too?" I asked and she nodded. This was ridiculous.

Benjamin sighed, "We had to," he said, "Meredith has intimate access to you and she is a highly trained operative."

I could only imagine the look on my face that made Von Bartham jump in.

"But we didn't suspect her in the least," he said, "It was just proper protocol."

"It doesn't make it right," I said.

"Maybe not," Meredith said, "But it was necessary. We wouldn't be doing our jobs if we didn't look at everyone involved. Both Carlos and Daniel had to be investigated too."

I growled at that, but could see their point. It didn't mean I had to like it.

"So who else is in line to the throne?" I asked.

A tablet was handed to me with a long list of names. I skimmed down the list, noticing both Will and Jordan were on it.

"All of these people have a claim to the throne," Von Bartham went on, "And will more than likely challenge you before your coronation."

I raised my eyebrows, "Really? Is there no clear succession?"

"After the Duke of Monterey, no."

"But if I'm killed, won't he automatically step in?" I ask, confused.

Meredith shook her head, "He has his own Duchy to think of, as does Frédéric. Anybody on that list could successfully challenge him on that fact alone."

This was all so confusing. I didn't fully understand how succession worked outside of my own family.

"So pretty much, if I'm gone, the throne is open for a hostile takeover?"

"Yes."

CHAPTER 10

THIS dining room was smaller, more intimate than the one they'd used for the ball. It was still over the top with formality, though. At least this time I actually got to sit at the table with my guests, instead of at a different table like a wedding reception.

On my right was Uncle Charles, Lord Bingham, Duke of Monterey and Meredith's father. He wasn't really my uncle, well I didn't think so. We were related though, so maybe cousins? Anyway, he was my father's best friend and I called him uncle because of that. He was also my godfather.

On my left sat, Jordan's father, Major General Elijah Wicks. He had also been a friend of father's, although not familiar enough to be called uncle. He had always been, and would always be, The General. He was retired now, of course, but I would never be able to separate him from his rank.

We had made fun of him as a kid, Jordan leading the way. He was an imposing man with a great Hulihee beard that was white now, as was his hair. He reminded me of the major general from Pirates of Penzance and every time I saw him, the song ran through my head on repeat.

Further down the table were Will and Jordan, although I had made sure they weren't seated next to each other. Having them both at the table made me uncomfortable, but for very different reasons. When I looked at Will, I was embarrassed by what I overheard him saying about me and when I looked at Jordan, I couldn't help blushing at the memory of the kisses we'd shared. It meant I spent most of the meal flushed or avoiding their eyes altogether.

Thank God Frédéric was also there to rescue me when conversation stalled. Which it did, often. I was the only female in attendance and it was an odd experience, but one I would no doubt have to become accustomed to. This was another one of those situations in which I was to serve as both king and queen. This afternoon I had spent time with the wives, sisters and daughters of these men, in which I was playing the role of queen, and now, tonight, I was playing the king role as I entertained them. Maybe I could combine the garden parties and these dinners to avoid this very situation.

But that was an issue for another time. Right now, I needed to get through tonight and maybe win some favour. These were my father's supporters and for me to win over Parliament, they needed to be mine too. The problem was, we had so very little in common. These men were old school, well, most of them anyway, and they didn't know how to talk to a young woman like me without coming across as condescending. It didn't help that most of them hadn't lain eyes on me since I was fourteen years old. I'm sure they still thought of me as that little girl.

I was more than happy when the formal dinner came to a close. I may have even rushed through eating the last few dishes in order to speed it up, and we all rose from the table. This was the part where the king would take the men into the drawing room and they would share brandy and cigars. I neither drank brandy nor smoked cigars and my father's drawing room had been a male only dominion all my life. I had never set foot across the threshold.

The men either didn't realise that fact or thought to continue the evening without me, because they all headed in that direction after leaving the table. Like a herd of old cows that made their way to the milking shed without needing the farmer's encouragement, the dukes and earls and viscounts all migrated towards, what would colloquially be known as, the man cave.

I hung back, unsure of whether to follow or not. I knew that the real deals went down in that room and that what happened around the table was mere façade. But would they accept me in that room? A room that had been, for generations, a gentleman's club?

"What's wrong princess?" Frédéric whispered in my ear.

"I've never been in there," I admitted to him, "I have no idea how to navigate this."

He chuckled and put a hand on the small of my back, guiding me forward, "Don't let them smell your fear," he said quietly, "You need to treat them like a pack of dogs. Your father was the pack leader. Right now there is a void and you need to be the one to fill it. You need to go in there and take charge."

"But I've never done anything like that before. I don't even know the types of things they discuss in there." I knew it was important to garner their respect, but I had no idea how to go about doing it.

"It's like a game of chess," he counselled me, "Everyone is trying to manoeuvre their piece closest to the king and they're all thinking several moves ahead."

"I suck at chess," I whined, "And the only reason they want to get close to the king is to knock him over."

Frédéric shook his head, "Not necessarily," he said, "Sometimes they want to get close to protect the king."

"Is that what you're doing?" I asked.

He smiled a brilliant smile, "I got your back Lys," he said.

I rolled my eyes and took a deep breath before crossing the threshold into my father's world.

THE STEWARDS HAD ALREADY BEGUN DISTRIBUTING THE BRANDY AND cigars. I took a brandy, but declined the cigar. I would make do with passive smoking. The men had broken off into little groups and I was reminded of a similar scene on a school yard playground. That hadn't worked out well for me either.

Deciding to start small, I headed for Jordan. He was, at least, a friendly face. He was talking to a viscount and an earl and they were discussing, of all things, sports. Another area in which my general knowledge was lacking.

"Who do you fancy for the MFA Cup this season?" Jordan asked the earl.

MFA. Merveille Football Association. I knew that, of course. Football was our national sport. The one with the round ball, not to be confused with the other types with odd shaped balls.

"Calanais looks good," the earl replied, "Although, Mersey look to have a strong team this year."

"Yes, but they lost their manager end of last year. The new one doesn't look like much chop."

"What about you, Your Highness?" Jordan asked with a sparkle in his eye, "Who do you have your eye on?"

I swirled the brandy in my glass for a moment, trying to remember a name of a team. Jacob had been a massive fan of...Genervé?

"I believe I'll be following the fate of Genervé," I responded, completely unaware of if the team was any good.

The men chuckled.

"A die-hard fan like your brother?" Jordan asked with a smile.

I shrugged a shoulder, "I was inspired by his passion."

"Not your father's beloved Royal Guards?" the viscount asked.

I swirled my brandy again. I was reminded of my father's and brother's loud disagreements whenever they watched a match.

"I think my father may have been blinded by loyalty in their regard," I replied, remembering that it was one of Jacob's most touted phrases when arguing the merits of their respective teams.

The earl and discount chuckled and then bowed and moved away leaving Jordan and myself alone.

"You did well," he said.

I huffed out a small laugh, "Are either of the teams I named any good?"

He laughed, "No," he said, "Your brother and your father were both blinded by their loyalty."

I blushed, hoping I hadn't just made a complete fool of myself.

"Do you have plans tomorrow Alyssa?" Jordan asked.

"Church, of course," I replied, "And then I'm going to spend some time in my father's office."

"Oh?" Jordan raised an eyebrow at me, "You haven't done that yet?"

I shook my head, "I haven't been able to face the memories. But I have a Parliamentary meeting coming up and I can avoid my father's business no longer."

"And Jacob's?"

"Next week," I said, "I can't do them both at once, it would be too much for me."

He nodded sagely. "Will you have time for a picnic?" he asked.

I smiled and felt myself relax, "That would be lovely," I said.

He raised my hand to his lips and brushed the skin above my knuckles delicately, "Until tomorrow then," he said before moving off.

I turned around to find another group to talk to and came face to face with Will. He had a mean scowl on his face that he wasn't quick enough to blank before making eye contact with me.

"Lord Darkly," I said haughtily.

He bowed, "Your Highness," he replied.

"I do hope your sister enjoyed herself this afternoon," I said, grasping for small talk.

"Indeed, she did," he replied, his face softening at the mention of his sister.

"I hope she will come and have tea with me sometime soon."

"I'm sure she would be delighted to," he replied.

We stood awkwardly for a moment, unsure of what to say next.

"You spend a lot of time with Wicks, do you?" he asked.

I raised an eyebrow at him, "He works in the palace," I replied, "We sometimes have lunch together."

Will sipped his brandy, his eyes darkening. "Not alone, I hope."

"Of course not," I replied, offended, "I always have my security detail with me, they are chaperones enough."

He nodded sharply, "I would caution you to keep it that way."

I took a moment to bite back my angry retort and said instead, "What is it you have against Lieutenant Wicks?"

He clenched his jaw and his eyes glittered hard and cold and for a moment I didn't think he would reply. "I have a problem with duplicity, Your Highness."

"I have noticed that," I replied, "You do tend to run hot and cold Lord Darkly."

His eyebrows lowered and his face became like a thundercloud, "It is not my duplicity that concerns me," he hissed before turning and walking away.

I watched him go, wondering what he meant. Was he implying that Jordan was the one with the duplicitous nature? I hadn't seen it, myself. Jordan had been the more consistent of the two of them since I had returned to Merveille. Each encounter with Will had left me feeling adrift in a leaky boat, whereas Jordan made me feel safe.

My attention was drawn to a round of loud laughter. A rather large group of men had gathered around The General and he seemed to be holding court. Frédéric was right, nature abhors a vacuum and in the absence of a leader these men seemed to be gravitating toward the very authoritative major general.

Making a split second decision, I wandered over to join the group, interested to hear what they were saying. As I approached, the conversation died and an uncomfortable silence was left.

"I hope you're finding the brandy and cigars to your liking, gentleman," I said.

"Your father always did have impeccable taste when it came to the little luxuries," The General replied.

"How is the leg, General Wicks?" I asked referring to the injury he sustained when my father was killed.

"Much better, Your Highness," he replied, "The surgeons did a remarkable job to save my leg."

"And no doubt, your life," I added.

"And my life," he conceded.

"It was a tragedy, what happened that day," another of the gathered lords said and there was a murmur of agreement from the group.

"Your father was a great man," another said.

"He will be sorely missed," The General said, "Merveille has lost something great."

My father was a great man, but I couldn't help but feel like these men were trying to subtly imply that I could never fill his shoes, and that worried me greatly. If they wouldn't support me, then who would.

"King Edward will indeed be sorely missed," Lord Bingham said from beside me, "But he left a wonderful legacy in Princess Alyssabeth."

I inclined my head in acknowledgment of his support. If anyone held more sway over the assembled men than The General, it was Charles Bingham.

"Thank you for a wonderful evening," I said, suddenly tired and wanting to be as far away from this room as I could possibly get, "If you will excuse me, I think I will retire for the evening. It has been a rather eventful day."

The men bowed as I turned to walk away. I didn't look back as I strode across the floor with more confidence than I felt, realising for the first time just how much of a mountain I was going to have to climb to win their favour.

I MADE IT THROUGH THE CHURCH SERVICE WITHOUT FALLING ASLEEP and embarrassing myself, for which I am sure both Priscilla and Jeanette were thankful. Savannah had dressed me in a lovely pale pink dress and matching hat paired with nude pumps. I felt pretty and feminine and ever so much grown up.

The service was boring and the bishop droned on in his awful croaky voice, but to amuse myself I people watched. This was greatly facilitated by the fact that we were seated in a royal box above the rest of the congregation and it gave me a rather good view of everybody in attendance.

The front rows were filled with the who's who of nobility and money, but the rows further towards the back were filled, somewhat sparingly, by the everyday people of Calanais. It was like an ombré effect; the closest to the front wore the most expensive clothes, hats, jewellery and shoes and each row backward the quality and cost of the outfits diminished. Not that the people in the back were wearing rags, by any stretch of the imagination. Merveille was a wealthy country with a good employment rate and very low numbers of people on the poverty line. But it was interesting to note the way the citizens arranged themselves. Merveille was very traditional and there was very little mixing between the classes. Wealth, power and title were the benchmarks and the higher you scored in each, the higher up the food chain you were.

There were some noticeable absences, Will and his sister Georgina being two of them. It didn't surprise me, really. Will didn't strike me as a man that was all too concerned about appearances, and let's be honest, the only reason these people came to church was to be seen. Also, if what Jordan had said about his father's fall from grace was true, I doubt he would want to be in close company with some these congregational members. Being at a formal gathering was a different kettle of fish; those were for political manoeuvring. Being in church meant opening yourself up to a more personal inspection. These people were very much concerned with your soul, even more so than their own.

At the conclusion of the service, I did the bare minimum of social-ising that Priscilla demanded and then I made my escape. I'd had quite enough of being surrounded by people who I didn't know were enemies or allies and I really needed some time on my own. Spending a couple of hours in my father's study seemed like just the place to escape to, despite the onslaught of memories that were bound to assault me.

I listened to my entourage discuss the fashions and the attitudes of the congregation. They were universally agreed on who they liked and who they didn't. I kept out of it, preferring to keep my own council about such things, but happy to listen in on their thoughts.

When we arrived back at the palace, I practically ran to my room, causing Jamie to chuckle as he kept up with me, and dug through my hidden treasures to find my Levi's. I changed into them and a sloppy t-shirt, grateful to be rid of the haute couture for the time being. My next destination was my father's study and blessed solitude. I figured I could get a couple of hours work done before my picnic lunch with Jordan.

But my plans were derailed when Alex knocked on the door to inform me that I had a visitor and they wished me to meet them in the stables. Deeming that my jeans and t-shirt were suitable enough, I pulled on my riding boots and headed out.

A commotion in the stable yard had me coming to a halt. A grey stallion reared on its hind legs, screaming in indignation. Jamie placed a hand on my shoulder, keeping me from moving towards the melee and I was happy to oblige. I had complete confidence in my stable hands and Master of Horse to corral the unhappy animal.

"Alyssa!" Jordan's happy greeting had me turning towards him with a smile. "Do you like your gift?"

"My gift?" I asked, confused.

He nodded in the direction of the horse, "Mistborn. Magnificent isn't he?"

I looked towards the distressed horse. He was no longer rearing, but his ears were flattened and his eyes were wild.

"You bought him for me?" I asked.

"It's my coronation gift to you," he said.

"It's still three months until my coronation," I replied.

"So? You're going to be receiving a lot of gifts over the next three months and I wanted to be the first."

"I don't know what to say," I said to him, my eyes taking in the dapple grey Arabian. "He is beautiful." And he was. Dark mane and tail and a gorgeous grey and white dappled coat. But he also had a look about him that I didn't like. I was an experienced rider; I'd learned when I was just a toddler, but I wasn't a horse whisperer. I liked my mounts to be well behaved and calm, not feisty.

"I bought him from a Sheik friend of mine. He has a royal blood-line and is a much sought after breeding stallion."

"What say Cliff?" I called to the Master of Horse.

Cliff spat in the dust, his eyes not leaving the stallion who danced and huffed his annoyance.

"He's gonna be a pain in my backside," Cliff grouched, "But he sure is pretty."

CHAPTER 11

"WHAT were you thinking buying a horse like that for me?" I asked Jordan, "You know I'll never ride him."

We were sitting on a grassy knoll near the stable yards eating an early picnic lunch and watching Jed work Mistborn. Jed was one of our best trainers, despite his young age, and he carried an authority about him that I could see Mistborn already respected. Not that that horse was giving an inch.

Jed was tall and wide at the shoulders, a big man with large capable hands and a steady stance. He was soft spoken and his silken Texas drawl seemed to comfort animals and people alike. Not native to Merveille, Cliff had lured him away from his beloved America with the promise of stellar horse flesh and a chance to work as head trainer. I hadn't met him before coming back to Merveille myself as he was only a recent transplant, but I liked what I'd seen so far and he had an undeniable gift with the horses.

He lunged Mistborn in a wide circle and the sight was mesmerising. It had taken a while for Mistborn to settle and he'd had a good go at biting anyone who got too close, but Jed now had him moving like a dream. His head was lifted and proud, his steps high and his tail held aloft arrogantly. I knew he was going to be a lot of work, as horses like

Mistborn would not be content to graze in the pasture. He would need to run and run hard. But for now, he and Jed had reached some sort of agreement and I could see what an amazing horse he was.

"I don't think he's that bad," Jordan said as he chewed on his panini, "He was just unsettled by the long trip. Once he gets used to you all, he'll be a dream."

"Jordan, it took four experienced stable hands to get him out of the float and one of them nearly had a finger bitten off."

Jordan laughed, "You worry too much," he said, "Look at him, he moves like silk. You will look spectacular on him."

I shook my head but didn't respond. If Jordan thought I was ever going to climb up onto that beast, then he didn't know me at all.

Jordan leaned back on his elbows and cast a long look over at me. "So what are you up to this afternoon?" he asked.

I sighed and reclined next to him, "Going through my father's study," I replied.

"Oh, that's right," he replied, "You told me that. Don't you have staff to do that though?"

"Yeah, I do," I said, "But I'd really like to get a feel for the way my father worked. I want to see where his heart was."

Jordan nodded in understanding, "You've got your Parliamentary meeting this week."

I exhaled harshly, "Yep." I popped the 'p', communicating my apprehension.

He chuckled, "They're all just big teddy bears," he said, "They'll bluster and carry on for a bit, but they'll come around. Nobody wants to see anyone but a St. Benét on the throne."

"Maybe," I conceded, "But they're not going to make it easy on me."

He reached over and threaded his fingers through mine, "If you need help with anything, you know I'm here for you, right?"

I smiled up at him, wishing we were alone so I could kiss him again. "Yes," I said.

His eyes darkened as they roamed over me and I felt heat flush through me under his gaze.

"Feel like going for a walk?" he asked, his voice gruff.

I wet my suddenly dry lips, running my tongue along the bottom and then the top, Jordan's eyes followed its path.

"Sure," I said, my voice breathy.

He stood to his feet and held out his hand to me. I took it and he pulled me to my feet and into him, our bodies brushing briefly, causing my breath to hitch. He kept hold of my hand and we wandered away from the stables, my security detail following at a discreet distance.

"I've been dying to kiss you again since Friday night," he murmured softly as we walked.

I smiled and my cheeks heated, "Me too," I replied.

He broke into a jog, pulling me with him and startling a laugh out of me. We headed towards the hedge maze and I knew my body guards would not be happy with either of us. He pulled me through the entrance and down the long, straight avenue before ducking around one of the corners. He'd pulled me into a dead end, and there was a stone bench and a marble statue filling the alcove.

Jordan stopped and pulled me into his chest. He looked down into my eyes and lifted his hand to brush an errant lock of hair off my cheek.

"I know Benjamin is going to be mad," he said, his voice low and husky, "But I really needed a moment away from all the prying eyes."

His head dipped and he fit his warm lips over mine. He kissed me softly at first and then gently coaxed my mouth open, deepening the kiss and causing me to lose all brain function. One hand cupped the back of my neck, under my hair, and the other slid around my waist and pulled me against him. I could feel every hard ridge and furrow of his body through our clothing and I melted into it. I could kiss him all day.

All too soon, he lifted his head and I became aware of footsteps heading towards us on the crushed gravel of the maze's path. I stifled a giggle as Jordan grabbed my hand and pulled me out of our hiding place and back onto the avenue. We raced through the maze until we reached the centre where Jordan pulled me to him once again and kissed me deeply, his tongue sliding silkily along mine and causing my skin to erupt in goosebumps. My knees turned to jelly and I leaned into him, letting him support me and keep me upright.

Jordan lifted his head and smiled at something over my shoulder and I knew we'd been found. I burrowed into his shoulder, embarrassed but delighted. Having a security detail and boyfriend was always going to be tricky and I had to trust that they would keep my confidences. But that didn't make it any less embarrassing knowing that they were going to be privy to nearly every new step in our relationship.

"Come on Jamie," Jordan called, "You couldn't give us even a half hour alone?"

"Boss' orders," Jamie said.

I sighed and turned around, giving Jamie a smile.

"It's okay," I said, "I have to get going now anyway." I turned back to Jordan and raised up onto my toes to press a chaste kiss to his cheek. "Thank you for lunch and for that ridiculous horse," I whispered in his ear.

He wrapped his arms around me in a brief, but tight hug, before letting me go. I walked backwards, towards Jamie, giving Jordan my sweetest smile.

"See you next week, Lieutenant," I said with a wave.

A FEW HOURS LATER I WAS SURROUNDED BY PILES OF PAPER, MY hand clenched around a fresh cup of coffee and a perplexing frown on my face. My father had been a good king, but he hadn't been a very innovative one. In the twenty-five years or so that he had reigned, he hadn't initiated a single thing. All he had done was keep the status quo. Merveille had been trundling along, secure in its wealth, but without any clear direction. Research and development had not been encouraged and from what I could tell, we were losing some of our smartest and most talented people to other countries.

The only person who seemed to persevere with the king was Will Darkly. I came across several letters and emails and proposals requesting grants from the crown to further develop the breed that Will had created and I couldn't, for the life of me, understand why my father hadn't jumped at the chance.

But we had missed the boat. Will had patented his breed and was in the process of petitioning for it to become recognised by the Livestock Association of Europe. If that happened, then Will would become a very wealthy man.

I noticed that he'd also had several grant requests denied to help with the expansion of his cheese factory. It just didn't make sense to me; we should have been fostering this kind of innovation. If we could support our own people in building successful industries and businesses, then we would be less reliant on the rest of the European Union.

I'd learned about micro-financing in my international relations studies and how it had helped developing countries grow their economies and improve their standard of living. Merveille was far from being a third-world country, but the principals still applied. Investing in our own people could only benefit us and that the king had turned down such an amazing opportunity confounded me.

Would all of Parliament be this conservative? Were they so mired in tradition that they failed to see the potential in our own people? We had aligned ourselves with the EU and had taken on board the Euro as our currency, but did that mean we had to lose our entire identity to them as well?

Or was I just being naive? I had to admit that I knew very little about our political standing in the EU or, for that matter, the political agendas of our own Parliament. I knew we were a wealthy country, but what were we doing to ensure that wealth continued? Surely initiatives like Will's could only strengthen our economy, so why weren't we encouraging that?

I pushed away from the desk and stood, gripping my coffee cup tightly. I paced the office, my eyes drifting over the detritus of my father's life. He had always been a conservative and a traditionalist. His resistance to me studying at university was proof of that, not that I'd needed it. He had very much endorsed the patriarchal society of Merveille, believing that men were born to lead and women were born to support their men. I really didn't think he realised how much of his political wrangling was dependent on my mother's sway with the other wives. They had worked as a team, even if he hadn't known it.

All of that left me wondering if the rest of the men in government were similarly unaware of their wives' assistance. How many of the backroom deals that these men brokered were actually born over a cup of freshly brewed tea and some fresh baked scones? Most of them, probably.

The women had done themselves a disservice in this way. As long as they allowed their husbands to believe that they were solely responsible for leading, the women of our country would never get a fair hearing. Backroom politics had its place, but not at the exclusion of women.

And so it had fallen to me to change the well-established mindsets of the powerful men of government. And that was going to go over like a lead balloon. Turning this tide was akin to steering the Titanic away from the fatal iceberg and I had to wonder whether I was too late in the game.

What chance did I have when I couldn't even sway my own father's opinion? I had been the apple of his eye, as long as I conformed to his idea of appropriate gender roles. He didn't care what my grades were or whether I was contributing to society in a responsible way. He only cared whether I could read aloud, pen elegant missives, play the piano, dance the traditional waltzes and be able to carry on a decent conversation with the other ladies at court. He hadn't taught me how to debate political strategies or how to understand the machinations of Parliament. Those lessons he had saved for Jacob alone.

I picked up a silver framed photograph of myself and Jacob. He had been about ten at the time, me a mere six. Jacob was staring confidently at the camera, a wide grin on his face, a sparkle in his eye. I was staring at Jacob. My small round face tilted up with a look of adoration for my big brother. He had been my hero and I had idolised him. I had followed him everywhere and he had let me, encouraged me, almost. That was until he started lessons with my father. Then for an hour a day, Jacob would be kept out of my reach. I didn't understand then and I certainly didn't understand now. If my father had had the foresight to include me in those lessons, maybe I wouldn't be floundering now.

I replaced the photograph on the shelf and turned to survey the mess I had made of my father's office. Stanley, my father's assistant, was going to hate me, but it was something that I'd had to do. My search had been fruitless, but I had gotten to know my father a little better. Unfortunately, I didn't like what I had seen. I had always thought my father a brave and astute man who led the country with wisdom. But from where I was standing, it looked more like he was just marking time and that was disappointing. It made me wonder whether my brother would have been the same.

I sighed and sat back down in my father's chair. I had loved him with all my heart, I still did, but now some of the shine had tarnished on the memories I had of him. Had my father been a mere figurehead? A puppet that bowed to the whims of the prime minister and his cronies? And is that what they expected of me too?

One thing was for sure, there was no way I would be just a puppet. If I were to become queen, then I wanted to be all in. Now I just had to get Parliament to agree with me.

BENJAMIN, JAMIE, CODY AND AIDEN ESCORTED ME ACROSS THE property to my mother's chalet. We travelled in two golf carts, Benjamin and I in the first followed by Cody and Aiden in the second. It wasn't far to the chalet; too far to comfortably walk but too short to drive. The golf carts were ideal, if a little odd.

"So things with you and Jordan are serious." It was a statement, not a question. Benjamin's soft but firm voice broke the stillness of the evening.

"I know you don't like him," I began, but Benjamin cut me off.

"You don't need my opinion," he said, "But I need to know of any potential suitors so that we can do background checks."

I huffed, "He works in the palace and I've known him my whole life."

Benjamin shrugged, "Be that as it may, I would still like to check up on him"

"Aren't you doing that already, with the investigation?" I asked softly.

"We are limited in our search criteria," he said, "But if you are serious about a personal relationship with him, then I'd like to dig deeper."

I sighed, "Do you really think that's necessary?" I asked, looking out at the passing scenery, "He was a close friend of Jacob's and his father and my father were also close."

"If you're not worried about what I will find, then you shouldn't have a problem with me looking into it." Benjamin kept his eyes forward and I watched the tick in his jaw as he clenched his teeth.

"Fine," I said with resignation, "I suppose I should've expected it."

Benjamin let out a harsh breath and shook his head slightly, "This is new territory for all of us," he said, "In all the years I've been on your detail you haven't even dated. We haven't had to have 'the talk'."

"Oh my God, Benjamin. You do not need to give me the sex talk." My face flushed with embarrassment.

Benjamin chuckled, "That's not what I meant," he said, "Well, not exactly what I meant." He sighed, "You don't get much privacy and so navigating a sexual relationship is going to be tricky."

"Stop, please," I said, completely mortified.

"No, we need to talk about this. That little stunt he pulled this afternoon, that can't happen again. We need to know where you are at all times. We're paranoid like that, and if we can't have eyes on you, then we at least need to know where you are and who you're with, if not what you're doing."

"God." I covered my face with my hands, wishing that he would just shut up.

"What I suggest is coming up with a signal. Something so that you can signal to us that you want alone time. We will back off and give you space, but we won't be too far away."

"So you want me to come up with a hand signal to let you know I'm going to have sex?" I asked, mortified.

He full out laughed and I continued to blush furiously.

"God, no," he said, "Maybe you just want to sneak into the maze for a few minutes, like this afternoon, or maybe you want to go for a walk in the moonlight in the rose garden."

His idea had merit, even if it was embarrassing to talk about.

"Okay," I conceded.

"And we should also have a signal so you can let us know if things are going further than you're comfortable with." His voice hardened and became dangerous.

"I don't think…"

"No, no one ever does, but it's better to be safe than sorry." He looked over to me as he pulled to a stop in front of the chalet. "We just want to keep you safe, princess, whatever it takes."

The seriousness in his eyes brought the reality of the situation into crystal clear relief. I nodded and rested my hand on his arm for a moment in acknowledgement. These men wouldn't hesitate to give their lives for me if they needed to and I needed to remember that. Taking off with Jordan this afternoon could've been dangerous and I had exposed us all to potential disaster without thinking.

"Thank you, Benjamin," I said softly before sliding out of the cart.

I walked down the short path and greeted Phillip, one of my mother's security detail. He opened the door for me and I walked inside, taking in the changes my mother had had done.

The chalet had been my grandmother's home before she died and I hadn't been inside since she'd lived here. It may be considered a cottage, but for the greater populace, it was an above average size home. Four bedrooms, four baths, chef's kitchen, formal dining and lounge, library, sitting room and, of course, a conservatory.

I was led by one of the house staff into the sitting room where I found my mother watching television. I smiled to myself and wondered what our people would think of the queen watching her soaps. Except, she wasn't the queen anymore, I was. The smile fell from my lips as she looked up at me.

"Oh, Alyssa," she said, her face lighting up, "It's good to see you."

I bent down and kissed her cheek, "Sorry to barge in on you," I said, "But I was hoping for a little motherly advice."

"Sit," she said, patting the couch beside her, "What can I help you with? Is it about Jordan?"

I laughed and shook my head, "No," I said and then sobered, "I'd like some advice about how to approach Parliament."

Her face blanked and she turned away from me, her eyes seeking the flickering screen across the room.

"Mama?" I asked when she didn't say anything.

She turned back to me, her face sad, "I can't help you," she said.

"But you've been dealing with them for years," I said.

"No," she corrected, "I've been dealing with their wives." She sighed and looked away again. "Do you think you should do this?"

"What? Do what?"

"Go through with the coronation."

That stopped me in my tracks.

"You don't think I should?" I asked.

"You're smart and capable, Alyssa, but politics is a man's game. Surely you don't want to get mixed up in, what is undoubtedly going to be, a long drawn out fight that you may lose anyway."

"You want me to abdicate without a fight?" I asked, disbelieving.

"If you choose to step aside, we will be looked after, maybe given a quiet duchy somewhere and you could finish your studies and get a job like you have always wanted. You wouldn't need to have your reputation dragged through the media and every aspect of your life judged by armchair warriors. You could live the life you've always wanted."

"What about daddy's legacy? What about the St. Benét name?"

"You father's legacy died with Jacob," she said flatly, refusing to look at me.

It was a punch to the gut.

I stood and walked out of the room, moving like a zombie. Was it my mother's grief that made her speak this way or did she really not believe that I could do this?

CHAPTER 12

I went through the next few days like an extra from 'The Walking Dead.' I smiled when I was told to, I met with people I was supposed to meet. I ate food that turned to sawdust in my mouth and I generally put on a show for all and sundry, but inside I felt dead. Not even my daily ride on Monty could lift my spirits. I often found myself sitting near the stable yards and watching Jed work with Mistborn, wondering if the stallion felt as out of place as I did. It was worse than when I'd first heard about the deaths of my father and brother. That had hurt, but what my mother had said to me was soul destroying.

Did all of the women of Merveille think like my mother? Were we, as a country, so far behind the rest of the western world in our attitudes towards women in leadership? There were no women in Parliament, no women in local government and I ventured to guess that the majority, if not all, of the corporate and small businesses were run by men. I had been away so long that I hadn't realised how stunted Merveille's growth was. After looking through my father's office, it was no wonder why.

It was Wednesday before I started to feel something and that something was anger. I was angry with my mother for her dismissive attitude towards me and I was angry at my father for his lack of initiative. And I was angry at myself for letting it get the better of me.

I pressed the intercom on my desk, "Alex, could I please see you for a moment?"

The door to my office opened almost immediately and Alex stepped in, tablet in hand ready to take notes on whatever it was I wanted to talk to her about. I liked this about her, she was always prepared and never thought a job was too small or beneath her.

"Take a seat," I said to her, indicating the sofa in the corner.

She sat primly on the edge and I pushed back from my desk and walked over to join her. She waited with her stylus poised.

"I would like to meet with as many female leaders in the community as you can find," I said.

"When you say leaders..."

"Business owners, women in high-placed roles in corporations, women with political aspirations, women who are innovative and who want to make a difference," I said as Alex scribbled furiously on her tablet.

"And I'd like to find out, as discreetly as possible, what women, in general, think of their next head of state being a female instead of a male."

She looked up at me, "Has something happened?" she asked, concerned.

I sighed and turned my head to look out the window behind my desk.

"I had a conversation with my mother the other night and it caused me to wonder whether the people even want me to be queen." I looked back at her, "Am I making a mistake by pushing ahead with this or should I just move aside and let Parliament choose someone from the list of male heirs?"

Alex searched my eyes before putting down her stylus and tablet and folding her hands on her lap.

"You and I have not lived in Merveille for a long time," she said, "We've seen what it's like out there in the big wide world, we've seen the possibilities for women, we've seen the good, the bad and the ugly of women's rights. Many of the older residents of Merveille have only seen the ugly. They see only what the media portrays, and let's face it, the media like to sensationalise. Any women who have wanted more, have either given in or left to seek their fortunes elsewhere because their cause hasn't had a champion. But now you have an opportunity to be that champion. It's not going to be easy and it's going to get dirty, but can you, in good conscience, walk away from the fight? I'm sorry if I'm being blunt, Your Highness, but the fact is that if you turn your back on this, then you are no better than those who openly oppress the women of our country."

I sat back in my seat and stared at her. She was absolutely right. If I did nothing, then I was condoning the patriarchal society of Merveille.

"A lot of the world wouldn't think we had it too bad," I said, "We aren't as misogynistic as places like Afghanistan or some of the other Arab states."

"No," she said, "But it is just as damaging. We are basically telling our young women that they have no value outside of marriage, that they are not intelligent enough or savvy enough to survive without the guiding hand of a man. We are telling them that they are only fit to breed and to gossip and to make things pretty. We are telling them that they are morally bankrupt and can never achieve anything on their own or for themselves."

I quirked a smile at her passion. Alex was normally so controlled and mild-mannered, but I liked this feisty side of her and she was absolutely right.

"Thank you, Alex," I said warmly, "I really needed to hear that."

Alex flushed and dropped her eyes, "I'm sorry," she said.

"Don't be," I replied, "I want you to be straight with me, always. I don't need or want to be surrounded by yes-men. If you think I'm being an idiot, I want you to tell me, I need you to tell me. Changing the long held beliefs of this country is not going to be easy and I'm going to need as many people in my corner as I can find."

She nodded and stood, and I could see a small smile on her face, "I'll get started on this list," she said.

"WE HAVE A PROBLEM," SAVANNAH SAID AS SHE BREEZED INTO MY office a couple of hours later.

I looked up from my computer screen and raised an eyebrow.

"And what problem is that?" I asked.

She slapped down one newspaper after another on my desk until it was fairly wallpapered with broadsheets.

"This," she said pointing a perfectly manicured fingernail at the headline.

"A Swing and a Miss - The Princess' Fashion Faux Pas," I read and then looked up at her.

"They're all the same," she whined, "Apparently your fashion sense is boring, unoriginal and ages you by ten years." She flopped on the sofa dramatically, "I've failed you."

I rubbed my eyes and looked over the offending papers. Every photo was awful, chosen to specifically humiliate and degrade me.

"It's not a big deal, Savannah," I said.

"But look at this one," she said, getting to her feet and shuffling through the pile. She pulled out one of the more reputable tabloids and shoved it under my nose. "They're comparing your first week in public with your mother's...*and she looks better.*" Savannah flopped back down on the couch.

I had never been a fashionista, I like comfortable and serviceable. Savannah had been trying her best with me, but I just didn't care enough about it. There were more important things in the world than what I wore.

"Seriously, Savannah, it's not a big deal."

"But it is," she said, sadly, "Don't you see? They are more concerned about what you wear than who you meet or the things you discuss. What you wear shouldn't over-shadow who you are or what you do."

I slumped back in my chair, amazed at what she was saying and surprised that I agreed with her. I had kind of written Savannah off as the air-head of our little group. Don't get me wrong, I liked her, a lot, but because of her preoccupation with hair, clothes, shoes and makeup, I had dismissed her.

I sighed, "You're right," I said, "And I owe you an apology. I've never thought of it like that."

She sat up and blinked at me, "Really? You're apologising to me?"

"Well, yeah," I said and shrugged, "I haven't been taking your advice seriously because I didn't think I needed to worry about what I wore. I mean, they never wrote headlines about what my father or brother wore."

"It's a double standard, to be sure," she said, "But they are always going to comment on what you wear. My job is to make it more of a byline than the headline."

"So how do we fix it?" I asked, having a rather surreal moment when I realised that what I wore was going to play a part in getting my country to accept me as their leader.

Savannah's eyes popped wide, "You're serious? You want to fix this?"

I smiled, "Of course I do," I said, "Why does that surprise you?"

She shrugged and looked down at her lap, "Nobody's ever taken me seriously before."

I got up from my desk and walked over to sit with her on the sofa. I took her hand in mine and waited until she looked up at me.

"Savannah, I chose you to be on my team because you are so much better at all this fashion stuff than I am. You know I would rather get about in my old Levi's and a t-shirt. But I can't do that and be taken seriously, so I need you. I need you to guide me and bully me if you have to because you're right, my fashion sense shouldn't be the headline."

"So, you'll listen to me?" she asked hopefully.

I laughed, "I'll try," I said and then gave her a hug.

She hugged me back and then jumped to her feet and I could almost hear the cogs turning in her brain. She paced my office, tapping a finger on her chin as she thought. I stood up and went back to my desk, knowing that when she was ready, she would speak.

"I'm going to have to re-think your whole wardrobe," she said.

I looked up at her, "Do you know any local designers?" I asked.

"Ooh, that's a great idea." Then she turned to me, "And I think you need a bit of a makeover. Hair, nails and makeup."

I huffed out a breath, but I couldn't turn her down now that I had just spent time assuring her that I would take her suggestions seriously.

"Okay," I said.

"Tonight," she said, "So that tomorrow when you go to Parliament we can reveal the new you."

I sighed, but agreed. I probably wouldn't be able to sleep tonight anyway, not with that meeting looming over me. Spending the night with the girls sounded like a great way to forget, just for a little while, that my future as head of state hung in the balance.

BRIDGETTE CUT SEVERAL INCHES OFF MY LONG DARK HAIR. IT NOW fell to the middle of my back, rather than to my waist and the heavy bulk of it had been lightened by a few choppy layers. I also now sported three different colour foils, all expertly blended so that they gave my hair movement and highlights, well that's what they told me anyway. The effect was a subtle brightening overall - darker underneath with lighter highlights on my crown.

Annette had been experimenting with different makeup looks and we had all had too much to drink and way too much to eat. But we laughed and bonded and for the first time in a long time, I felt like my old self. It was nice to have girlfriends that I could trust.

Along with the makeup and hair, I'd gotten a manicure and pedi-cure. Savannah wanted me to try acrylic nails, but I put my foot down. We compromised on a manicure with shellac to keep my polish looking fresher for longer.

Jeanette had taken the opportunity to educate me on social media and, although I wouldn't be allowed to actually post anything myself, we agreed on how to brand my public identity. I wanted to be taken seriously, but I didn't want to come across as elitist or out of touch. I was still a twenty-four year old woman, after all, albeit a powerful one.

Priscilla schooled me on how to approach Parliament and everyone weighed in on their opinions regarding a female head of state. I was happy to know that these women, at least, supported me. All of the women present, except my maids Bridgette and Annette, had been living outside of Merveille and had grown up with the belief that women could have equality.

"What do you think?" I asked, turning to my two, quiet maids, "Do you think the queen should be able to rule in her own right?"

They shared a look before Bridgette spoke up, "It's what we all dream of, isn't it? As little girls we imagine what it would be like to be queen. But the reality is that there can only be one."

"Yes, but little girls can grow up into scientists and scholars and prime ministers and CEOs and small business owners," I said.

"And some of them just want to be mothers and wives," Annette said quietly.

"But that's my point," I said, "We should have the choice. If you want to be a wife and mother, then I want that for you without judgement. But if you want something different, then you should have that choice. One is not better than the other. We need the wives and mothers, but we need the business owners and scientists too. The most important thing is that everyone, whether male or female, get the same opportunity to achieve whatever it is they dream of."

The room was quiet when I finished my little speech and I looked at each one of the women in my circle. It was a sobering moment, and not the first one I'd had that day. The issue of me being queen was bigger than just me, it would have far reaching effects for years to come - whether I succeeded in the ascension or not. I may not even see a significant change in my life time, but I would sow a seed and be a catalyst for change.

It was why I'd wanted to work at the UN, so that I could be part of the change for the oppressed and down trodden. I had never thought that my own small, *wealthy*, European country would need it, but the more time I spent here, the more I looked into what it would take to rule this country, I realised we did. Merveille needed an intervention and I was best placed to initiate it.

But first I had to convince Parliament that I was the queen they needed and I still didn't have a clue about how I was going to do that. These men were set in their ways and undoubtedly enjoyed their way of life. For all intents and purposes, I was an outsider. Yes, I was born here and, for the most part, grew up here, but I had never shown any indication that I wanted to make Merveille my home. I had left to pursue my own career and had left the office of princess in my wake. Now I had to convince them that I was prepared to stay for the long haul and I was under no illusion that they would be putty in my hands.

When I finally climbed into bed and the darkness of the night stole over me, I said a small prayer. I just needed the wisdom to say the right things to convince them that my gender didn't have any bearing on my abilities and that they would be open to hearing it.

CHAPTER 13

I started the morning with my usual jog around the grounds accompanied by my security detail. I timed it, as always, to coincide with Will's cheese delivery. I don't know why I did it, but for some reason I wanted to see him, even if it was only from a distance.

It was a miserable day and by the time we made it back to my suite, I was thoroughly drenched. The forecast was for heavy showers and possible thunderstorms for the afternoon, which about suited my mood. I was full of nervous energy and gut clenching anxiousness which in turn made me short-tempered.

Experts in reading body language, my security detail had picked up on my sour mood and were keeping their distance. Even Meredith was quiet, not pushing me or demanding I pull my head in. I knew I was being rude and obnoxious, but I didn't have the brain capacity to care.

I took a long, hot shower, letting the steaming water warm my rain-chilled body, and I felt marginally more human when I emerged. The meeting was at ten and I had a little over an hour before I needed to leave. Bridgette had delivered a breakfast tray to my suite, but I only nibbled at the fresh fruit, my stomach too uneasy to accept anything else other than coffee.

Savannah came to supervise my dressing and Bridgette and Annette did my hair and makeup. I wore a fawn coloured, knee length pencil skirt with a crisp white shirt that had a big collar and a deep neckline that skated the edge of sexy. Over the top I had a long, knit cardigan that hit mid-thigh and was the same colour as my skirt and on my feet I had nude Louboutin pumps. My accessories were silver - a thin belt on my skirt and a chunky bangle on my wrist that complimented the silver bangle I always wore. My hair was left down but with a tousled look (thanks to the new layers) and my makeup was subtle but with smokey eyes.

The overall effect was corporate but not stuffy. There was definitely a youthful look to it without compromising my need to be taken seriously. I liked it and finally felt that Savannah and I had reached an agreement on my image.

The room was practically silent as I was dressed and made up. Everyone was either nervous themselves or picking up on my mood and it was an odd thing to be part of. I wanted to break the tension, reassure them that everything was going to be fine, but I couldn't find the words, which didn't bode well for the upcoming meeting. Being struck dumb in front of all those men was not part of the plan, but if I didn't snap out of the funk I was in, that's exactly what was going to happen.

Priscilla and Dominique breezed into the room when I was finally dressed and instead of making me feel better, it only amped up my anxiety. They would accompany me to the meeting, although they wouldn't speak, and it should've been a comfort for me. Instead it just added pressure and made me feel completely out of my depth.

I had fifteen minutes until we had to leave and I shooed everybody out of the room. I needed a few minutes to myself, to find my equilibrium. I stood at the window looking out over the grounds and took a deep breath. From where I stood, I could see the separate stable and yard that Mistborn had been housed in. He stood in the yard, his head held high like he was surveying his kingdom. He moved his head slightly and I felt like he was staring right at me, daring me, egging me on.

I turned from the window and shook my head, damned horse. Cliff was right when he said he was going to be a pain. It was just like an

Arabian to think that he was the ruler of his new home and his silent challenge of me rankled. Why was it that all the men in this damned country wanted to make my life difficult?

There was a soft knock on the door before it opened and Jordan walked in. He smiled at me and I felt a small measure of peace invade my heart. He looked good in his military dress and even though I saw it all the time, I still admired the cut and fit of it on him.

"You need to relax Lys," he said coming over to me and taking my hands, "It will all work out, I promise you."

I exhaled in a huff and dropped my eyes.

"Do you really think so?" I asked, "Do you think I would make a good head of state?"

"You'll make a great queen," he said without hesitation.

I looked up at him and narrowed my eyes, "But that's not what I asked," I said, "I asked if I would make a good head of state."

He sighed and shook his head as he ground his teeth together. He dropped my hands and walked over to the sideboard that held a crystal decanter and matching glasses. I watched, confused, as he poured himself a finger of scotch and downed it.

"You don't think I can do it," I whispered.

He turned to me and shrugged, "You're very bright and personable," he said, "And so very beautiful. Everyone will love you."

"But, again, that's not the question," I said, this time through gritted teeth.

"What does it matter what I think?" he asked, "I'm not the one making the decisions."

"Maybe not," I replied, angry now, "But I thought you supported me in this."

He walked over to me and took my hands in his again. "I do," he said, "I do support you, but I worry about you. This is not going to be an easy thing and I'm concerned that the stress of it all will be too much for you."

I snatched my hands out of his and walked towards the door. I turned back to him before I stepped through and said, "I am not some fragile, porcelain doll, Jordan, and I won't have you or anyone else tell me that I am."

I walked out the door without looking back. At least now I felt the determination that had been lacking earlier and I could thank Jordan for that.

I WALKED INTO THE HOUSE OF LORDS CHAMBERS AND TOOK A DEEP, steadying breath. I had never been here before and the atmosphere of centuries of tradition was palpable. The smell of leather, wood and cigar smoke permeated the room and the high sandstone walls and stained glass windows had the desired effect of intimidating me even more.

The meeting was not yet in session and the sixteen lords, the speaker, the bishop and the prime minister mingled, the low murmur of male voices a reminder that I was probably the first woman to step foot inside the chamber in its entire history.

The members wore their robes and wigs and I, with my entourage and bodyguards, was immediately noticeable as an outsider. Yet another tactic to intimidate me, no doubt.

The House of Lords was made up of the peers of the realm, the sixteen lords appointed by the crown, along with the bishop. The speaker and the prime minister straddled both the House of Lords and the House of Commons. The prime minister would get to vote on any of the bills that were brought to the floor, but the speaker refrained except in the event of a tied vote. The role of speaker was to keep everyone in line, ensuring that no one spoke out of turn and that the code of conduct was adhered to during sessions.

The office of speaker was currently held by Lord Charles Bingham, the Duke of Monterey and Meredith's father, which was of benefit to me because I would be sure to be given a fair hearing. It was also a problem because he couldn't support me by voting in my favour.

The House was brought to order and the members moved to take their seats. I was ushered to a visitor's bench and sat uncomfortably on the leather seat to await my turn. I watched in terrified fascination as the lords argued one point or another in their attempt to get different bills passed. They were nasty, degenerating to name-calling on several occasions and frequently theatrical. Lord Bingham had his hands full in trying to maintain decorum among these privileged, but immature, school boys.

All too soon, it was my turn to speak. I was to make a case for myself to ascend to head of state, as every heir was required to do. Usually it was a simple formality, but in my case nothing was simple. I stood and walked towards the podium. I spoke the traditional words of petition and then the speaker opened the floor for discussion and questions.

The prime minister was the first to speak. "I have to make it known that I have reservations about this situation," he said, "We have never had a female head of state and there is no precedent for such a thing. We need a stable, firm and reliable leader and I do not believe that a young, twenty-something girl fits the bill."

There were murmurs of ascent from the ranks of men, regardless of what side of politics they fell on. It may be the first time that these two parties had agreed on anything.

Lord Bingham motioned for me to make my rebuttal.

"While I understand your concerns," I began, my voice wavering with nerves, "I can assure you that neither my age nor my gender has any bearing on this appointment. I was born and raised a St. Benét and I have the experience of centuries of forebears to fall back on, not to mention the very real experience of being raised by arguably one of the best kings to have ruled our small country. I am also university educated with studies in international relations and have a good under-standing of the political climate of our region. I may be twenty-four and a female, but I am also capable, intelligent and reliable."

"But you have not lived here in over four years," another of the members yelled from his bench.

I nodded, "That is correct, but Merveille is in my blood and I want the best for her."

Jordan's father, Major General Elijah Wicks, stood to his feet and waited patiently to be acknowledged by the speaker.

"Princess Alyssabeth," he began, "You have certainly gown into a fine young lady, I'm sure we can all agree. You are indeed intelligent and educated, and while you are young, no one denies that you have had a stellar upbringing. But the fact remains that you are female and we have never had a female head of state. While we don't deny your fervour for our dear country, being that you are female puts some restraints on the role you can successfully hold. The idea of becoming our head of state may be a pretty bauble for you right now, but what about when you change your mind or something else comes along to catch your eye? What about when you meet someone and fall in love? Men have the ability to keep their feelings separate from their business, but we all know that that is not the case for a woman. I bet every man here can attest to a time when his wife's emotions got the better of her. And if you do successfully fall in love and marry without it affecting your role as head of state, what about when you have children? Surely your interest will wane then and you will want to spend as much time with them as possible. And what of your husband? Even without the children in the equation, what role is he to play? Is he to fulfil what would traditionally be the queen's duties? Meeting with the ladies of the court while you discuss crown business with the lords? And how is he meant to be the head of your household, as all good husbands should be, when you are, in effect, in authority over him?"

I stood there completely dumbfounded. The man spoke with eloquence and aplomb, but his words were condescending and patronising. His disdainful view of women was medieval and draconian.

"On the other hand," he went on after a small pause in which the entire House was silent, "If you were to marry and were willing to allow your husband to take the role of king and therefore our head of state, then there would be no reason for us to deny your ascension to queen."

You. Have. Got. To. Be. Kidding. Me.

There was a rousing clamour of agreement from the other lords as the General took his seat. I made a pretty good impression of a gold fish as I tried to make sense of what he was saying. The speaker banged his gavel to bring the House to order and I cleared my throat as I took to the podium again.

"So, what you are saying," I croaked, "Is that if I marry a suitable man who can fulfil the footsteps of my father and brother, you will approve my petition to be queen?" I threw up my hands in defeat. "And if I refuse?"

The General smirked at me and shrugged his shoulders.

"Shall we take a vote?" Lord Bingham asked, "All those in favour of granting Princess Alyssabeth her petition of ascension, say aye..." there were a couple of half-hearted ayes of which Lord Bingham noted, "All those opposed?" This garnered a far greater reaction and I felt my stomach drop.

Lord Bingham banged his gavel once more to bring order to the ensuing noise.

"Princess Alyssabeth," he intoned, "You have thirty days to appeal this decision or to provide us with your intent to marry." He banged his gavel and then moved on to the next order of business.

JORDAN WAS WAITING FOR ME WHEN WE ARRIVED BACK AT THE palace. I raced past him, up the stairs and in through the doors, jumping into the elevator before he could stop me.

I was mad. So mad I wanted to scratch someone's eyes out. I stormed into my suite, through the sitting room and into my bedroom. I pulled off my clothes and pulled on my Levi's and t-shirt, along with my riding boots and a hoody. I needed to go for a ride. I needed the wind through my hair and the fresh air in my lungs.

"Alyssa," I heard Jordan call from the sitting room.

"I don't want to talk to you," I yelled back.

He came to the door of my bedroom and leant against the door-jamb, "Please, Alyssa, tell me what happened."

"You know very well what happened," I ground out, "They denied my petition because I am a woman. So unless I can come up with a reason why that shouldn't matter in the next thirty days, or get married, then I won't be queen."

His lips tugged in a small smile, "So, let's get married."

I stopped my tantrum and looked at him like he was insane, "What did you just say?"

He walked towards me and took my hands in his, "I said," he lifted his hand and brushed a stray hair from my face, "Let's get married."

"Are you kidding me?" I yelled, pulling my hands from his and step-ping away from him, "Don't you understand?"

He looked genuinely puzzled, "No, I don't understand what the problem is. You need a husband and I can be that for you. I love you Lys, don't you know that? If we get married, we both get what we want."

"No," I said, "We don't. If I get married, I have to give up being head of state and let my husband have that role. That is not getting what I want."

"Don't you love me?" he asked.

"That is not the point," I growled at him, "The point is that I am the heir to the throne and I should be the one to sit on it."

"But you still get that," he said, "You get to be queen and I'll even change my name to St. Benét so that the tradition of your family continues. I don't see the problem."

"The problem," I said, "Is that I will be handing over my birthright to you and that is not what I want. Why should it matter that I am a woman? And why the hell can't you support me in this?"

"I'm offering you a solution," he said, his anger finally becoming known, "That *is* being supportive."

"No Jordan, that is serving your own political agenda. Is that what this whole relationship has been about from the start? You just want me because of what I can do for your career?"

"Don't be ridiculous," he scoffed, "I thought we were heading down the aisle anyway, so why not achieve two things at once? You need to get married in order to become queen and I can do that for you."

He came towards me again, but I batted his hands away, "Leave me alone, I need to think," I said, racing out of the room.

I ran past my body guards, who looked a little worried, but I signalled them that I needed some space, so they stayed where they were. I raced down the corridor and opened the first door I came to, it was a stair well. I jogged down the stairs, rounding each landing and continuing down until I came to the bottom. I pushed out of the emergency door and found myself in the yard near Mistborn's stable.

The wind whipped through my hair and pulled at my clothes, the sky rumbled with thunder and the rain beat down. I ran across the lawn to the stable and walked inside the dim space, taking a big breath of hay and horse. Mistborn stood tethered and saddled, an unusual occurrence, but one I didn't think too much about. I gathered the reins and swung up onto his back. He snorted and danced under me, not happy that I had taken control of him.

I turned him towards the stable doors and urged him on. He jumped out into the storm like a racehorse from a gate and we took off towards the paddocks. I gave him his head, gripping with my thighs and threading my fingers through his mane. He was fast and his thundering hooves combined with the stormy weather had a cathartic effect on me.

I had been angry enough to spit bullets when I left Parliament, but after talking to Jordan, my fury had consumed me. How dare he offer to marry me like he was sacrificing himself on the altar for me? He knew what was in it for him, he'd probably known before I had even left for the meeting. He and his father had most likely discussed the best way for things to go and had come up with this plan weeks ago. And I had fallen hook, line and sinker for it.

I couldn't believe how gullible I'd been. I had leant on Jordan after losing Father and Jacob and he had taken advantage of me. I should have listened to Carlos when he tried to warn me, but my damn stupid heart had betrayed me. I thought I was falling in love with Jordan, but now I was finding out it was all a lie.

A bolt of lightning streaked through the sky followed almost instantaneously by a loud crack of thunder. Mistborn, spooked by the sudden brightness and loud noise, reared, throwing me from his back. I tumbled through the air and landed hard, hitting my head and then the world went dark.

CHAPTER 14

I was dreaming. It wasn't the first time Will's face had appeared to me in a dream. It was the first time though, that he had been dripping wet. His face filled my entire vision, the edges soft and blurred. The light was soft, like the tail end of twilight and a soft breeze ruffled the dark curls that haloed around his head.

"Will," I whispered and smiled, reaching up to touch his face.

His eyebrows were pulled together in a frown and his clear, blue eyes full of concern. I preferred the dreams when he smiled, when he looked at me like I was his everything. Now he looked at me like something was wrong and I didn't like it at all.

My hand cupped his jaw, the rough whiskers rasping against my palm. He closed his eyes and leaned into my hand. This dream was much more tactile than anything I'd previously experienced and I relished the warmth of his skin on mine. My eyes fluttered closed and I sunk back into darkness.

"Lys," his voice was urgent and I felt him jostling me.

I cracked an eye open, "Hmm?"

"You can't go back to sleep," he said, but that didn't make sense because I knew I was already sleeping.

"Is okay," I slurred, the words feeling like cotton in my mouth, "Jus' need to close my eyes for..."

"No, Lys," he jostled me again, "You need to stay awake."

"I'm sleepy," I murmured, closing my eyes again.

I felt the warmth of his body press alongside mine and realised how cold I was. I snuggled into him and sighed.

"You feel good," I whispered.

"God, Lys," he groaned, "Stay with me sweetheart, don't go back to sleep."

I giggled, "You're silly. I'm already asleep."

"Come on, Lys," he said as I felt his strong arms gather me to him and then lift me from the ground.

I frowned as my body hurt and my head spun, the sudden movement causing nausea to roil in my gut.

"Ow," I hissed.

"God, sorry," he murmured before pressing his warm lips against my temple.

I felt the motion of him walking while he carried me and I grabbed his wet shirt in my fists to steady myself. I began to think that maybe this wasn't a dream at all.

"What were you doing out here, Lys?" he asked as he kept moving forward.

"Don't...remember," I replied, my head beginning to pound painfully. "What happened?"

"I have no idea," he said and I felt him put me down. "Do you think you can sit up and hold on to me."

"I'll try," I said as he manoeuvred me so I was sitting astride his ATV. He slid in front of me and pulled my arms around his waist tightly.

"Hold on," he said as he started the engine.

I gripped his shirt in my fists and bit my lip as we bounced along. It was raining and I shivered with the cold. Will's back was hard and warm and I pressed into it in order to steal some of his heat. My teeth began to chatter and I moaned against the pain in my body as I was we hit bump after bump.

I still didn't know what had happened, I couldn't remember how I'd gotten to be in the middle of the rain. I didn't even know where I was. The only thing that made sense was the man who I now clung to desperately.

The ATV slowed and we entered a barn. The comforting smell of hay and the brush of warmth on my chilled skin was welcome. Will parked the four-wheeler and gently unclasped my hands from around his waist. He slid off the bike, not letting go of my hands and, when he was standing, he slid his arms around my waist and under my knees and picked me up like I weighed nothing.

He walked out of the barn and jogged through the rain until we reached his house. He climbed the stairs and shouldered the door open and I was hit with the heat of a well-tended kitchen fire. The shock of the warmth startled me into uncontrollable shaking and Will held me closer, whispering comforting sounds in my ear.

"Will? Is that you?"

The female voice sounded familiar but in my barely conscious state, I couldn't place it.

"Oh, God, is that the princess?"

"Georgie, grab some towels, will you?" Will said gruffly as he sat on a chair and held me in his lap.

"Of course," Georgie said as she scurried away.

"I don't understand," I stammered through my chattering teeth, "What happened to me?"

"I was hoping you could tell me," he said as he rubbed my back with a strong hand. "What's the last thing you remember?"

I tried to think back to the last thing that was clear in my abused brain, but everything was scrambled. I didn't know what was real or a dream.

"Here, Will," Georgie said, saving me from answering, "Let me get her out of these wet clothes and warmed up. Why don't you call the palace and let them know she's here."

I could feel Will tense before reluctantly letting me go. He stood and then sat me down on the chair. He squatted in front of me and framed my face with his big palms. He stared into my eyes for a moment before leaning forward to place a soft kiss on my forehead. I let my eyes close with his touch, but then he was gone and I was left with Georgie.

"HERE, LET ME HELP YOU OUT OF THOSE WET CLOTHES," GEORGINA said, kneeling beside me and handing me a fluffy towel.

"Thank you," I replied, through my still chattering teeth.

Together we wrangled the wet clothes from my body and she handed me some clean, dry, *warm*, sweats. I pulled them on thankfully and she wrapped a blanket around my shoulders and urged me closer to the fire.

As I began to thaw out, I gazed around the room. We were in the kitchen and it was so very different from the one in the palace. I hadn't been to the Pemberton Estate since I was a little girl and I doubted very much that I had ever been in the kitchen. It was a large room with a slate tiled floor, a monstrous wooden island bench that wore the scars of time like badges of honour, gleaming copper pots hanging from the ceiling and the huge fireplace that I now sat practically on top of. It also had the modern conveniences, fridge, gas range, microwave, but held true to its period features. And it was dark, apart from the flickering light of the fire.

Georgina filled a large black kettle with water and then hung it over the heat of the fire.

"The storm knocked the power out," she said apologetically, "But I can make tea and maybe heat some soup if you're hungry."

I nodded, "Tea sounds wonderful," I replied.

We sat in silence and watched the flames, their hypnotising dance calming my nerves as they heated my frozen body.

"What time is it?" I asked.

"After seven," she replied and I gasped. How long had I been missing? The palace must be going crazy.

"I need to get to a phone, I need to let everyone know I'm okay," I said, struggling to get up.

Two large, warm hands settled on my shoulders, halting my progress.

"Take it easy, princess," he said, "The phone lines are down, probably knocked out by a tree, and I'm pretty sure I saw lightning hit the closest cell tower, so they're out as well. Once I've warmed up a bit, I'll head out and go over to let the palace know where you are."

"It's too dangerous, Will," Georgina pleaded with her brother.

I finally took in the raging storm outside. The wind howled and the thunder peeled and it sounded like hail was hitting the tiled roof of the portico outside.

"You can't go out in this," I croaked, my throat feeling like I'd swallowed razor blades.

"I have to let them know you're okay and that you're here," he said sitting down beside me. "Why wasn't someone with you? Where is your security detail?"

I rubbed my aching head. Whenever I tried to remember what happened, pain lanced through my brain. "I don't know. I can't remember anything about today."

The fire began to hiss and spit as the kettle boiled and sent hot water onto the coals beneath. Georgina grabbed some thick pot holders and removed the kettle from the heat and took it over to the big island bench. She poured the steaming water into a big teapot and waited for it to brew.

"Is it just the two of you here?" I asked, curious about this family who I had lost touch with over the years.

"I sent everyone home when the storm reports started coming in," Will said, rubbing his hand through his damp hair. He had changed out of his wet clothes and wore faded denim jeans and a long sleeved t-shirt that skimmed his torso almost like a second skin.

"How did you find me?" I blurted out, "How did you even know to look for me?"

"I didn't," he said, "I was checking on my cows, making sure they were all under shelter when I found you lying in the paddock."

"I was in your paddock?" I asked.

He nodded and then cursed under his breath, "I thought you were dead," he said harshly, "Your lips were practically blue and your skin was so pale. I saw the blood in your hair and I near had a heart attack."

"I'm bleeding," I whispered in horror as my hand went to the tender place on my head.

"Not now," he said, reassuringly, "But you were."

Georgina placed a warm mug of tea in my hands and I sipped it gingerly. The hot, sweet and spicy chai scalded my tongue, but felt so wonderfully warm as it burned down my throat that I didn't care. Will took his own mug from his sister and then she sat down next to us with one of her own.

"Was there any damage to any of the buildings?" Georgina asked before taking a tentative sip from her mug.

Will shook his head, "No, it seems we were lucky. All the repairs to the out buildings have held and the generator has kicked in over in the factory, so we're good."

"You have a generator?" I asked dumbly.

Georgina snorted, "To look after his precious cheese," she smirked.

He sighed and shook his head, "I know, I know," he said patiently but with a smile for his sister, "I'll get around to fixing up this place when I have a spare minute."

She smiled, "It's okay," she said, "I don't mind that we live in only five rooms of this massive thirty room monstrosity. Less for me to clean."

"Like you do any cleaning," he laughed.

The easy banter between the siblings had a comforting effect on me. Jacob and I had had a similar relationship, although not as close as Will and Georgina obviously were. I sat quietly and sipped my tea, letting it and the company soothe me. My eyes started to droop and I leaned my head to the side to rest it on Will's shoulder. I was so tired and now that I had thawed out and felt warm and snug, weariness tugged at me.

I felt the now empty mug being pulled from my fingers and I let it go easily. Before I knew it, I was being lifted by strong arms and I burrowed into the strong chest that held me. With a sigh, I drifted off into the welcoming darkness.

THE NEXT TIME I OPENED MY EYES, I WAS IN A DARK ROOM. A FIRE flickered in a hearth across the room, but it was the low, banked ember type fire rather than the roaring one that had been in the kitchen. I lay on a leather couch that was soft and cushioned my aching body. I was covered with a fluffy crocheted blanket and my head rested on something harder than a pillow but softer than a rock. I looked up to see Will above me, his head leaned back against the sofa, exposing his long neck, and his eyes closed. My head was in his lap and I had the overwhelming desire to snuggle back into it and fall back asleep.

But the silence of the night was suddenly loud in my ears. The storm had passed and I needed to get home. I couldn't imagine what Benjamin and Meredith and the rest of them must be thinking. They would have no idea where I was and there would be panic - controlled panic, but panic none the less.

I tried to sit up, but the blinding pain in my head caused me to gasp and freeze. I felt one of Will's arms tighten around my waist and the other one gently stroke through my hair.

"Shh, princess," he whispered, "Take it easy. You've got a nasty bump on your head."

"The storm's gone," I croaked, my throat on fire, "I have to get home."

"It's okay," he said, his voice rough with sleep, "They know you're here, they know you're safe."

I relaxed back down into the couch and breathed through the pain in my head. Will continued to stroke his fingers through my hair and it felt wonderful. I closed my eyes and relished the decadent feeling of it.

"Thank you Will," I murmured.

"For what?" he asked softly.

"For taking care of me."

He chuckled and the sound rumbled through me causing my stomach to flop and my insides to warm.

"It has been my pleasure, Lys," he whispered.

I loved hearing my nickname fall from his lips in his husky, sleep ravaged voice. Being here with him in the dark, surrounded by his strength and his warmth made me feel safe and I relaxed even more into the softness of the couch.

"Do you remember anything from yesterday?" he asked softly, his fingers still playing with my hair.

"No," I replied.

"Well, it seems you had a bad day in Parliament and then had a fight with Wicks."

I groaned as pain speared through my brain, but the memory of the day came back in a flash. I swore and scrunched my eyes shut.

Will's hand stilled in my hair, "Did he hurt you?" he asked, and I could tell that his jaw was clenched tight.

"No," I said and I felt the tension in him relax, "Not physically anyway."

He exhaled sharply, but his fingers resumed their stroking through my hair.

"Parliament won't approve my ascension unless I'm married and sign over my role as head of state to my husband," I said, feeling again the hurt and anger of the previous day.

"Then they're idiots," he said.

I huffed out a laugh at his immediate response.

"What?" he asked.

I smiled, "You're the only one to think so," I said.

"Merveille needs someone like you," he said, "We've been stagnating too long in a cesspool of nepotism and backroom handshakes. If something doesn't change soon, we are going to lose everything that is great about our country."

"I agree," I said softly, "But what can I do? I can't even step into my inheritance because of the boys club that is our House of Lords."

He sighed, "I know," he said, "Jacob and I had discussed his plans for change. He wanted to get some new blood into the chamber, maybe open it up to more than just the peers."

"I saw your applications for grants in my father's office," I said softly, "I can't believe he denied them."

He snorted, "I loved your father," he said, "But the man had no backbone or foresight. The Parliament controlled him and I was not a favoured person around here after my father disgraced himself."

"But you've proved them wrong," I said, "Look at what you've achieved without their help or influence."

"I know," he said, "But I couldn't have done it without Jacob in my corner. God, I miss him." His voice was raw with emotion and I felt the pickle of tears behind my eyes and my throat clutch.

I sat up slowly, gritting my teeth against the pain, and moved so that I was practically sitting on Will's lap. I wound my arms around his neck and burrowed into his shoulder as tears flowed out of my eyes. I hadn't cried for my father and brother since that first time on the plane, but hearing Will's grief broke the dam on mine.

His arms held me tight and he pulled me onto his lap. His strong hands petted my hair and rubbed my back making nonsensical noises to comfort me.

"I wish to God I had gone with him that day," he said harshly, his voice rough with emotion. "Maybe I could have..."

"No," I said, lifting my head to stare into his eyes, "You probably would have been killed too. What happened was out of everyone's control, even his security detail couldn't stop him from dying."

His jaw firmed and his nostrils flared, "But I knew something they didn't," he ground out. His gaze softened and his hands came up to cup my face, his thumbs brushing the tears from my cheeks, "I'm so sorry I failed him and you," he said before dipping his head and brushing his lips against mine.

Sensation washed over me in waves as his lips continued to slide over mine. I threaded my fingers through the hair at his nape and responded to his kiss, opening my mouth and tasting him for the first time. The smell of wood smoke and the sandalwood of his cologne infused my senses and he tasted like cinnamon and star anise from the tea we'd had earlier.

He angled my head so that he could delve deeper into my mouth and I whimpered. His hands skated down over my shoulders, down my back and came to rest on my hips. His large hands spanned the small of my back as he pulled me closer, pressing my soft places against his hard ones and it felt so wonderful that I lost myself to it.

His tongue slid against mine as he continued to kiss me, deeper, more urgent. My hands slid from his hair to grip the rounded muscles of his shoulders and my short nails dug into the flesh as I pulled myself against him. No one had ever consumed me like Will did now, not even Jordan's kisses had ignited this deep burning desire within me.

The sharp rap of a brass knocker against wood pierced through our fog of lust and we pulled apart. I was breathing heavily and my lips felt swollen and tender. I looked down into Will's eyes and saw the desire banked there, turning his clear blue ones dark and stormy. His lips were wet from our kisses and his cheeks flushed. We just stared at one another, breathing hard, minds blank until the knock came again and spurred Will into action.

He lifted me gently and sat me on the couch as he stood and ran a hand through his hair. He didn't look at me as he straightened his clothes and took a deep breath. He strode out of the room and I heard the front door open followed by his harsh, "What the hell are you doing here?"

CHAPTER 15

"I'M here for Alyssa," I heard Jordan's hard voice echo down the hall.

"The hell you are," Will replied with heat, "I told you that if you ever darkened my doorway again, I'd kill you. Now get off my property before I get my rifle."

"Not without the princess," Jordan's voice was firm.

"She's not going anywhere with you," Will answered, his voice had risen in volume, but deepened in timbre.

"That's my goddamned fiancé in there and I'm not leaving without her."

Fiancé? If I was Jordan's fiancé then I was still missing a significant portion of my memory.

I heard Will swear in a low growl and then I heard footsteps as Jordan must have barged past Will. He strode into the room searching for me and when he found me a weird look crossed his face before he schooled his features into a look of concern.

He stepped over to me and knelt down at my feet.

"Oh, God," he said, his voice rough, "We were so worried about you."

Will walked into the room behind him and stood in the doorway, blocking it. His large arms crossed in front of his chest and a look of steel on his face. His eyes were cold and whatever warmth had been between us before had now disappeared with the arrival of Jordan.

"I-uh-I don't remember much of what happened," I said.

Jordan cradled my face gently in his hands, "You were upset about what happened in Parliament and we had a fight. You took off into the storm on Mistborn."

"Mistborn?" I croaked. That, I didn't remember.

He nodded. "The horse came back, drenched and wild looking and we couldn't find you anywhere."

"Who is Mistborn?" Will asked, well, growled.

"An Arabian stallion that Jordan gave me," I answered automatically still in shock that I had ridden the beast.

"You gave her an Arabian stallion?" Will asked before swearing under his breath, "Were you trying to kill her?"

"Don't be so dramatic," Jordan waved Will's comment away, "It was a coronation gift."

"A coronation gift that very well nearly killed her," Will reiterated.

Jordan jumped to his feet, "Well I didn't expect her to be stupid enough to ride him in the middle of a storm," he growled, his fists clenched at his sides.

"Excuse me?" I asked, my body going cold. Is that what Jordan really thought of me?

He whipped around, panic on his face and knelt in front of me again, "I didn't mean to say that," he said, "I'm just so upset and worried about you."

Will snorted and looked away from Jordan's display. I was so confused, I didn't know what to think or feel or believe. Moments before I had been locked in Will's embrace with his lips scorching mine and searing my veins with need. Now he could barely look at me. Meanwhile Jordan was playing the devoted fiancé, even though I couldn't even remember him proposing to me.

"Come on Alyssa," Jordan said, "Let's get you home."

"No," Will said, his voice low and hard, "She's not going anywhere with you."

"You don't have that kind of authority," Jordan said, standing to his feet and staring Will down.

"I told Benjamin that I would stay with her until he arrived so, yeah, I do have that authority."

"I'm her fiancé," Jordan said, drawing himself up, "I am not a threat to her."

"I know who you really are," Will said dangerously, "I know all about you Wicks and there is no way in hell that I am letting the future queen of Merveille leave here with you."

"I am no threat to her," Jordan repeated through gritted teeth.

"I'm not so sure of that," Will responded in kind.

Jordan swung at him and I gasped, my hands flying up to cover my mouth. Will blocked his swing with one arm and then drove his fist into Jordan's gut with the other. Jordan doubled over with a woosh of air leaving his lungs and dropped to one knee. I jumped to my feet and, despite the pain, moved over to crouch beside him.

"What the hell, Will?" I yelled at him.

"He started it," Will said.

I shook my head at his childish display as Jordan groaned. I helped him up to sit on the couch beside me and heard Will's curse as he turned and stomped out of the room.

"Stay here," I said to Jordan as I followed Will out and down the hall to the kitchen where we had been last night.

Will stood with his back to me, his hands braced on the island bench and his head bowed. I stood in the doorway and crossed my arms over my chest.

"What the hell was that?" I asked.

He sighed and shook his head, but didn't answer me.

I ran a hand through my hair, wincing as I skimmed over the lump where I'd hit my head.

"I don't understand," I said, "You, Jacob and Jordan were all such good friends. First Carlos tells me that Jacob and Jordan hadn't spoken for three years and now this. What the hell is going on between you?"

"Leave it, Lys," he said harshly, "Just stay the hell out of it."

"No," I said, "I won't. After everything Jordan did for you after your father died, how can you treat him like this?"

He turned to face me, his face a mask of horror, "After everything he did for me?" he asked softly and then shook his head. "You have no idea what Jordan did to my family. I think you should leave, the two of you deserve each other."

Will stomped out of the kitchen and I heard the back door slam and then his boots on the stairs. What the hell had just happened? I stood there frozen until I felt Jordan come up behind me and rest his hands on my shoulders.

"Let him go, Lys," Jordan said softly, "He's hurting still and he's just lashing out at whomever he can."

Jordan was right, but it still hurt to see Will so angry. I turned into Jordan's arms and let him hold me for a moment before he led me out of the house and into his car to take me home.

PANDEMONIUM. THAT'S WHAT ENSUED WHEN JORDAN BROUGHT ME back to the palace. He wasn't supposed to come and get me, he was supposed to have waited for my security detail to come get me. Apparently Benjamin and the team had thought me perfectly safe with Will until the morning.

Jordan had obviously disagreed and he was prepared to tell everyone and anyone, quite loudly, that I was his fiancée and he felt it was more prudent for me to be home in my own bed and tended to by the royal physician.

I just wanted to crawl into bed and ignore everyone for the next forty-eight hours at least.

I didn't want to talk about what happened. I didn't want the doctor prodding and poking me and sticking a tongue depressor down my throat or shine a light in my eyes. I didn't want to explain to Benjamin why I had purposely taken off from my security detail. I didn't want to explain to Jed and Cliff why I was stupid enough to jump on Mistborn, a horse I barely knew and one that was too dangerous for me anyway, and ride off into a storm putting both the very expensive horse and myself in danger.

And least of all, I didn't want to hear the word fiancé come out of

Jordan's mouth one more time or I might finish what Will started with him.

But, of course, being a crown princess, I didn't get anything I wanted. I had to sit through the doctor examining me, poking at my sore bits and prodding at my even sorer bits. And while that humiliation was in progress, I had to sit through a lecture from Benjamin and Von Bartham who tag teamed me with their berating. And, try as I might, I couldn't seem to get rid of Jordan.

When the doctor had finally completed his consultation and declared me banged and bruised but essentially unharmed, I did the only thing I could think of to get rid of everyone. I threw a tantrum.

"Get out! Everybody get out of my room NOW!"

It was so out of character for me that it managed to shock everybody into shutting up, which helped my headache no end. I ushered everyone out the door amid protestations and questions about press releases. When everybody was over the threshold and in the hallway, I blocked the door and looked each one of them in the eye.

"I don't want anything said to the press about any of this until I have managed to talk to each and every one of you and that won't be until the morning. So go about your day and leave me the hell alone."

I slammed the door and took a deep breath to calm the uncontrollable shaking that had taken over my body. I leant my back against the door and slid down to the ground, burying my head in my hands.

This was my life now. Well, it would be if I continued to be part of the royal family. I had been careless, I could freely admit it, but every other twenty-four year old woman on the planet got to be careless sometimes, didn't they? And they didn't have the whole damned household coming down on them like a tonne of bricks.

Emotion sometimes got the better of me; was Parliament right to block my petition? My tantrum yesterday and today had certainly proved one of their points right, so how could I blame them for their hesitancy?

I took a deep breath and leant my head back against the door. Is this what I wanted, really? I had been given the perfect out. I could go back to America, resume my studies and get a job at the UN. I would be normal, live a normal life without having to worry about what clothes I wore or being followed by body guards. I could live the life of obscurity that I always craved.

But what would happen to Merveille? Would the next head of state just continue on in the same vein as all the previous ones? Or would they look to change and a way to keep Merveille fresh and relevant? Surely I wasn't the only one that wanted to see change, Will had as much admitted that he too thought we needed fresh blood.

God, I was so tired and I just couldn't face any of this right now. I got to my feet slowly and moved into the bedroom, discarding clothes as I went. I crawled beneath the sheets and hit the button to lower the shades, dousing the room in darkness. I sighed and closed my eyes, surrendering to sleep.

THE DREAM STARTED INNOCUOUSLY ENOUGH.

I was running through the hedge maze and I was laughing. The day was bright, the sun shining gaily in the sky, I was laughing as I ran, holding up my billowing white skirts. I was in a wedding dress and I was happy, deliriously happy. I took a turn and ended up in the small alcove where Jordan had kissed me that time and I came to a stop to catch my breath. Strong arms wrapped around me from behind and spun me around. Will smiled down at me, his blue eyes sparkling with mirth and then he dropped his head and kissed me.

When he lifted his head, his eyes clouded as he saw something over my shoulder. I turned to see Jordan standing there in all his military regalia. He reached for me and pulled me away from Will, crushing me against his chest and kissing me roughly.

"You're mine, now," he said harshly when he lifted his head, "You're my wife Alyssabeth and he can't have you."

I looked around frantically for Will, but he was gone. I turned back to Jordan, but he was gone too.

I stepped out of the alcove and back into the maze, and tripped over something. I looked down to see a body in a black suit. Jamie stared up at me with dead eyes. I stifled a scream and started running down path after path searching for Will. I came across other bodies as I searched, my mother, Benjamin, Carlos, Aiden, Daniel. My whole security team had been wiped out. I tried to run faster, my panic to find Will growing.

I called out his name, but there was no sound except the howling wind. The weather had turned and black clouds roiled overhead. The walls of the maze drew closer, the branches catching and tearing my dress, scratching my arms and legs as I ran past.

As I neared the centre of the maze, I saw the bodies of my father and Jacob and then Meredith. But I couldn't stop to mourn, I had to find Will, the need to do so forcing me forward, forcing me away from the people that I loved and who had died for me.

I finally made it to the centre of the maze and I saw Jordan standing there, his eyes intense, his face like the storm. His hands hung at his sides, straight, with fists clenched and in his hand he held a bloody tusk. As was the way of dreams, I knew it was a boar's tusk without having to examine it too clearly, and couldn't tear my eyes away from the ivory drenched in and dripping with blood.

I heard myself cry out and fell to my knees on the rough gravel path. The wind tore at my hair and dress and the crash of thunder boomed overhead. My eyes followed the slow, syrupy drip of blood as it fell languorously from the end of the tusk and landed with a splash on the pure white gravel, the bright red a harsh contrast to the pearly white stones. It trickled, leaving a red path behind it as it joined a much larger pool of blood. The surface of the blood shimmered as lightning rent the sky and even though I tried hard not to look, I couldn't help turning my head to see what had caused the bloody puddle.

Two bodies lay at Jordan's feet, a bride and a groom. The groom wore a dark tuxedo and his dark hair was ruffled by the wind swirling through the maze. I crawled closer and looked down into the dead blue eyes of Will, their sparkle dimmed and lifeless.

A keening cry broke the silence and I knew it was me. I clutched at Will's chest, trying to put pressure on the wound and my hands were coated in his sticky, cold blood. I begged him to live, I pounded on his lifeless body demanding he not leave me until I finally threw myself across his body and sobbed.

The fluttering of white out of the corner of my eye caught my attention. I turned to look and saw the second body lying beside Will. Their hands were clasped and I saw the sparkle of a diamond ring on her finger. My gaze drifted up her arm and over her shoulder, finally falling on her face. My face.

I sat up in bed, dragging in a deep, cleansing breath. Movement across the room startled me and I was just about to scream when I saw

Meredith's face peering into mine. She clicked the bedside light on and sat on the bed next to me.

"What the hell was that?" she asked, grabbing me and checking me for injury.

I took a few more deep, ragged breaths and let her presence soothe my jangled nerves.

"Nightmare," I finally croaked. I grabbed her, throwing my arms around her and pulling her to me.

"God, Lys, you're crying," she whispered as she returned my hug.

I sobbed into her shoulder as the illusive wisps of my dream faded and scattered.

"What the hell did you dream about?" she asked when I finally let her go.

She handed me some tissues that were on the bedside and I wiped my eyes and blew my nose.

"I-I don't..." I couldn't seem to grasp any of the fleeting pictures.

"Jordan was there and, and Will," I said.

"Lord Darkly?" she asked, frowning, "Did he hurt you."

I scrunched up my face and shook my head, "No," I said, "I think he was hurt or...Oh God, I can't remember."

"Shh, it's okay," she said, rubbing my back, "It was just a dream."

My pulse rate slowed, but the awful feeling of fear wouldn't let me go. I needed to know what happened in my dream, it felt like a warning of some sort, not that I had ever put any stock in dream theory before. But this had felt different, had felt more real, more urgent.

"Stay with me," I pleaded with Meredith and she smiled and climbed into the massive bed with me.

"Are you okay, Lys?" she whispered as we huddled together under the covers.

"Yeah," I said, blowing out a breath, "I think so. It was just a dream, right?"

"Yeah," she whispered and I shivered.

CHAPTER 16

I was back into the swing of things the next day but the strange pall of the dream still hovered around me. It was a Saturday, which didn't really mean much to my workload, but it did mean that there was an afternoon tea in the garden. Afternoon teas and garden parties were generally reserved for weekends and leant a more festive air to the palace than the usual Monday to Friday operations.

But first on the agenda was a very awkward staff meeting with my entourage and Jordan. I had to do some damage control.

They sat in the conference room waiting for me. I took a deep breath to steel myself and twisted the silver bangle on my wrist three times before entering and taking my seat. There was coffee and morning tea set out along the side board and one of the servers automatically placed a full cup and a plate of food in front of me. I picked up the cup and took a fortifying sip of the scolding beverage before I called the meeting to order.

"First off," I said, "I want to apologise to you all." I could tell by the stunned expressions around the table that they had not been expecting that. "I should never have run off without letting someone know where I was going or what I was doing. I understand that a lot of you were out in that storm searching for me when it was discovered that I was missing and I shouldn't have put your lives in danger like that. It won't happen again." I made eye contact with Benjamin and he inclined his head in acknowledgement. I had never done something as foolish or reckless before and I didn't want him to think that I was going to make a habit of it. "Secondly," I went on, "What to tell the press."

"There are already rumours, Your Grace," Jeanette said, "The media know that the doctor was called."

I nodded in understanding, "Okay, I figured as much. Let's just say that I went riding and had a minor fall but that I am fine with no injuries."

I watched Jeanette make a note on her tablet and then her eyes lifted to mine again.

"And what do we say about the engagement?"

I clenched my teeth together and stared at each of them until I reached Jordan. His cheeks reddened and he looked away from my gaze.

"I thought I told everyone to keep that quiet until we had spoken today." My voice was steel.

"There was a leak," Jeanette said, "Unidentified source, close to the palace."

There were rumblings of swearing from the security team and some unhappy faces from the rest of the assembled group. Nobody liked a leak. I shot a look at Jordan again, but he kept his eyes steadfastly down, refusing to meet mine.

"Considering I have no memory of a proposal let alone agreeing to it, I think it is a tad premature to make a formal announcement to the press."

"So, you're not engaged?" Margaret asked.

"No," I said shaking my head, "The group in this room will be amongst the first to find out if that ever happens."

Jordan clenched his jaw and his cheeks reddened, but he still didn't look up at me.

"So what do we say to the press?" Jeanette said.

"Ah, no comment?" I replied, unsure.

She made a noise in the back of her throat and shook her head, "No, we need to say something. Let me work on it."

"Make sure you run it past me before you post anything. For all the rest of you, if the press asks, it's no comment." I waited for everyone to nod in ascent before going on. "Lastly, if you haven't already heard, the House of Lords denied my petition for ascension. I have thirty days to appeal their decision."

"Or show intent to marry," Jordan spoke softly, but in the quiet room, everyone heard him.

I rolled my lips between my teeth and exhaled before I spoke.

"Parliament don't think a female can handle the office of head of state and want me to abdicate to my husband."

It wasn't a surprise to those assembled, so I assumed that Priscilla had told them the gory details.

"So what are you going to do?" This from Alex.

I sighed and fiddled with the handle of my cup, "I'm not sure," I said, "I don't want to abdicate. If I'm going to be queen, I want to be head of state. I believe that we need change in Merveille and I think that the boys' club days are over. But, I don't exactly know how I'm going to be able to do it."

The room was quiet as we all thought about the challenges ahead.

"We believe in you,"Alex said. She looked around at the rest of the group, "And I think we'll all support you in whatever capacity we can."

Meredith nodded, "And I'm sure there are more people out there who will support you too."

I smiled at them, "Thank you," I said, "I'm going to need all the help I can get."

The meeting broke up after that and I was ushered into my suite to get changed for the afternoon tea. This was the first of many to be conducted over the next few months. The agenda was to meet with the up and coming female leaders of our small country to garner their support. I just hoped that I could inspire the same amount of confidence in them that my team seemed to have.

THE GATHERING WASN'T LARGE, JUST TEN WOMEN PLUS MY entourage. We all dressed in our prettiest tea party dresses and wore polite society smiles as we sipped tea from delicate china cups and ate dainty petit fours. There was polite conversation but there was also a fair bit of wary looks and sizing of one another up.

Some of these women had grown up titled and were experts at the parlour games that were played at court, some of them had not been exposed to such machinations but were smart and experienced in holding their own in hostile situations and then there were the ones who were completely out of their depth.

I mingled, making sure to speak to each person in attendance. I needed to get a feel for who I could rely on and who would be a problem for me. And I hated every minute of it. I was not adept at the pointed conversations that said more than the words you could hear and I was not a fan of subterfuge and underhandedness. I was really no match for some of these women, but I knew I would need them in my court if I were to mount a significant defence for my crown.

I currently sat at a table with four very unlikely allies. Lady Isabella de Vaughn sat opposite me and eyed me over the rim of her tea cup with a shrewd eye. This was a woman I wanted on my side. As head of the Women's Caucus, a group dedicated to furthering the political aspirations of women in Merveille, she knew the law and had tangled many times with both the prime minister and the major general. She was very vocal about women's rights and the need for more women in Parliament. But she also tended to be a bit abrasive.

"So, Your Grace," she said to me across the table, "It is a very interesting mix of guests you have here today."

I smiled serenely, "It is," I agreed.

"It's not what I expected when I received your invitation," she went on.

"No?" I inquired with a raised eyebrow, "What did you expect?"

She shrugged an elegant shoulder and sipped her tea, "Well I certainly didn't expect to see Catherine here, not that I'm complaining."

Catherine Maddison smiled tightly at Lady Isabella. She was not titled but she was the head of the Women's Business Association. I had been pleased to discover that there were quite a few female business owners in Calanais and they had banded together to form this association to support one another.

"It definitely isn't the usual crowd," Lady Poppy Della Sabina added with a slight turn up of her lip. She was probably the 'one-of-these-things-is-not-like-the-other' guest. Lady Poppy loved everything about being titled and privileged and was President of the Merveille Women's Society. She took it as her personal mission to ensure that each and every well-bred lady was properly introduced to society and that they had impeccable manners, etiquette and deportment. She had taken it as a personal affront when I decided to go stateside for my university degree and therefore miss out on my debutante ball. I didn't think she had forgiven me yet.

"I think it's wonderful," Georgina spoke up. Will's sister and I were close in age, although she seemed younger and more...*fragile*...than me. I put that down to the hard times her family had been through in recent times. Nevertheless, Alex assured me she would be a good fit with what we were trying to build. She was studying abroad, law, and despite her seeming naiveté, she was very active in various women's advocate groups.

"May I speak bluntly?" I asked.

"Of course," Lady Isabella said.

"I would like to form a mastermind of sorts," I said. I looked at each of them to gauge their reactions. Isabella looked skeptical, Georgina looked eager, Catherine looked intrigued and Poppy looked almost horrified.

"And what would this mastermind be in aid of?" Isabella asked.

"I believe that the women in Merveille deserve a higher profile. We have a country of smart, savvy women who are looking outside our borders because of the lack of opportunities. I'd like to see that change."

"It is not exactly a supportive atmosphere for women with ambition," Catherine said.

"And I'd like to change that," I said.

"How?"

"I have no idea," I said truthfully, "But that is what today is about. I want to see who is interested in forming this mastermind and then together we can form a plan of action."

"I don't exactly know why I'm here," Poppy said, "I'm not known for my love of the women's liberation movement." She made a face as the words crossed her tongue like they tasted bitter.

I smiled, "This is not about the women's liberation movement," I said, "This is about choice. I want all our girls growing up knowing that they have a choice. They can be boardroom CEOs or politicians or housewives without being afraid of judgement or being ostracised for their choices. That is what I believe true equality is."

"Well, I think it's vulgar," Poppy said, getting to her feet, "Merveille is the last bastion of gentle society and I refuse to see it destroyed by some upstart who has barely spent any time in the country. I don't agree that our children should be abandoned to fend for themselves so that their mothers can chase after a career. I think seeing women in the Houses of Parliament is unseemly and I will not support any such changes."

She stomped off and there was a moment of shocked silence.

"So that's a 'maybe' then Poppy?" Isabella called after her.

"I can't say I'm surprised," Catherine said, "She organised a boycott of all the businesses that we represent because she didn't think that women should run a business."

"I knew it was a long shot," I murmured, "But I didn't want to dismiss her out of hand. At least we know where she stands now, what about you three?"

"I'm in," Georgina said.

"The idea has some merit," Isabella conceded.

"I'm interested," Catherine said, "But my business comes first, so I don't know how much time I can contribute."

"Wonderful," I said, "I will have Alex contact you all with more information when we have it."

I smiled to myself, despite Poppy's reaction, I thought the day was going well.

By the end of the afternoon, I was having second thoughts. So many of the women I had spoken to were resistant to see any change in Merveille's policies in regards to women. There were times when I'd wanted to grab the particular lady I was talking to and give her a good shake. We were living in the twenty-first century and they were behaving like it was the nineteenth.

Not only were they reluctant to see more equality for women, some were also opposed to my becoming head of state, some stating their opinions quite loudly and rudely. Oh, they didn't mind if I became queen, that was fine, as long as I was married and my husband took over all my head of state duties.

I also had to tactfully dodge the gossip about my engagement to Jordan. These women were surprisingly adept at social media and despite the palace's 'no comment' on the leaked information, they all took it as gospel truth, nodding and winking in a conspiratorial way when I denied that there would be an upcoming wedding. If not for my years of training, I may have lost my temper and given a few of them a tongue lashing. But I kept my mouth shut, even if it meant literally biting my tongue at times.

So it was with relief that I bid each of the women goodbye. Those that had shown interest in the mastermind would be contacted by Alex to set up a more intimate meeting and the rest would stay ignorant of our plans.

"Thank you so much for inviting me," Georgina said as she was leaving.

"I'm so glad you could come," I said honestly, "I haven't had a chance to thank you and Will for saving me the other day. Maybe we could get together for dinner sometime soon so I can thank you properly."

"Oh, that would be lovely," she said, smiling, "But Will is away on business for the next couple of weeks."

"Oh?" I said feeling disappointed, "When did he leave?"

"Yesterday," she said, "Right after you were picked up. It was an unexpected trip and one he couldn't avoid."

I battled with feelings that I didn't quite understand at this news. Will had left, without saying goodbye, without checking that I was okay. Instead of voicing these thoughts I plastered a smile on my face and pretended it was fine.

"Well, when he gets back then. I'll have Alex send you my personal email and you can let me know when he returns so we can get together.

I really am grateful for what you both did and I'd like to somehow show you my appreciation."

"Thank you," she replied demurely, "But you really don't have to. We only did what any good neighbour would've done."

"Maybe," I said, "But I'd still like to say thanks."

I watched her walk away and my thoughts were filled with Will. Why had he left so suddenly, did it have anything to do with our kiss? With the fight he had with Jordan?

I went through my remaining duties by rote until I could escape to my rooms. I had my dinner in my suite and sat alone pondering Will's sudden departure. And his kiss.

Things had moved so quickly after Jordan had brought me home that I hadn't had time to really examine my feelings about what happened. It was kind of funny that I had spent four years in America among men who were much more forward and demanding of physical affection and yet it had taken me coming home to our oh-so-very conservative country to experience my first kiss.

Laying hands on a royal was highly impolite, kissing one was beyond offensive, but I hadn't minded. When Will had kissed me, it had felt like the most natural thing in the world. We were just two people with a mutual attraction and it hadn't mattered that I was the queen in waiting and that he was an impoverished duke. We seem to fit together and his soft lips on mine had set me on fire.

Kissing Jordan had been exciting and a little scandalous. The combination of it being my first kiss and that it was out in the open and at a royal function had all combined to make it something magical. And then again when he had coaxed me into the maze and away from my security team, the adrenalin of doing something forbidden had heightened the experience. It had all felt like a wonderfully fun game.

But kissing Will had been an entirely different matter. Kissing Will had seemed more real, more intimate. Where Jordan's kisses had been showy and almost like he was making a public claim or statement, Will's had been private and sincere and made special because of it.

The two men were polar opposites, how could it be that I was attracted to both? They both had qualities I admired and they both equally frustrated me at times. Will could be cutting with his remarks and his standoffishness, Jordan too cavalier. But I liked Jordan's sense of fun and his easy smile. I was similarly drawn to Will's softer, thoughtful nature and the intense way he looked at me.

But perhaps my attraction to Will was moot anyway. He left, without a word to me. Maybe he found my kisses inexperienced and bland. Maybe it was just a spur of the moment thing to kiss me by the firelight and hadn't meant anything to him at all. I know that Jordan stormed in spouting off things about us being engaged, but surely if he really felt something for me then he would fight for me.

I was so out of my depth. I had such little experience with men and relationships that I had no idea what to do. Being with Jordan seemed so easy. From the very moment I had stepped off the plane, he had been there for me. I liked spending time with him, I liked talking to him and despite his resistance to my desire to be head of state, and I did like him. I could even see myself falling in love with him.

But there was something about Will. Our relationship had started out rocky, right from when we were kids. When I had returned to Merveille, it had been awkward with him, but I couldn't deny the attraction I'd felt in spite of that. And then the other day when he had rescued me and taken care of me and then kissed me...that made me want to melt into a puddle of goo.

Jordan's kisses were playful and exciting and I enjoyed them. Will's kisses were deeper, more intense and I found myself craving more of them.

CHAPTER 17

I T was Sunday morning and that meant church. I groaned and
rolled over, turning off my alarm and trying very hard to go back
to sleep. I didn't want to go and sit through another long and
tediously boring scripture reading by a man for whom I had such little
regard.

Unfortunately, the ever efficient Alex, foiled my plans to avoid
mass. She had me up, fed, dressed and walking out the door on time as
usual. I loved her organisation and capability but sometimes I wished
she was a little less so - especially on Sundays.

The road outside the church was packed with paparazzi and of
course we had arrived in the palace cars complete with their little royal
flags on the front that always reminded me of cocktail picks. Security
had been set up and the photographers and reporters were being kept
well behind barricades. I had been warned that they would be here.
There was always some form of press whenever I left the palace
grounds, and church was easy pickings. They knew I would be there
and what time, so it was pointless to try and avoid them. Their usual
numbers had swollen today, though, probably due to the accident and
the leaked engagement.

Meredith stuck close to me as we exited the car. Benjamin led the way, Jamie and Aiden brought up the rear. They were followed by my ladies in waiting and Alex, who were in turn followed by Carlos and Daniel. Scott and Cody would already be inside and that rounded out my ridiculously large security detail all for a simple church service.

The press shouted questions to me, which I ignored. I waved regally and smiled graciously and moved as quickly as was appropriate into the vestibule.

There were the usual niceties and hobnobbing with the peerage as we moved through the antechamber and towards our seats in the balcony. The church seemed fuller today as well, probably more due to my appearance than to the bishop's prepared sermon. I suppose I could think that they were here to see for themselves that I hadn't sustained any serious injury, but I was certain that it had more to do with the more enticing gossip of possible nuptials. Everyone wanted to see if I had a big rock on my finger and I was increasingly thankful that we had denied Jordan's request to sit with us today, as it would've only added fuel to the fire.

The hymns began and seemed especially pious today. I had experienced a Pentecostal church service while in the States and I had to admit I found them more to my liking. The songs they sang were much more upbeat and you didn't need to be an opera singer to reach the range of notes. I'm sure the bishop would rather be burned at the stake than allow such music to be played within these hallowed walls.

I should have paid more attention to the songs being sung though and then I might not have been so blindsided by his sermon. A particularly scathing one, no doubt aimed at me, using the scriptures to disparage the value of women who were without a husband. It seemed to the bishop that a woman was only saved from the evils of sin if she were appropriately married and kept under the thumb of her mate. The bishop had obviously been coached by Parliament to pressure me to marry, thinking that I would cower from this public humiliation. They didn't know me very well. If they had, they would have realised that by trying to force my hand, they had only caused me to redouble my desire to rebel.

How dare they try and embarrass the crown in this way? It had become more and more apparent that my father had been walked over and a little part of me died with the realisation.

I wasn't the only one who was disgusted by the bishop's blatant soap box sermon, if the rustles and fidgeting in the congregation was any indication. Even the perfect society ladies in their perfect dresses and perfect hats seemed uncomfortable under the raging of, what I was sure, was an increasingly unbalanced man of the cloth. The scriptures he used to illustrate his points were taken out of context and wielded like a blunt object. And by upsetting even the most devout in the congregation, he overplayed his hand.

I was in an atrocious mood by the end of the service and wanted nothing more than to disappear back behind the palace gates. But Jordan foiled my escape by stopping me in full view of congregation and paparazzi alike.

"Your Highness," he greeted me with a bow, "I was hoping we could share a picnic lunch this afternoon."

I smiled, my public façade in place, "I was intending to eat in my room," I replied, "And read."

Our voices were low so as not to be overheard and to the outside world we were having a pleasant conversation, our faces open and friendly.

"I would really like the chance to talk to you, in private, and apologise."

His eyes were soft and pleading with me and I felt my anger towards him melting away. How could I stay mad at him when he had been so good to me and had helped me through one of the toughest times in my life?

I sighed and nodded, "Okay," I said, "A picnic on the grounds."

He smiled and bowed again to me before moving away. I watched his back as he retreated, lost in thought, until Meredith nudged me. I can just imagine the shots the photographers had gotten of me while I had zoned out and no doubt they would be plastered across the front pages of tomorrows newspapers.

WE RODE HORSES ACROSS THE LUSH GREEN FIELDS, MY EVER PRESENT security detail trailing us, two in a golf cart, two on ATVs. Jordan and I didn't ride fast, we took our time, enjoying the warm sunshine and the bright summer day. We made polite small talk as we crossed the paddocks and I relaxed in his company.

Jordan was easy to be with, he made small, insignificant things fun, and he made me laugh. I felt genuine affection for him and valued our close friendship. Whether we could be more than that? I didn't know.

Jordan found a spot for us on the same grassy knoll that we had picnicked on before, overlooking the lake. The bright sun glinted off the crystal blue waters of Lac Merveilleux and the gentle breeze made the green grass swish softly. I flopped down on the blanket he spread out and lay on my back, staring up at the clear summer sky.

Jordan settled beside me after hobbling the horses and his hand sought mine out, clasping it in his.

"I'm sorry Alyssa," he said, "I'm sorry for telling people we were engaged. I was just so worried about you and it seemed like the best course of action for people to take me seriously."

I sighed. I could understand his actions, but he had acted without thinking about the long term ramifications and that was a problem for me.

"Do you know how it got leaked to the press?" I asked, not ready to let him off the hook yet.

He was silent beside me for so long that I turned to look at him.

"No," he said, "But most of the staff in the palace heard me say it so it could've been anyone."

That troubled me more than anything. We had iron-clad non-disclosure agreements for all our staff and they were paid well to keep this sort of thing from happening. But mostly, I felt betrayed. The staff got to see us at our most vulnerable and if I couldn't trust them to keep my private life private then I would never have a moment's peace. I couldn't imagine living my life in such a way that I had to watch every single word that came out of my mouth, even in the sanctuary of my own home.

"There'll have to be an investigation," I said, turning back to look at the sky. "If I can't trust my staff then I can't trust anyone."

"You can trust me," Jordan said, squeezing my hand and shifting so that he was laying on his side facing me.

I rolled over to face him and searched his eyes for any guile. I wanted to trust him, I really did, but there was always something holding me back from letting my walls down completely around him.

"And although I went about it in completely the wrong way," he went on, "I really do want to marry you."

I sat up and stared down at him, shocked by his words. "You want to marry me?"

He sat up to and twisted so that he was facing me, "Yes," he said, reaching out to take my hand, "I do. I have loved spending time with you these last few months. You're beautiful and smart and fun to be with, and I want more of that, more of you."

He leant forward to kiss me and I flashed a hand signal to my security detail telling them to back off. Jordan and I needed privacy for what was about to happen.

His lips brushed softly across mine and he cupped my cheek, tugging me towards him. His lips felt nice against mine and I let myself melt into it. He laid us back down on the blanket and he rested on his elbow, while he let me lie flat. His head leaned over me and he continued to kiss me as his free hand caressed my neck with small, gentle circles.

His lips nudged mine open and his tongue slipped into my mouth, sliding along my tongue. It was nice, but it didn't heat my blood like Will's kiss did.

Jordan's hand trailed down across my shoulder and down my arm before coming to rest on my hip. He continued to kiss me, alternating long slow open mouthed kisses with small, soft pressing of lips to cheek, jaw, eyelids. He rolled towards me, half lying on me and I felt the heat of his body along my length. His hand began to move again, playing with the hem of my shirt, his fingers dipping underneath to tease the exposed skin. I sucked in a breath at the intimate touch and he plundered my mouth again, deepening the kiss. He slid his hand under my shirt and up along my ribs while his kisses became hard and demanding.

I tried to pull away, to take a breath. This was further than I had ever gone with someone and I didn't think I was prepared for it, especially not out here in the open. I brought my hands up, trying to get them between us to push him away, but he levered himself up and over me, taking my hands in one of his and raising them above my head, holding them down.

His other hand continued to roam under my shirt and I wriggled, not welcoming his touches and feeling more and more uncomfortable with his attentions. I pulled away from his harsh kiss and sucked in a breath.

"Jordan," I said, breathlessly, "I...uh..."

"Shh," he whispered, "It's okay Alyssa. You want this as much as I do. I'm going to make you feel so good."

His hand grasped my breast over my bra and I hissed out a breath.

"No, Jordan," I said, louder this time, "I don't want this."

His mouth crashed back down onto mine, silencing me, but I continued to struggle. He held my wrists tightly and my focus went to getting them free. He was covering my entire body with his now and I bucked my body against his trying to dislodge him but he just ground himself into me.

Panicked now that he would take this further, I bit his lip, sinking my teeth into the soft flesh. He reared back and roared, his face red and angry. I scrambled out from under him and watched as he clenched his fists as if trying to keep himself from lashing out at me. I dragged my hand across my mouth, wiping away his kisses and sucked in oxygen. He turned to me and I held up a hand.

"*Arrêtez*," I said loud enough for my security detail to hear. The French word for stop was my sign for them to come running.

I stood tall and took a deep breath. Jordan turned away from me, his hands on his hips, his posture stiff. Carlos strode into sight and I acknowledged him with a tilt of my head.

"I think I'd like to go back to the palace now," I said, hating the tremor in my voice.

"Right away, Your Grace," he said in a monotone, "Will you be riding your horse back or would you prefer to accompany me in the cart?"

"The cart please," I said weakly and walked towards him without looking back at Jordan.

WE RODE IN SILENCE. I COULDN'T EVEN PUT INTO WORDS WHAT I was feeling. Had I given Jordan signals that I had wanted that? In my inexperience had I inadvertently led him on?

What he did was completely out of line and illegal if I wanted to argue semantics. He had laid his hands on the royal person without permission or invitation, and I could have him charged. His attentions had been completely unsolicited and yet...I still felt responsible, like it was somehow my fault.

I hugged my arms close to my body, feeling chilled despite the heat of the afternoon. All my self defence training had deserted me when I had needed it most and I was left feeling shocked, betrayed and violated. I had let my guard down around him, had been lulled into a false sense of security because of our friendship and it had been to my detriment.

Any relationship we'd had, and feelings of friendship and affection had been wiped away by his callous act. I couldn't trust Jordan, that had become abundantly clear, and it left me feeling so utterly alone. I had thought he was the one person who had liked me for me, not for what I could do for him. But he was just like all the rest; he only wanted me because he thought he could sleep with me. All these months he had been whittling away my reticence, getting closer to me. And it had all just been about sex.

I was an idiot. A naive idiot. I had so little life experience, was it any wonder that Parliament saw me as a joke? How could I possibly lead this country if I couldn't even see through the apparent affection of a man who just wanted to get into my pants?

The cart came to a stop and I jumped out, not waiting for Carlos. I strode into the palace and headed straight for my brother's office. I needed to be surrounded by familiarity, by memories of the last person who I could trust implicitly. I couldn't even trust my ladies in waiting, not completely. They all had their own reasons for being here and I was pretty confident that if push came to shove, they would choose their own agendas over me.

I walked into the office and the first thing that hit me was the scent of my brother's aftershave. It permeated the room and I was overwhelmed by the onslaught of memories. I slumped down in his chair, pulling my feet up and wrapping my arms around my knees. I dropped my head onto my arms and felt so completely abandoned.

I don't know how long I sat there, but when I finally raised my head, the room was dark and my cheeks were wet from crying. I missed Jacob so very much and wished I could have one more conversation with him, one more afternoon to just spend with him, talking and joking and feeling secure and protected by him. He had always made me feel that way and I suddenly realised that it was missing from my life. Maybe if I'd recognised the hole in my heart I wouldn't have been so quick to fill it with Jordan.

I had latched on to Jordan because of his relationship with my brother. The association had made him safe and I had tried to replace my brother with a cheap substitute. But nobody could ever replace Jacob in my life. I would forever have this gaping hole where he should be. The challenge was to learn how to live with it, like an amputee learns to live without a limb.

With a sigh, I reached over the desk to flick on the lamp. For the first time I noticed the disarray of the room. When I had stumbled blindly in here, I hadn't taken notice of anything except the memories that assaulted me. But now I took the time to look around.

I had spent a lot of time in here with Jordan whenever I was home. Jordan's desk was always relatively tidy and I had expected it to look like he had just stepped away for a minute and would be back at any moment. But that wasn't what was before me. Papers were strewn across the dark mahogany of the desk, drawers where pulled out of the filing cabinet and his hard drive was missing.

"Carlos?" I called, "Are you there?"

The door opened and Carlos stepped into the room. His eyes widened at the sight.

"Did you need me, Your Grace?" he asked.

"Has anyone else been in this room? Has it been searched by the authorities or by our own security team?"

He shook his head, "No, Your Grace," he said.

"Then why the hell does it look like this?" I jumped from the chair.

"You didn't do this?" he asked, taking a more intense look around the room.

I shook my head, "No," I said, "I was sitting in his chair, crying. I didn't notice anything until now."

Carlos clicked his cufflink mic and spoke into it softly.

I took in the complete disarray of the room and wondered how I had missed it when I first walked in here. I picked up random bits of paper, reading their contents, trying to understand what had happened in here.

"I don't think you should touch anything," Carlos said, "Not until Benjamin and Von Bartham have had a chance to see it."

"Right," I said, setting down the piece of paper in my hand. Why would someone do this? What reason would they have for ransacking Jacob's office?

Benjamin strode into the room, closely followed by Von Bartham and they both pulled up short.

"What happened in here?" Von Bartham exclaimed.

"I was hoping you could tell me," I said, "I found it like this."

Benjamin ran his hand through his hair and turned to Carlos, "Was Jacob working on anything of any importance that you know of?"

Carlos waited a beat and his eyes slid to me before he answered, "There was something he was looking into, but he wouldn't give us details. Said he didn't want to tip anybody off."

They shared a look and I wanted to stamp my foot in frustration. If they knew something, why wouldn't they tell me?

Benjamin stuck his head out of the door and spoke to someone on the other side. Meredith stepped into the room and her eyes widened before she could school her reaction.

"Your Highness, why don't you go with Meredith? She can take your statement as to what you found in here and I would also like you to debrief her about the incident this afternoon."

I rolled my eyes. I hadn't really expected to get away without explaining what happened with Jordan, had I?

"Fine," I said, crossing my hands over my chest and giving them my best royal look, "But I want a complete update about this in the morning."

"Yes, Your Highness," Benjamin replied and I swear he was trying to hide a smile.

CHAPTER 18

W E met in the conference room the next morning. The mood was somber and no one would look me in the eye. I knew that what I had told Meredith about Jordan wasn't in confidence, I knew that she would tell them what happened and I knew they would be disappointed in me.

But this morning wasn't about that. This morning was about why Jacob's office had been ransacked. His death and now this invasion of his personal space were not good omens. If his death hadn't already been suspicious, then this would definitely make it so.

"Tell me what you know," I said, refusing to cower before them, refusing to let my naiveté become a reason for them to lose respect for me.

Benjamin blew out a harsh breath, "We know very little," he said, "Jacob's secretary assures us that nothing appears to be missing, but someone was definitely looking for something."

"Who and what?" I asked.

"I don't know," Benjamin replied, shooting a look at Carlos.

I looked between the two men. There was something being said without words and I couldn't decipher it, but I very much wanted to.

"Look," I said, standing, "I know that my actions yesterday have shown me to be a silly girl." They began to protest, but I held up a hand to stop them. "But," I went on, "I don't intend to let it derail me. I intend to be a good leader...to *learn* to be a good leader. And for that to happen I need to have people around me that can be honest with me. I don't need yes-men and I don't need to be molly coddled. Please," I paused to look at Carlos and Benjamin, "Tell me what's going on."

Carlos grit his teeth, the muscle in his jaw jumping and he stared hard at Benjamin. Benjamin returned his stare and then turned to me with a sigh.

"Jacob was having someone in the palace investigated," he said.

"Who?" I asked.

"They exchanged another look.

"We don't know. He asked Sebastian to look into it."

"Sebastian?" I knew the name but couldn't place it.

"He was one of the body guards killed in the attack," Carlos said, resigned to telling me the whole story. "Whoever it was that your brother was investigating, it was someone close to him. He asked Sebastian to do it because he was relatively new and it would be less likely to tip off the target."

"He didn't confide in you?" I asked.

He shook his head. "He told me he had suspicions about someone who had recently taken up a position in the palace but he didn't tell me who."

"So is it safe to say that whoever broke into Jacob's office knew they were being investigated and was looking for the documents that revealed his, or her, misdeeds?"

"That was our conclusion," Benjamin said.

"But we don't know if such documents even existed or whether or not our thief found them."

"Correct."

I exhaled harshly, frustrated at both my brother's subterfuge and that the intrepid thief may have just covered his tracks.

"There's something else we think you need to know," Meredith said placing a small box on the table.

I picked up the small red leather box and ran my fingers over the gold embossed design on the lid. Cartier. I flicked the lid and nestled amongst the red velvet was a platinum and diamond engagement ring. I looked up at Carlos.

"Was my brother seeing someone?" I asked, surprised.

Carlos nodded, "Yes, Your Grace. He was going to ask Lady Darkly for her hand."

I slumped back in my chair and gazed at the gorgeous ring that sparkled in the halogen lights of the room. Jacob was going to ask Georgina to marry him. I wonder if she knew? She hadn't mentioned anything, and neither had Will.

"I take it this wasn't common knowledge," I said, not taking my eyes from the ring.

"No," Carlos said, "He was waiting for Lady Darkly to graduate."

"Did..." I cleared my throat that was suddenly thick with emotion, "Did Will know?" I whispered.

"I believe the prince asked his permission to court her," Carlos said softly.

"Your brother was also working on something with Lord Darkly," Benjamin said, "A project of sorts."

"Oh?" I said, raising my eyes to him, "What project?"

Why had Will never mentioned any of this to her? Had he thought she wouldn't honour any promises her brother had made?

"It's probably better if you look through the paperwork yourself," Benjamin said, "The prince's secretary is waiting for you in his office if you have time now."

I stood, "Now is perfect," I said.

All of my appointments for this week had been cancelled so that my things could be moved to my father's wing. The renovations on his rooms had been completed and the security team had been persistent in their urging to get me to move. All of the palace's rooms had secrets, but my father's rooms had been the best kept. I knew that there was an escape tunnel from his bedroom to a small cottage on the edge of the property but there were other secrets that I had yet to be made aware of. No doubt I would be fully briefed when I had been completely moved in.

"Let's go," I said, leading the way out the door and towards Jacob's office.

As we walked I turned to Meredith, "I need to speak with Georgina Darkly as soon as possible," I said. Alex was busy coordinating the move, as were the rest of my ladies in waiting, and that left Meredith to fill in as my assistant.

"I will call her today," she replied.

"Good," I replied, "Can you also let Alex know that I will be working from Jacob's office for the rest of the week? If anything comes up and someone needs to see me, send them there."

Meredith nodded.

JACOB'S OFFICE WAS IN A MUCH BETTER STATE WHEN I ENTERED IT this time. His secretary, Jeremy, stood by his desk waiting for me. He bowed low as he greeted me.

"Your Highness," he said, "I am sorry for your loss."

I took his hands in mine and looked him in the eye. I had hardly spent any time with the personal staff of my brother and my father since I had been back and now I felt bad for it. These people were hurting too and I had pretty much abandoned them.

"Thank you Jeremy," I said, "And I am sorry for yours."

He nodded and swallowed. "Thank you," he said and then cleared his throat, "Please let me know how I can be of service."

I smiled at him, "I want to know everything my brother had been working on. I understand he had a project underway with Lord Darkly."

"Yes, Your Grace," he said, snapping into professional mode, "The prince was working with Lord Darkly on a way to export his cheese products."

That made me irrationally happy and I was at a loss to make sense of it. It was cheese, for God's sake, but it was really good cheese...and it was Will's cheese.

"Show me," I said and he led me into the office. A laptop sat on the desk that hadn't been there last night. "Whose laptop is this?" I asked.

"It was the prince's," Jeremy answered, "He had me lock it up in the wall safe every night."

"Is there anything else in the wall safe that we should know about?" Benjamin asked.

Jeremy shook his head. "If you're talking about the secret investigation he was conducting, no. He wouldn't even tell me what was going on."

Benjamin nodded and then looked around the room. I indicated for Jeremy to show me what Jacob and Will had been working on.

The next few hours passed quickly as I read through the documents and emails that Will and Jacob had shared. They had put together a strong business plan and had gone into the venture as equal partners. By the looks of the financial reports, the business was flourishing and Will was no longer the impoverished duke that everyone assumed he was.

Pemberton Cheese and Dairy had indeed broken into the international market and had won several notable awards. Will had repaid the debts of his father and had restored his fortune tenfold. He was now a very rich man, and yet he didn't flaunt it like so many of the other peers would have.

I looked through the articles of incorporation and, though not a lawyer, I understood the majority of it. Jacob had been named as an equal, but silent, partner and upon his death the proceeds of his share would pass to Georgina. I smiled at his forethought for the woman he loved, but I wondered why this hadn't been included in the reading of his will.

"That was Lord Darkly's doing," Jeremy said when I asked him. "Lord Darkly insisted that the prince's shares remain with his estate. The prince hadn't yet declared his intention publicly and Lord Darkly didn't want the private matter of his promise to Lady Darkly to become tabloid fodder."

Will continued to amaze me. I had often thought him standoffish and cold, but he was a deep thinker and held his cards close to his chest. I feared that Will felt very deeply and kept such things bound up so as not to be hurt. My heart melted a little at the thought of how he had been protecting his sister and Jacob from public scrutiny. Will was loyal to a fault and I had misjudged him.

Meredith knocked on the door and I looked up at her.

"Lady Darkly is here," she said, "Would you like to take tea in the salon?"

Hearing Meredith behave like a court secretary brought a smile to my face and I nodded. She poked her tongue out at me before turning and walking away.

I stood and stretched. Despite the circumstances that resulted in me finding all this information out about my brother and his close association with the Duke of Pemberton, today had been a good day. It was nice to see that my brother had not intended to be a king like our father. He'd had a vision and a plan for Merveille and I felt a close connection to him because of it.

I walked out of the office and made my way through the palace to the salon. Georgina stood as I entered and I went to her and pulled her into a tight hug. When I let her go and stood back, she had tears in her eyes.

"You know," she said simply and I nodded.

We sat down and a few stray tears fell from her eyes.

"Why didn't you tell me?" I asked.

She shrugged, "He hadn't made it public, I don't think even your parents knew. It wasn't my place to say anything."

"Oh, Georgina," I whispered, "It was absolutely your place. You have been grieving all this time on your own."

She smiled sadly, "Not alone," she said, "I've had Will."

"Your brother loves you very much."

"Yes," she said, "He has always been my protector and my champion."

"How...how did you and Jacob come to be...close?" I asked cautiously.

"There was some trouble a little while ago," she began.

"Your father?"

She nodded, "And...and another man."

"Jordan?" I asked kindly.

She looked away from me, staring out the window for a moment and then she seemed to come to a decision.

"Will would kill me if he knew I was telling you this," she said, "But I think you need to know."

"Go on," I said and a heavy feeling settled in my gut.

"I, uh, I overheard you and Will fighting the other day," she said in a rush, "And I want you to know the truth about what happened between Jordan and I."

"Okay," I said slowly.

"Jordan did come to us, that is my father and I, when Will was away at school. My father wasn't coping with the death of my mother and he was drinking too much and not looking after the estate. Jordan offered to help and for a while, things seemed to get better." She took a breath. "I fell in love with him, well," she shook her head, "What I thought was love anyway and he...he took advantage of it. He insinuated himself into my father's business and into my affections. He proposed to me and I said yes and then the estate took a turn for the worst. It was leaking money and we had no idea how or why. Jordan got angry and he..." she closed her eyes and swallowed, "He tried to rape me. He said if there was no money to be had in the estate then he would at least get something out of it. Jacob stopped him."

"Oh, God," I said, my hand flying to my mouth in horror, "Oh Georgina, why didn't you press charges?"

She laughed hollowly, "No one would've believed me. We were engaged and Jordan has friends in the police. He is a high ranking soldier with an exemplary record and a father who sits in the House of Lords. I was the daughter of a disgraced Lord with no money or prospects. I knew how it would go."

"But Jacob could have testified on your behalf," I said.

She shook her head, "I would never have asked him to put his neck out like that for me. I wasn't harmed, a little shaken up maybe, but not harmed. Jordan called off our engagement and disappeared for a few months. Will was livid when he found out and would probably have shot Jordan on sight if he had been here."

"Surely Jacob didn't leave it at that," I said.

She shook her head again, "No, he was wonderful. He started

keeping tabs on Jordan, making sure he couldn't do to someone else what he's done to me. He had vehemently opposed Jordan's appointment at the palace, but he wasn't in a position to block it."

"Oh God," I said, "I didn't know." I stood and shot a glance to Meredith who had been sitting nearby listening intently. Her eyes were dark with anger and I nodded to her. She would need to report this to Benjamin especially in light of what had happened to me yesterday.

Jordan was a wolf in sheep's clothing. No doubt he was the man that Jacob had been investigating, but did that also mean that he was the one to murder my brother and father? It didn't seem possible.

I sat back down and clasped Georgina's hands in mine, "Where's Will?" I asked.

"He's in France, I think," she replied, "But I'm not sure how long he will be there. He had a long list of places that he had to visit."

"Is he keeping in touch with you?" I asked.

"Yes," she nodded, "He emails me daily."

"Okay, good," I said aware that I was scaring her. I smiled and softened my voice, "I came across the business agreement he had with my brother and I'd like to honour it."

"Oh, no, you don't need to do that," she said, "It wouldn't be right."

I pulled the Cartier box out of my pocket and put it in her hands, "We found this among Jacob's things. I know he loved you and had spoken to Will about proposing to you. We would've been sisters."

She opened the box and gasped at the ring inside. "It's beautiful," she whispered tracing the lines of the platinum band with a finger.

"I want you to have it," I said, "He bought it for you and it's only right that it be given to you. I also want you to have the share of the business that you had been promised."

"No, I couldn't," she said, "And I can't accept this ring." She held it out to me, willing me to take it.

I closed her fingers around the box, "You can't refuse me," I said, "I'm to be your queen, you have to do what I say." I smiled, "And I want you to have both the ring and the shares."

"But it's too much," she said.

"No, it's not," I said, "Besides, I have plans to show the people of Merveille that women can be a force to be reckoned with. Your brother's business has seen tremendous growth and I know that you have helped so why shouldn't you reap the benefits?"

"I...uh...I don't know what to say," she stammered.

"Say yes," I replied.

WHEN I RETURNED TO THE OFFICE I OPENED JACOB'S LAPTOP AND pulled up an email he'd sent to Will. I copied the address and opened my own private email program and started a new email.

DEAR WILL,

We need to talk.

I believe I owe you both my thanks and an apology.

Thanks for rescuing me in the storm and for taking such good care of me, and an apology for the things I said to you afterward. I was out of line and I hope you can forgive me.

But that isn't all we need to talk about. I was going through my brother's office and came across some very interesting information. I would like to discuss this more with you at your earliest convenience.

This is my personal email address and is not accessed by anyone except me. Will you write me?

Yours always,

Alyssa

I REREAD THE EMAIL SEVERAL TIMES BEFORE HITTING SEND. I DIDN'T want to give away all my secrets if he was still angry at me, and I knew he had been angry after that day in his kitchen. But I didn't want to play games either, I was no good at these court machinations and much preferred to just speak plainly. Hopefully I said enough for him to forgive me and make him curious enough to respond.

Now all I had to do was wait.

CHAPTER 19

M *Y dearest Alyssa,*

IT HAD BEEN SEVERAL DAYS SINCE I HAD SENT THAT EMAIL TO WILL and I had checked my incoming mail obsessively waiting for his reply. The rest of my days were spent learning the new aspects of my more secure lodgings (tunnels, secret hallways and panic rooms) and delving into the work my brother had been doing. But finally he had replied.

AFTER MUCH ADMONISHING FROM MY SISTER, I MUST ADMIT TO YOU that I should have been honest that day...more to the point, I should have been honest with you from the start.

As you may have gathered, Jacob and I remained close. He had been my greatest supporter and my closest confidante. We were brothers, in a fashion, and I miss him dreadfully. He stood by me when we were disgraced by my father's actions and he offered me a sounding board when I first conceived of my ideas for the estate. He backed up his encouragement with action and his singular support of my fledgling business is the reason it is such a success now. I owe him everything.

Jordan, on the other hand, has been a thorn in my side. You know our history, you know that as children the three of us were inseparable, but what you might not know is that Jordan was never really one of us. That may sound callous and unkind, but what started out as childish fun between the three of us became a competition. Jordan had this need to always win, to be on top and he was prepared to tread on whoever he had to to get there. We allowed him a place with us, if only to ensure we could keep an eye on him and keep his bullying to a minimum.

My sister has told you how he stepped in when I moved away, but she doesn't know the full story. Yes, my father became desolate after my mother passed and he turned to drinking to medicate his pain and loss. And yes, Jordan did step in, but not for the reasons he may have you believe. Jordan saw my absence and my father's inability to function as an opportunity. What you may not know about Jordan is that he has a terrible gambling addiction. He needed money and he saw my father's weakness as a way to get it. He set his sights on my sister in the hopes of marrying into a title and as a way to get to my family's coffers. He offered to help my father run the estate while I was away and proceeded to bleed us dry to furnish his addiction. When he could get no more out of my family, he tried to ruin my sister and if not for your brother, he would have succeeded.

I fervently wish I had been honest with you from the very moment you returned to Merveille, but the moment I saw you with Jordan, I could barely contain my anger. He betrayed me and my family and he betrayed your brother and I saw your association with him as yet another betrayal. I now realise that I was wrong to have so carelessly labelled you. You had no knowledge of the things that man was responsible for, but I was blinded by my anger and jealousy. Can you ever forgive me for that?

As for the matters of business that you alluded to, I have no wish to change my earlier decision. I owe so much to Jacob and for the store of trust and belief that he put in me. I know his wishes were for my sister to inherit his shares, but I want to assure you, my sister will not want for anything. The estate is once again profitable and I have already made provisions for her should anything happen to me.

Although at times I may have seemed unaffected by your renewed presence *in my life, I want you to know that the few times we have spent together have meant a great deal to me. I am glad that you have come home to Merveille, tragic though the circumstances are, and I hope that we can forge a friendship from our mutual loss.*

Your friend,

Will

I READ AND REREAD HIS EMAIL TIME AND AGAIN. JORDAN'S BETRAYAL had gone beyond anything I could imagine and I was beginning to see him in a whole new light. His affections towards me were no doubt a duplication of what he'd tried to achieve with Pemberton. If what Will said about Jordan's gambling addiction was correct, then no doubt he needed money and had set his sights on the crown's treasury this time.

It was like a stab to the heart to realise I had been so thoroughly taken in by his charm. Jordan was a snake in the grass and I had blithely let him into the house. I had so much to lose, and if things had gone differently the other day, Jordan would be in line to become the next head of state. Which made me wonder if that hadn't been his endgame all along seeing as though it was his father who had spear-headed the attack on me in the House of Lords. Had they been working together?

Jacob had known the duplicitous nature of Jordan and I now believed that the man he was investigating was none other than Jordan Wicks himself. Carlos had been telling the truth when he had revealed to me the falling out Jordan had had with my brother. Looking back now I can only assume that that falling out had come about because of Jordan's treatment of Will and his sister. In light of that, it was only natural that when Jacob learned of Jordan's appointment to the palace he would have tried to stop it.

But the major general was a powerful force in Parliament and had more pull than the crown prince. The king would have been useless and would've bowed to the major general's demands without a whim-per, so Jacob had needed hard evidence that couldn't be disputed or explained away. Had Jordan somehow become privy to Jacob's investi-gations? The ransacking of his office suggested he had.

I stood and began pacing the office, thinking through the events that had led to this moment. I would've been of no value to Jordan as the heir presumptive. Although I would have provided him the necessary funds to finance his gambling, there would have been no power and authority. As heir presumptive I would have been given an allowance, but even more than that, as heir presumptive, I wouldn't have even returned to Merveille. My future had already been determined and it didn't involve any royal duties. My life as an international relations consultant with the UN would've held no interest to a man like Jordan.

So had his plan to woo me come together in the hours following my father's and brother's deaths or had it been formed earlier?

My brain screeched to a halt before I could even think of the possibility that Jordan had had a hand in the deaths of the two most important men in my life. It seemed too unreal to be true and I refused to let my mind wander down that path until I had irrefutable evidence.

Sleep did not come easy that night. I was restless and fidgety, tossing and turning until the blankets were a twisted mess. After a few hours of frustration, I finally got out of bed and grabbed my laptop. I hadn't replied to Will's email and at least doing that small thing might shunt my brain off the singular track it seemed to be on.

My dear Will,

I am so glad of your reply, although not so happy with the subject matter. I do wish you had come to me earlier and explained the situation with Jordan. He has since proven himself to me to be a man of very little character and if I had known sooner, I would not have been so quick to allow his easy access to my life. But I also understand your desire to protect your sister from the wagging tongues of idle gossips and that your decision was made because of your love for her and not because of any ill-will towards me.

My other regret is that perhaps our own renewing of acquaintance may have been less awkward had I known the truth about Jordan. I can't help but feel that we got off on the wrong foot since that very first meeting and I dearly wish that things had gone differently. Our friendship has been strained at times because of unsaid things and it is an awful lot of pressure to put on such a fledg-

ling relationship. May I suggest we start again without all the baggage that has held us back prior to this?

Hello, Will, you may not remember me but I am Jacob's little sister Lys. You used to pick on me dreadfully when we were children and I do so hope you have grown out of that. I am much impressed by your success and I have to admit to being quite partial to your brie. I hope I won't embarrass you by saying that it is the finest cheese I have ever tasted. I also hear that you have developed a specialised breed of cow to provide the milk for your award winning cheese and I have to say how incredible that is. As the future queen of our small country, it gladdens my heart to see such innovation coming from our very own populace and if there is ever anything the crown can do to further bolster your success, know that the door will always be open to you.

There, now, is that a better introduction than the one we had? I fear it may be a tad too formal and not at all in the vein I had intended. I am really very bad at this and have had such little experience in communicating with normal people that I'm afraid I may just scare you off. I hope I don't. I have really enjoyed the very few times we have had together and I look forward to you returning so that we may have more.

If it is not too forward to say...I like you, Will.

Yours,

Lys

I FRETTED OVER SENDING IT. I WANTED HIM TO KNOW THAT WHEN he kissed me, I felt something more, something deep, something that I want to explore further. I want him to kiss me again. But would he laugh at my admission? Would he think of me as nothing more than a child? Had the kiss we shared meant as much to him as it had meant to me?

I hit the send button and then jumped up and paced frantically. I may have spent four years in another country, but I had still led a sheltered existence. My woeful lack of experience with the opposite sex was never more evident than in how I allowed Jordan to manipulate me. All he'd had to do was show me a little kindness, flatter me with his attention and dare to kiss me and I had been putty in his hands. And look how that had turned out.

I slammed the lid on the laptop and crawled back into the bed. I had to believe that Will was worthy of my trust and I had to admit that he had done nothing to make me doubt him. I had been grieving and alone when I had returned to Merveille and Jordan had seen the weakness and pounced. Will had never tried to manipulate me or ask more of me than I could give. He could have marched into the palace and made demands on his sister's behalf, but he didn't. The trappings of nobility and fame had no interest for him and I had absolutely no reason to worry that any of our private conversations might end up in the tabloids. Unlike with Jordan.

I shook my head at my own stupidity. Jordan had played me and I had let him. The signs were there, the leaked date that meant we were inundated with paparazzi, the way he made sure to be by my side whenever a photographer was around, the leaked engagement. I was pretty sure now that Jordan was the leak and everything he had engineered with me was so that he could make our relationship seem more than it was. He wanted the public to think that we were a couple headed for the altar so that I would have no choice but to accept his marriage proposal. But then he had tipped his hand and pushed just that little bit too far.

There was no point in beating myself up about it. What was done was done and now I just needed to keep moving forward. I had an appeal to win and I would not let Jordan's underhandedness rob me of my inheritance. He may have thought to cower me, but instead he only made me more resolute. I was going to win that damned appeal and I was going to be queen and there was nothing he could do about it.

I WAS SLUGGISH THE NEXT MORNING AS WE RAN OUR USUAL TRACK throughout the grounds. I hadn't slept much and what little sleep I did have was fitful and unhelpful. I suppose I could have stayed in bed and begged off, but I knew the fresh air and exercise would be good for me and help me to get through the day.

Jeanette as waiting for me when we returned and by the look on her face and the pile of newspapers in her hand, the news wasn't good.

"What is it now," I asked tiredly as I sat down at the small breakfast table.

She slapped down newspaper after newspaper and on the front page of each was a grainy photograph of me and Jordan in a very compromising position.

I stared at them in disbelief. The photo had been taken from a distance with a telephoto lens, probably from one of the boats on the lake. It was grainy, but there was no doubt who the two subjects were. Jordan lay on top of me, one hand holding my wrists above my head, the other disappearing under my shirt. It looked like a romantic tryst, not like the near rape that it was.

I swore. Loudly. I used every swear word I knew in all four languages that I spoke. I called Jordan every name under the sun and even made up a few of my own. My tirade was so loud and so absolute that I garnered a crowd of onlookers, staff drawn to the raising of my voice and the vulgar things I was saying. Eventually the spectacle brought Benjamin and Von Bartham to the room and they cleared it of all non-essential personnel so that I could have my meltdown in relative privacy.

When I finally calmed down enough to form a coherent thought, I turned to Jeanette and asked the obvious question.

"How do I respond to this?"

"Before I can tell you that," she said carefully, "I need to know what happened."

"Nothing!" I cried, "Nothing happened. He took liberties which I rebuked. That photo shows him pinning me down and not letting me up even though I told him no and demanded he set me free." I looked helplessly at Benjamin. "What can we do about this?"

"Do you want to press charges?" he asked and in his eyes I saw him say something different. He would do what I asked, but he wanted his own brand of justice on Jordan. I couldn't say I blamed him.

I sat down and took a breath to think about things logically. This had to be another ploy of Jordan's. I had shut him out since the incident and this was his warning to me. He would not be denied. If the palace was to come out and say that Jordan had acted inappropriately, Jordan would no doubt have his response already prepared. There was enough evidence already in the media to show that we had been in a relationship and it would look like the palace was just trying to save face and use Jordan as a scape goat. The last thing I needed was to give the public any reason to doubt me. But if we didn't respond at all, people would make up their own minds.

"I should probably tell you about some information that I discovered yesterday about Jordan," I said and took a breath, "You know that he tried a similar thing with Lady Darkly, but there is more to the story. Jordan has a gambling problem and I have reason to believe that he is the one Jacob was investigating."

Von Bartham and Benjamin exchanged a look.

"What does that have to do with this?" Benjamin asked carefully.

"I think Jordan wants my crown," I said simply, "I think he wants the treasury to bankroll his gambling and I think he wants the power that comes with marrying me. This is how he thinks he can get it."

"By disgracing you in the media?" Jeanette asked, incredulous.

I shook my head, "It wouldn't be a disgrace if we were engaged to be married. This is his way of forcing my hand. If I turn him down now, I will ruin my chances to win the appeal."

Jeanette sat down with a plop onto a chair beside me.

"So what do you want us to do?" Benjamin growled.

"I want you to look into Mr. Wicks. I want you to dig up every little dirty secret he has. Maybe start with where he got that blasted stallion from. I also want you to see if you can link him or his father to the hunting accident."

The room got very quiet as they all thought on the implications of the bombshell I had just dropped. Jordan was no longer playing games, he was in all-out attack mode and I needed to know how deep his deception went. Even if that meant finding out that he and his father had instigated the plan to kill my father and brother. I had to take the blinders off and start seeing the world how it really was, warts and all.

"And in the meantime?" Benjamin asked.

"I think I need to have a meeting with him. If I can get him to state what it is he wants, maybe we have a better chance of nailing him. He is guilty of something, I'm just not sure what that something is yet. I intend to find out."

I shooed everyone out so that I could shower and dress. I would spend some time in my brother's office going through every little thing I could find to see if there was any concrete evidence that I could level against Jordan. I needed leverage, something to give me the upper hand. I just prayed that Jacob had left something for me to find.

CHAPTER 20

I buried myself in Jacob's office. I systematically went through every drawer, every cupboard, every hidey-hole I could find. I skimmed every piece of paper for clues, I crawled under the desk to check for secret compartments and I checked the drawers again, this time for false bottoms. I pulled every book off his book shelf to check behind them for a hidden safe or false back or a big arrow that would point me to something he wanted me to find. Where was the big 'x' to mark the spot?

I took my time putting the books back. Jacob had loved books, he collected them. Many of his personal collection were first editions and some were not even in print anymore. Whenever I walked past a used book store, I would always flick through the hardcovers looking for titles that he didn't have. It became a bit of a game between us. He would send me cryptic clues about a book he was looking for and I would try and find it for him.

He was a big Hardy Boys fan and had painstakingly collected the entire series. I flicked through them, breathing in the musky smell of old paper and ink. I missed my brother in so many ways and being surrounded by his most loved treasures bought it into stark relief.

My laptop dinged with an incoming message and I put down the book I was holding and stood. I looked around and stared at the office, I had made an awful mess. It looked like it had been ransacked again, which I suppose, it had been. I sighed and flopped down in the chair behind the desk, tapping the keyboard to wake it up.

I clicked on the new email notification and smiled as the email opened. It was from Will and it gave me a warm fuzzy feeling to see his reply. It also made me nervous about what he might say to my late night declarations.

My very dear Lys,

There are so many things that I wished I had done differently and I feared that we may never get past those first few halting steps.

I don't know if you realise this, but the reason I was so dreadful to you when we were younger was because I had a boyhood crush on you and I didn't know how to deal with it. You were my best friend's little sister who followed us around like a bad smell, but I liked that you did and was too cowardly to acknowledge it. I'm blushing as I write this, but I agree that there are so many unsaid things between us and I have a deep desire to bare my heart to you in the hopes that we can start again, on the right foot this time.

I like you too, Lys, so very much. I can't stop thinking about those few moments we shared that night. I hope that is not too forward to say. I regret leaving the way I did and letting Jordan get to me. I should have stayed and fought for you.

I hate knowing that Jordan has hurt you and that I am not there to protect you. I know that you are surrounded by men and women trained to protect your person, but I wish I was there to protect your heart, to tell you that everything will be okay. Know that, even though I am not there in person, my heart is with you always.

My business is almost concluded and I will be returning to Merveille in the next day or two. I would really like to ask you out on a date...how does one ask the next queen of Merveille on a date? If you are amenable to the idea of us... going out? Dating? Then I'm sure we will be able to make the necessary arrangements to satisfy Benjamin's safety concerns. If not, then maybe we can be friends at the very least.

As I sit here and think about the past, about my childhood spent with Jacob and with you, I am reminded of the very large tree that we would play in. I believe your brother demanded a treehouse be built in the tree and I remember so many wonderful times climbing and playing in that tree. Is it still there? Is the treehouse still standing? Maybe we could investigate it together when I return.

With love,

Will

OH. HE LIKES ME. HE LIKES ME! MY FACE SPLIT IN A GRIN AND I clasped my hands to my chest feeling like a giddy school girl. I hadn't realised how much I had been hoping that he returned my feelings and seeing them there in black and white was such a relief to me. I spun the chair in a circle and smiled like an idiot as I day dreamed about his return.

And then I remembered the photo in the paper. I didn't know if the photo would go international, but what if Will saw it? I had to let him know about it, let him know the circumstances of the photograph. I turned back to my laptop and hit reply.

There was a tap on my door and I looked up to see Meredith standing there with a perplexed look on her face.

"What happened in here?" she asked.

I blinked up at her and then took in the room realising what it must look like.

"Oh, that was me, I thought I should do another search of the office to see if I could find a clue that could help us."

She stepped into the room and picked up a red covered book, turning it over in her hands.

"Wow, this looks really old."

I stood and walked over to her, taking the book from her and reading the cover.

"The Magic Faraway Tree," I read and smiled. "This was one of our favourite books when we were kids. Our nanny used to read it to us every night." I flicked the cover open and checked the editor's plate. "Look," I said pointing to the type, "It's a first edition." I turned another page and stopped short. There was a hole cut out in the middle of the pages and sitting in the hole was an old fashioned iron key. I dug it out and held it up so Meredith could see, "What's this?"

She took it from me and turned it over in her hands, "It's not for any door here in the palace," she said, "All the locks have been updated to key codes or biometrics."

I took the key back from her and examined it. It was old with a large scrolled top. It seemed familiar to me, but I couldn't place it. I slipped it into the pocket of my pants to look at later.

"So, did you come in here for something in particular or just checking up on me?"

"Oh, right," Meredith said, shaking her head, "Benjamin wants to see you in your new suites. They need your fingerprints and retina scan for the security in the room."

I took one more look around the room and shrugged, "Okay, I suppose now is as good a time as any. I'll clean this up when I get back."

I spent an hour with Benjamin setting up the security in my new suite. The rooms looked so different to how my father had decorated them. Gone were the dark wood paneling and navy blue wall and window coverings and in their place were white and beige and the odd pop of pale pink and blue. The rooms that had been oppressive and heavy before, now felt light and airy. Gauzy curtains hung in place of heavy velvet and the carpets underfoot had been stripped back to reveal pale wood which had been refinished and shone with a high gloss. Textured and patterned rugs gave the rooms interest and the art on the walls were from a local artist who specialised in watercolour landscapes.

I had worried that the rooms would always remind me of my father and that the grief would be too much to bear, but the transformation was so complete that there were no lingering ghosts to haunt me.

"You should be right to sleep in here tonight," Benjamin said as he tapped away on his tablet, "The decorators have finished, all the security is in place. I'm sure your maids can organise to move your clothes and other personal effects in today." He looked up at me. "How does that sound?"

I walked around the living area and ran my hand over the plush sofa. The room felt good, like a new beginning. I turned and smiled at Benjamin.

"That sounds great," I replied.

Meredith, who had been standing nearby nodded and made a note on her tablet to alert the maids to the move. I wandered over to one of the casement windows and looked out over the grounds. This wing of the palace had a different view than the suite I had grown up in and it overlooked the gardens and maze. On the edge of the rolling lawn I spied the tree that Will had spoken about in his email and I smiled.

"Benjamin," I said, turning back to him, "I'd like to go for a walk on the grounds. Do you have someone to accompany me?"

"Of course, Alyssa," he said, "Meredith will go with you and I'll have Jamie, Cody and Aiden waiting for you at the back door."

I smiled my thanks and left the room with Meredith. We took the elevator to the ground floor and walked through the halls to the back door where we found the rest of the security team.

"Where to Your Grace?" Jamie asked.

"That big tree," I said, pointing to it.

"Walk or ride?" he asked.

I looked at the golf cart and shook my head.

"I'll race you," I said and took off running. I heard Jamie whoop behind me and Meredith curse. They could all outrun me, but I had the element of surprise and got a good head start.

I laughed as I ran, remembering the many times that Jacob and I and Will and Jordan would race across the lawn. The three boys had always tried to lose me, but I was determined to keep up with them. As a kid it had felt like it was miles away, but as an adult who regularly ran five kilometres every day, it took me no time to cross the grassy expanse and pull up at the foot of the tree.

I beat Jamie, but only by a handspan and I laughed delightedly at his scowl. Meredith arrived next, shaking her head at me and the other two arrived together in the golf cart, smug smiles on their faces.

"I haven't been here in years," Meredith said as she stared up at the tree.

It was an old European Plane tree with a thick trunk and spreading branches. It was currently flush with bright green, maple shaped leaves, which I knew would turn gold and then red as we entered the autumn season. I looked up into the branches and saw the floor of the treehouse and smiled. I searched the trunk to find the boards nailed to it that acted as a ladder and started to climb.

"Whoa, Lys," Meredith called, "That might not be safe."

"It's fine," I said as I continued to climb, finally reaching the trap door.

I had expected it to take some banging and strength to open due to the swelling of the wood over the years, but it opened easily on well-greased hinges. I climbed up into the treehouse and was immediately swamped with memories. It was just how I remembered it.

Meredith climbed up behind me and whistled as she looked around.

"Do you think the children of the staff play in here?" she asked.

"I don't know," I replied, taking note of how un-abandoned it looked. Someone had been here regularly and recently. There were no cobwebs or dust to speak of, no rodent droppings or water damage. The treehouse had been looked after and even modernised. It appeared to be watertight and had glass in the windows and even a television.

"Maybe Jacob spent time here," I said softly, running my hand over the bookcase that was stuffed full of well-read books. There was a wingback chair, which I couldn't even imagine how they had gotten into the room, as well as blankets and even a lamp.

"Carlos would know," Meredith said stepping up to one of the windows to look out.

"Jacob, Will and Jordan would spend hours up here," I murmured, sinking into the wingback and closing my eyes, "Sometimes they would let me in, but most times they would not and I'd sit at the base of the tree and yell at them or I would stomp back up to the house in a snit and Nanny would have to find me something to do."

"I remember," Meredith said and I could hear the smile in her voice, "I'm pretty sure your temper tantrums were the reason we first met."

I laughed and opened my eyes, "Probably," I replied, "The boys were sick of me following them around and Nanny was at her wits end with my protestations of being bored. I hope I wasn't too terrible for you."

She turned to look at me and smiled, "Never," she said, "And we had our revenge on the boys."

It was true. When Meredith had come to be my companion we had devised many and varied ways to get back at my brother and his friends.

"I miss him Mer," I said quietly, getting up out of the chair and walking over to a cabinet full of curiosities. I ran my fingers lightly over the treasures my brother had collected over the years. I wondered what would have become of this place had my brother lived...would he have brought his own children here and shown them the secrets of the treehouse?

There was an old metal strongbox sitting on one of the shelves. It was intricately decorated and patinated with age and looked not unlike a pirate's treasure chest. I tried to lift the lid, but it wouldn't budge, likely stuck with rust and age.

"Your Grace," Jamie called up from the ground, "The sun is starting to set."

I sighed, "Okay," I called down to him, "We're coming."

LATER THAT NIGHT AS I PUTTERED AROUND MY NEW BEDROOM putting things away and generally making it feel more like home, I couldn't help thinking about the treehouse. After we had come back to the palace, I had gone back into Jacob's study and put it back to rights before sending of a quick reply to Will telling him that the treehouse still exists and that it had been improved upon.

I felt closer to Jacob, somehow, after having spent time there and I could see that in the weeks to come I would find refuge there. The path ahead was going to be rocky and it was comforting to know that I had somewhere I could escape to when I needed to. No doubt that was what Jacob had used it for.

I was beginning to feel that I had allies, finally. Lady Isabella had contacted me with news that she may have found something for me to use in my defence at the appeal and we had made plans to meet later in the week. Hopefully she would have some good news for me.

I was weary and it had been a long day, so I trundled off to the bathroom to shower and change, looking forward to climbing into bed and surrendering to sleep. I unzipped my pants and let them fall to the tiles and I heard an unmistakeable clank as they hit the floor. I reached down into the pocket and pulled out the key I had found in Jacob's office. I turned it over in my hand, taking in the delicate scroll work of the bow, the long shaft and the simple, three pronged bit. It was an old key, discoloured with age and put me in mind of the box I had seen in the treehouse.

It was such a little thing, but I couldn't help feeling excitement over the discovery. The strongbox was likely empty or full of forgotten childhood treasures, but I wanted to find out. The key had been hidden in a book like a prize or a clue in a treasure hunt and I desperately wanted to find out if it qpened the treasure chest.

I pulled my pants back on, my shower and tiredness forgotten, and skipped out to the door of my suite where Carlos and Daniel were on duty. I pulled the door open and they both turned to look at me curiously.

"I need to go outside," I said, "I need to look at something in the garden."

"Can it wait until morning, Your Grace?" Daniel asked, reasonably, "It's late and dark out."

"I know," I said, trying not to sound bratty, "But I don't think I'll be able to sleep without having a look."

Carlos tried to hide his smile and looked away while Daniel looked decidedly put upon.

"Okay," he said resignedly, and I had to contain my desire to clap and jump up and down like a kid.

I followed them down to the back door where they collected two other guards, not ones I knew well, and we set off over the lawn to the treehouse (in golf carts this time). Carlos went up the ladder first and turned on the lamp, before I followed him up and into my brother's domain. I pulled out the key and went straight to the box. It slid in easily and turned with a click. I lifted the lid and discovered my bounty.

The box contained a hard copy of a dossier and a flash drive. I pulled them both out, pocketing the flash drive and flicking through the dossier. The information it contained was incendiary at the least and potentially incriminating for some very high ranking officials at worst. From the very quick look at the information inside the file, Jacob had been investigating corruption amongst the peers and he had found some very damning evidence.

"Ah, Carlos," I murmured, not able to tear my eyes away from the pages, "I think we need to get back to the palace and alert Von Bartham and Benjamin." I looked up and saw his eyes widen as he sneaked a peek at the pages I was looking at.

"Right away, Your Grace," he said.

We raced back across the lawn and up into the palace. I headed straight for Jacob's office with Carlos and Daniel on my heels. I turned to them both as we stood in the outer office.

"This information," I said, holding up the flash drive, "Is the key to everything." I handed the flash drive to Carlos. "Guard this with your life." I said and started pacing. "We need to keep this as close to our chests as we can, there is no telling how many leaks we have in the palace. Carlos, I want you to go and wake Benjamin, give him the flash drive and then head to the conference room. Daniel, I want you to go and wake Von Bartham and meet us there. I just need to grab a few things from Jacob's office and then I will follow you there."

"No," Carlos said, "We're not leaving you here alone."

I harrumphed, but nodded, "Fine," I said, "But I'm going to be a few minutes in the office. One of you can stay out here and wait for me."

They nodded and then Daniel stalked out the door, while Carlos took up a position beside the secretary's desk. I shook my head, but didn't say anything as I walked past and into the dark office.

I closed the door and let my eyes adjust to the darkness for a moment before moving towards the desk and reaching for the lamp.

"I wouldn't do that if I were you," a familiar voice said in the darkness as a hand clamped around my wrist.

"Jordan?" My voice shook with surprise and a little fear. I could smell alcohol and sweat as he neared me, his hand a vice around my arm.

"The one and only," he said, his voice low and sinister. I felt the press of something small and metallic against my ribs and gasped. "Don't scream now, princess," he sneered into my ear, "You might startle me and the trigger on this little baby is very sensitive."

"What do you want Jordan?" I asked, trying to keep my voice even and not screech or hyperventilate.

He stood behind me, his body an unwelcome pressure against my back, and he forced me forward so that I was pushed up against the desk, the mahogany tabletop pressed painfully into the tops of my thighs. He let go of my wrist snatched the dossier out of my hand, keeping the gun jammed into my side and his body keeping me prisoner against the desk.

"This," he said, shoving it into his jacket, "And you."

"You won't get away with this," I said feeling stupid for saying something so cliched, "Carlos is waiting right outside and Von Bartham and Benjamin are on their way."

"We'll be gone before they even know you're missing."

His arm snaked around me roughly and he dragged me across the room, the pain in my side a brutal reminder of the lethal force he was prepared to use to keep me quiet. The room was dark, but my eyes had had time to adjust and the ambient light from outside meant that I could make out rough outlines of the furniture in the room. Jordan pulled me over to the fireplace and pressed his hand against a wooden panel causing the section of wall beside the mantel to open soundlessly.

Crap.

I had been shown the secret panels in my new suite of rooms, not to mention the ones I grew up with in my childhood bedroom. I didn't even think that Jacob's office might also have a secret escape route.

Jordan pulled me into the dark corridor and the panel slid shut, encasing us in darkness. I took a breath, ready to scream regardless of the gun and then I felt a sharp pain in the back of my head and I lost consciousness.

CHAPTER 21

MY head hurt. It was my first cognisant thought as I swam up out of the darkness and towards consciousness. I couldn't remember what had happened or why my head hurt and the temptation to slip back into the nothingness of sleep was almost too much, except that there was a very real feeling of wrongness that buzzed in the back of my mind. Something was wrong, I just couldn't remember what.

I tried moving, but my arms and legs were both bound, which sparked panic in me. Being a princess, the threat of kidnapping and what I was supposed to do in the event that I was kidnapped had been drummed into me all my life. Panicking was not a luxury that I could afford. I needed to calm down and use my brain. Figure out where I was, who had me and what they wanted.

I took some deep breaths and slowly opened my eyes. The room was dim, but not fully dark. It was a small bedroom and I was on a bed. There were no pervading odours, like dust or mildew, and the room was a comfortable temperature, neither hot nor cold. I could hear a voice in the room beyond, but it was too soft to make out the words.

I wiggled on the bed until I could sit up and swing my legs over the side. My hands were tied together at the wrist in front of me, for which I was grateful, and my legs were tied at the ankle. My head pounded with my change of position and I gritted my teeth and took a few deep breaths until the dizziness passed.

I tried to think back to what had happened before I found myself in this predicament. I had been at the treehouse, had found the dossier. We'd gone back to Jacob's office and then someone had grabbed me.

Jordan.

It came back to me in a rush. Jordan had grabbed me and forced me at gunpoint into a secret room and then he'd hit me over the head. Pistol whipped, I thought was the correct term.

It took me a moment to let the reality sink in. Did Carlos know about the secret panel? How long would he wait before coming into the office to check on me? Where did the secret tunnel lead to? How long had I been gone? And what was Jordan going to do to me now?

The thoughts racing around my head triggered an attack of anxiety and my breath started to come in pants and my heart raced. I had no answers to these questions, and no idea how I was going to get out of this. Truth be told, I had never really taken the threat to my life seriously. I was only the spare, and not a very famous one at that. Jacob had always been the main target and although I had learned some self defence and martial arts, it had more been for fitness than my safety. I had always known that if there had ever been a credible threat, I had a whole bevy of body guards to save me.

Except that I didn't.

Jordan was the perfect person to instigate such an attack. He had unrestricted access to the palace, he was respected and well-liked by the staff and I had let him into my inner circle. He also had intimate knowledge of the security of the palace, being that he was responsible for visiting dignitaries and the like. He'd known about the secret passageway when even I hadn't.

He also hadn't given anyone reason to suspect him. Well, not until after he'd overplayed his hand with me.

I only hoped that he was also implicated on the flash drive that I had given to Carlos. The one I hoped he hadn't forgotten about. The one I hoped they would look at to see if they could find any clues as to who took me.

Would they even connect the two? They weren't stupid, but in the first initial panic of me going missing, would they think to look at it?

The only way out of that office without going through the outer office where Carlos had been waiting was through the panel in the wall. Logically that would be where they would concentrate their efforts first. I didn't know where that particular passage terminated, but Benjamin and Von Bartham would. The problem was that Jordan wasn't dumb enough to stay put where ever it was that the tunnel ended. They would need to know who took me in order to find out where I was.

Maybe I could find out where I was and somehow let them know. I had no idea how I was going to do that, not with my hands and feet bound and no access to a phone or internet or nautical flags. I would even use a smoke signal if I could or Morse code in a pinch. But I had no way to let anybody know where I was or who had taken me.

The panic gave way to hysteria and I had the overwhelming desire to laugh. I swallowed the bubbling in my throat, knowing that if I gave into it, I wouldn't be able to stop. I took a couple of deep breaths and stood to my feet. The dizziness and nausea from my head trauma took a moment to subside and then I shuffle/hopped across the room to the one window. It was covered by a heavy curtain, which I wrested out of the way to peer outside. It was still dark and I could see nothing beyond the glass. I thunked my head against the glass in frustration.

THE DOOR OPENED BEHIND ME, SPILLING LIGHT INTO THE ROOM.

"What do you think you're doing princess?" Jordan snarled.

I whipped around, barely keeping my balance. "I should be asking you that question," I said back, trying for my best princess voice.

"I thought you would have figured that out by now," he said leaning against the door jam. He looked me up and down with a sneer. "It didn't have to come to this, you know."

"No, it didn't," I said.

"But you just wouldn't cooperate."

"How is this my fault?" I knew I shouldn't be arguing with him, but I wasn't in control of all my emotions.

"If you had just married me, then we could have avoided all this...*unpleasantness*." He said the word like it tasted bad.

"Unpleasantness?" I couldn't believe what he was saying. He was kidnapping me and threatening me at gunpoint because I wouldn't marry him?

"Don't act so naive Alyssa, I gave you more credit than that."

"I'm sorry I'm not living up to your expectations, but I'm still trying to catch up and my head is killing me."

"Sorry about that," he said as if he were apologising for being late to dinner, "But I knew you were going to scream and I really didn't want to have to shoot you. Not yet anyway."

I took a breath. Talking to Jordan was like scrambling through a maze. When I looked at him, he was my old friend, the guy I had been dating, the guy who had helped me through the tragedy of losing my brother and father. I couldn't reconcile that man with the one who had kidnapped me, who was holding me bound. I didn't know which way to go, to appeal to the Jordan I knew or to treat him like a rabid dog.

"Jordan," I said, pitching my tone low and calm, "My head really does hurt and I would dearly love a hot cup of tea and to sit down."

He looked me over for a minute before giving me a sharp nod. He strode over and picked me up, putting me over his shoulder like a sack of potatoes and carrying me out of the bedroom and into the light. The room we walked into was a combined kitchen, dining, lounge room and I recognised it. It was one of the hunting cabins that we had in the woods along the lake. There were three in all and they were all exactly the same in layout and decor.

Jordan put me down on a chair at the table and busied himself in the kitchen making tea. The cabins were normally stocked with the bare essentials - nonperishable food stuffs and basic bathroom toiletries - but Jordan seemed to have spent some time stocking this one. Would somebody have noticed him bringing food out here? And did that mean he was preparing to stay a while?

The dossier I had found in the treehouse was sitting on the table and I tried surreptitiously to bring it towards me so that I could have a better look through it. I flipped the cover over and looked at the photograph on the first page. It was an official photo of Jordan's father, the major general.

I read the words of the report, not comprehending them at first. The General was in debt up to his eyeballs and to some very shady characters, if the report was to be believed. His estate was mortgaged to the hilt and his retirement fund had made very little dent in the amounts owing.

The General had been keeping his head above water by taking money from certain interested parties to block bills in the House of Lords. Unfortunately for him, the money was drying up and he would soon have to make good on his loans.

I turned the page to see the police chief staring back at me. He was implicated in taking bribes to quash arrests or to look the other way when certain titled men were caught in a compromising position.

Jordan's hand came down hard on the file and dragged it away from me. He replaced it with a mug of tea and then stalked to the other side of the table to take a seat. He closed the folder and watched me as I tried to pick up the mug with my tied hands.

"I have been looking for this damned report for months," Jordan said, self-deprecatingly with a rueful shake of his head. "Where the hell did you find it?"

"In the treehouse," I said. I didn't see any reason to lie, there were no other secrets hidden there, well, not that I knew of.

"The treehouse?" Jordan quirked an eyebrow at me before shaking his head. "Your brother and that damned treehouse. God, I hated that place."

This was news to me. Jordan had seemed to love it, he had been with Jacob and Will every time they'd climbed into the cubby.

"Will and Jacob never did like me. I knew they only tolerated me being around them because of the position my father had."

I kept my mouth shut and sipped my tea. I wanted him to talk, I wanted him to spill his guts to me and hopefully it would distract him long enough so that someone would find me.

"I tried everything to make them like me, but nothing I did was good enough." He smiled and it made me uncomfortable. There was something about his eyes that made me think that Jordan was a little unstable. "But look who has the upper hand now," he went on, "I do. I'm the one in charge now."

Jordan's phone rang and I jumped, spilling hot tea on my hands. Jordan didn't even notice my squeak of pain as he got to his feet and answered his phone.

"Yes father," he said and my heart sank. The General was involved and that could only mean bad things for me. "I have her, here with me," Jordan said and then I watched as his face turned white and his mouth twisted into a scowl. "No," he growled into the phone, "I've got this handled. I know what I'm doing." He listened for a bit, his jaw working and his eyes getting darker, his eyebrows lowering in a frown. "Shut up!" he suddenly screamed into the phone. He jabbed his finger at the screen and then threw the phone against the wall. I watched, dismayed, as it shattered, leaving no hope for me to use it to contact someone.

Jordan paced angrily, his jaw set and his lips pressed together into a thin line. His fists clenched and unclenched as he made his way across the small room. When he turned back towards me, his eyes looked wild; red rimmed and wide. Up until now I had thought that because I was with Jordan, he wouldn't really hurt me. We had known each other for years, he'd kissed me just days ago. Looking at the man before me now, I was afraid.

"Sit down Jordan," I said tremulously, "We can work this out. It's not too late."

He stopped and stared daggers at me. "You don't know what I've done, princess," he said with a chilling laugh.

"Whatever it is," I tried, "I can help you. If you take me back now, no one will even know I was gone. You've still got options."

He just shook his head and went back to his pacing. "It's too late. It's too late." His pacing became more agitated and his hands went to his head and he gripped his hair. His foot caught the leg of the coffee table and he tripped. He got up and kicked at the table, sending it towards the wall. It stopped short before hitting it and he walked up to it and began kicking it harder, smashing it to pieces against the wall.

That small bit of violence seemed to switch something on in him and he systematically went around smashing things, taking his anger and frustrations out on the furniture and anything breakable he could get his hands on. He threw lamps and vases, he used the fire poker to attack the bigger pieces of furniture that he couldn't otherwise lift.

I scrambled from the chair, falling painfully onto the floor. I pulled myself along the wooden floorboards and into the kitchen area, taking cover behind the counter while Jordan rampaged through the rest of the cabin. I huddled in the corner, praying for rescue. Everything I'd learned about defending myself, fled as fear invaded my mind. Jordan was out of control.

The was a loud smash and I jumped and then screamed as everything went dark.

"ALYSSA," JORDAN'S SING-SONG VOICE SENT CHILLS UP MY SPINE, "Princess Alyssabeth, come out, come out wherever you are."

I held my breath. Jordan's terrorising had come to an abrupt end with the loss of the light. It was deadly quiet and I had to suppress a shiver. I was night blind from the brightness of the cabin and I squinted my eyes closed hoping to get my pupils to expand as quickly as possible. I was tied hand and foot, I needed every advantage I could get.

"Alyssa," he called again in the dark, his voice not as cheerful as it had been.

I heard his shuffling feet come closer to the kitchen and I tried to shrink down to as small a target as possible. My heart pounded in my ears and I was sure he would be able to hear it. I kept my breaths even, I didn't want to give my position away with a badly timed noise. I had my back to the cupboard doors, my knees pulled up in front of me and my arms wrapped around my legs. If he was going to hit me with the poker, my legs would bear the brunt of it and I could tuck my head under my arms to give me some form of protection.

I knew I wouldn't last long if he found me, but I couldn't risk trying to move either. I didn't know where he was in the cabin and I couldn't move fast. I needed a miracle.

The scraping of a chair along the floor and a muttered curse alerted me to his position. He was just on the other side of the counter at the dining table where I had been previously sitting. There was only one exit out of the kitchen and it was right past Jordan.

The cabin had a wooden door in the front, which was on the opposite side to where the kitchen was, through the small lounge area. The dining room had a glass sliding door that led out onto a small wooden deck and overlooked the lake. The cabins were surrounded by dense forest and were hidden from the main thoroughfare by a long, wooded drive. There was no way anyone could accidentally stumble upon us and no one would know to come here looking for me. There was no escape.

"Princess," Jordan's voice had taken on a hard edge. "Where are you?"

I didn't answer, I didn't know if I could even if I wanted to.

The cacophony of splintering wood and broken china started up again and I could only imagine that Jordan had started swinging the poker around again in his frustration. I opened my eyes and was glad to see that I could make out shapes in the gloom. I had no idea what time it was or how long it would be until sunrise. I didn't even know why making it to sunrise was important, my situation wouldn't be any more improved by having sunlight.

There was a loud shattering and the sprinkle of glass as it fell to the hard floor. I jumped with the sound and my head hit the cupboard door hard. I yelped with the pain and silence descended like a fog. He'd heard me.

I held back the whimpers that threatened to escape from my throat and tried to change my position as quietly as I could, shifting along the cupboards, heading for the other corner. I saw his silhouette as he walked towards the kitchen, the glass cracking under his footsteps. He held the poker up over his head like a baseball bat, ready to strike. He felt his way around the counter and stopped in the gap, blocking my only escape. I was huddled in a dark corner, but just like me, he was getting his night vision and it wouldn't be long before he would be able to make out my shape in the darkness.

His eyes scanned the small square area, starting in the corner I had previously been huddled in. Maybe if I kept still long enough, his gaze would sweep past me without seeing me. I prayed that I was invisible, I begged God to please get me out of this situation. And then his eyes stopped, right on me.

"Alyssa, darling," he said taking a step towards me, "Why didn't you answer me?" He raised the poker higher and I dropped my head and covered it with my arms waiting for the first blow.

Noise behind him made him turn and a bright light clicked on.

"Freeze!"

CHAPTER 22

JORDAN looked startled for a moment and then he stepped forward and swung the poker at me. I ducked my head and heard the rapport of a firearm and then felt the glancing blow of the poker across my forearms. A dull thud followed and then the pounding of feet and voices yelling to one another. I stayed curled up in a ball, not yet ready to face the reality of the situation.

I felt a hand on my arm and smelled the familiar scent of the one person who had been a constant in my life.

"It's okay Lys," Meredith whispered to me, "You're safe. It's over. We've got you."

I began to shake with the acknowledgement of the trauma I'd just been through.

"Are you hurt?" she asked, her hands skating over me looking for injury, "Do you hurt anywhere?"

"Just my head," I mumbled.

Meredith checked the spot on the back of my head where Jordan had hit me and swore lightly before giving a report to someone standing behind her. Then she gathered me close to her, the harsh nylon of her kevlar vest scratching my face. I tried to wrap my arms around her and realised I was still tied up. I sobbed/laughed and held up my wrists to her. She smiled down at me and produced a wicked looking knife from a scabbard on her thigh and sliced through the bindings. I threw my arms around her as soon as I could and pulled her close.

I heard the noise going on around me. The commands from Benjamin, the moaning from Jordan as they secured him. He wasn't dead, but he had been shot. I listened to the rest of the team stomping through the cabin, systematically checking each room and opening every closed door. All the while I stayed buried in Meredith's shoulder, trying to stop myself from falling apart completely.

"Okay Lys," Meredith said, "It's time to move. Can you stand?"

I nodded and gathered my legs under me. She helped me stand and when I was secure on my feet, I looked up. There were torches to light up the darkness and I was surrounded by my security team, all kitted out in their kevlar vests and armed to the teeth. Their faces were drawn, more serious than I had ever seen them, except for the day they had stormed my lecture theatre. Jordan sat on the ground, his back up against the kitchen cupboards, his hands cuffed behind his back and his shoulder bleeding profusely. His face was a grimace of pain and as I looked at him, I felt nothing.

Meredith herded me out of the small cabin and into a waiting SUV. She climbed in behind me and leant forward to instruct the driver. I settled back into the leather seat and closed my eyes, allowing myself to feel safe. The car started to move and I had to hold back the tears that threatened to fall.

"How did you find me?" I asked wearily.

She tapped something on my wrist. The bracelet she had given me for my birthday.

"It has a tracking device in it," she said, "I'm sorry I didn't tell you."

"It's okay," I said. If it had been any other day, any other circumstance, then I probably would have been angry, but how could I be when it saved my life? "What happens now?"

She blew out a breath and slumped back into the seat beside me.

"Benjamin had time to have a quick look at the flash drive. From what I saw inside, it's an expanded version of the dossier. It has far reaching implications and there is going to be a lot to sort through."

She was holding something back and I thought I knew what it was. "Jordan killed Jacob," I said, a statement not a question.

She took a moment before answering. "We think it was the General's plan and Jordan was the one to execute it. There are a lot of inconsistencies in the police investigation, so we're pretty sure that if the police chief wasn't in on it, then he was coerced to cover it up.

"But why?" I asked the one question that had been plaguing me through the whole thing, "What did they have to gain?"

"Power. Money. They figured that if they could block your ascension by requiring you to be married, you would jump at the chance to marry Jordan. He would then have become the head of state and his father's puppet. Not to mention the royal treasury would clear both of their debts.

Money and power. The two things that had the potential to corrupt otherwise good men.

WHEN MEREDITH NUDGED ME, I REALISED I HAD FALLEN ASLEEP. I opened my eyes blearily to see that we had arrived back at the palace. The old stone building blazed with light and the front stairs were a mass of people. Police cars with their strobe lights lit the scene like a disco, flashes from cameras punctuated the early morning as reporters jostled for position behind roped off lines. My head started to throb.

"God, do I have to go out there?" I whined.

"Uh, there's something I didn't tell you," Meredith said uncertainly.

I turned to look at her and she swallowed before looking down at her lap.

"Jordan leaked a story to the papers that you were eloping with him."

"WHAT!"

"Yeah, and, um, we're pretty sure he was the source of all the other leaks too."

"Son of a..." I shut my mouth and breathed hard through my nose. I counted to ten in my head and closed my eyes briefly. "Okay," I said calmly when I opened my eyes. "They need to see me a little battered and bruised so that it will completely dispel the rumours. I assume we'll have a briefing and then a press conference?"

Meredith nodded as the car door was opened. She climbed out first and I took a breath before sliding out after her. I ignored the rise of voices as they saw me, lifting my hand and smiling tightly. I moved quickly, keeping close to Meredith as I was surrounded by more security and hustled into the palace.

The noise dimmed as the large doors closed behind me and I took another deep breath. There were a lot of people waiting in the entry way for me; my staff, my ladies in waiting, and they all wanted reassurance that I was alive and unharmed.

I hugged and greeted and made soothing noises, ensuring everybody knew I was okay. What I really wanted to do was have a scolding hot shower and then crawl into bed, but bed, at least, would have to wait.

"The doctor is waiting for you in your room," Meredith whispered to me, steering me away from the crowd. "He wants to check out that bump on your head. Your maids are waiting to help you shower and then Benjamin will be waiting in the conference room for you for a debrief."

"Great," I whispered back, "Please get me out of here."

She gripped my elbow and started to barge unceremoniously through the crowd. I let her guide me, following in her wake as she shouldered past people.

"Lys!"

I stopped, his voice arresting me. I turned and searched the crowd before my eyes landed on him. As soon as our eyes connected, he started making his way towards me. The crowd seemed to part around him, letting him through and I couldn't tear my eyes from his. And then he was there in front of me. Will.

I fell into his arms and he drew me close. I buried my nose in his coat, the smell of sandalwood enveloping me and making me feel safe. I gripped his lapels and felt his head dip to kiss my hair.

"Thank God you're okay," he murmured, "I don't think I could have survived losing you too." His arms tightened around me and I relished the feeling of him surrounding me.

Meredith tugged on the back of my shirt, "Come on, Lys."

"He's coming with me," I said grabbing his hand and pulling him through the crowd.

We finally made it to my suite and I relaxed with being surrounded by the familiarity. Bridgette and Annette were waiting for me with concern on their faces. When they saw me, the worry disappeared and they snapped into action, dragging me away from Will and Meredith and towards the bathroom. I let them fuss over me, grateful for the attention.

When I emerged from the ensuite half an hour later, I was feeling a lot more like myself. I walked out into the sitting area and was glad to see that Will was still waiting for me. I smiled tentatively at him and he grinned back.

The doctor was also there and I sat obediently while he examined me. Meredith was close by and Bridgette and Annette hovered, prepared to fetch anything that I might desire.

When the doctor was finished, he gave me the all clear and left. My stomach grumbled and I realised I had no idea what time it was. I looked around the room and noticed that the sun was starting to shine through the windows. It was morning, but it felt like it had been a week since I had left the room on a jaunt to the treehouse.

"Benjamin will be waiting in the conference room," Meredith said, breaking the silence.

"Will there be food?" I asked, "And coffee?"

Meredith smiled and nodded, "Yes."

I turned to Will, "Can you stay?"

His face softened and he smiled at me, his eyes crinkling at the edges. "I'll wait right here for you."

I nodded and stood. "Bring Lord Darkly some breakfast," I said to the two maids, "And make sure he has everything he needs to wait comfortably."

They curtsied and set about their duties.

I turned back to Will and picked his hand up in mine. "I'm so glad you're here," I said.

He squeezed my hand and then I let myself be dragged away by Meredith.

IT WAS THE SAME ROOM AS THE ONE WHERE I'D HEARD THE gruesome details of my father's and brother's murders. We knew they were murders now and not merely a hunting accident.

The same men sat around the large mahogany table, with one exception. The police chief was not present. The looks on the faces of the men around the table were the same though.

"Were there any casualties?" I asked after the usual greetings had been done.

Benjamin shook his head, "No. Well, apart from Wicks."

"He'll survive?" I asked dispassionately.

"Yes."

I nodded and swallowed harshly. I hadn't wanted him dead...okay, if I was completely honest with myself, part of me wanted him dead.

"Meredith told me the basics," I said, "What else can you tell me?"

Benjamin and Von Bartham shared a look and I held back the desire to roll my eyes at them.

"Look," I said, tired, hungry and severely lacking in caffeine. "I need to know the truth. Please don't try and spare my feelings, I think we are beyond that. From my own investigations I know that my father was a figurehead at best, but more than likely he was little more than a puppet. I don't intend to be like that, to rule like that. Please don't do me the discourtesy of thinking that I am too fragile to know what is really going on."

A cup of coffee and a plate of pastries was plonked down in front of me and I looked up at Meredith, my lips twitching. I picked up the coffee and took a generous sip of the hot bitter liquid, closing my eyes and relishing the hit of caffeine.

"You're right about your father," Von Bartham said on a sigh, "He was little more than a mouthpiece for the major general, but things had begun to change. The king had been handing a lot more work on to the prince and the major general no longer had as much influence over him. I'm ashamed to say that the corruption goes deep, possibly to the prime minister."

"He will need to resign, regardless," I said, "It was happening under his nose and he would've had to've been blind not to see it."

Von Bartham nodded, "The next few months are going to be destabilising for the country," he said, "You are going to need to establish an interim government as quickly as possible."

"I need to speak with the Lord Chancellor and Lord Bingham," I said and turned to Meredith, "I also want to speak to my Mastermind group." She nodded and tapped out a note to Alex on her tablet.

"Do we know how many of the Lords are implicated? Will there even be enough of them left to form a quorum?" I asked, looking around the table.

Benjamin ran his hand through his hair and looked to the ceiling. "Not many of them were involved criminally," he said, "A lot of them were being blackmailed into keeping quiet or coerced into assisting the Major General in his endeavours. I'm sure once we get access to his records, the whole thing will be blown wide open."

I picked up a Danish and bit into it absentmindedly. My coffee cup was empty and I needed more plus the sugar rush from the Danish to keep my brain alert.

"Whose idea was the tracking device?" I asked.

Meredith and Benjamin looked guilty and the others in my personal security team refused to look me in the eye.

"Mine," Benjamin finally admitted, "Meredith wanted me to tell you about it, but I thought it would be better kept a secret."

"That's why you didn't panic when I got caught in the storm at Lord Darkly's estate."

Benjamin nodded. "Lord Darkly had been vetted and his estate was well known because of the time the prince had spent there. We knew you would be safe with him."

"And what about Jordan?" I asked, "Hadn't he been vetted too?"

"He had been," Von Bartham said, "But it was the king that had vouched for him. At the time we didn't realise that your father's decisions had been compromised."

"So, the boars?"

"We are investigating a new lead," Benjamin said, "The chief of police had frustrated our efforts and given us bad intel. We expect to find a link between the boars and the major general."

"And the gunshot that killed my brother?"

"We believe that came from Lieutenant Wick's weapon," Von Bartham replied.

The confirmation of my greatest fear wasn't accompanied by gnashing of teeth or wailing. It landed with a dull thud in my heart. I had been carrying on with my brother's murderer. I had let him into my personal space, he had hugged me, kissed me. I felt like I needed another shower.

"Do you have proof?" I asked, my voice trembling, "Do you have irrefutable evidence?"

"Not yet," Von Bartham said.

"Then get it," I said through gritted teeth, "I want Jordan Wicks stripped of all his military rank and I want him incarcerated for the rest of his natural life."

I stood and walked from the room. I didn't care if they were finished or not, I was done.

CHAPTER 23

WILL was waiting for me right where I had left him. He was sitting on the couch in my sitting room, his ankle crossed and resting on his opposite knee. He had a pair of reading glasses on and he was engrossed in a folder. An empty tray sat on the coffee table in front of him and a half filled coffee cup was in his hand as he read the file that rested on his lap.

I had seen farmer Will in his plaid shirts and dusty jeans, I had seen Lord Darkly in his formal tux and bow tie, but this was the first time I had seen the businessman Will. His overcoat had been laid over a wingback chair, as had his suit coat, leaving him in a crisp white business shirt. He wore a steel grey tie and silver cufflinks winked at his wrists.

He looked up when he heard me walk in and a smile broke across his face. He was happy to see me and I had to admit that I was happy he had waited for me. I walked over and sat down on the couch beside him. He uncrossed his legs, took off his glasses and placed both them and the document he was reading on the coffee table and then angled his body towards me. I liked that he was willing to give me his full attention even though he was obviously working.

"Am I keeping you from anything?" I asked. I laid my head back against the couch cushions and looked up at him.

"Nothing important," he said. He lifted a hand and traced a line across my forehead and down my cheek. "Are you okay? Truthfully?"

His eyes were concerned, his voice soft, and the warmth of his body welcoming. I felt tears well up in my eyes and before I could answer him, he pulled me in to his lap, enveloping me in his arms.

"Shh," he whispered into my hair, tenderly kissing my temple as I leaned against him. "I've got you Lys, you're okay."

He let me cry, rubbing my back in firm, but comforting circles and murmuring soothing nonsense noises. I let all the fear and anger and grief coalesce like a ball in my stomach and then expelled it through my sobs and tears.

"I'm sorry I wasn't here for you," he said when my sobs had quietened, "I'm sorry I didn't speak up about Jordan earlier."

I tilted my head up so that I could look at him.

"You can't blame yourself for this, Will," I said, "You weren't the one who kidnapped me, you weren't the one to set the wild boars loose in the forest and you weren't the one who pulled the trigger and shot my brother. None of that can be laid at your feet. Jordan and his father are the ones to blame, not you, never you."

"But maybe if Georgina had pressed charges..."

"It wouldn't have made any difference," I said, "The chief of police was up to his neck in this. Georgie would have been put through that harrowing experience for nothing and knowing Jordan like I do now, he probably would have dragged her through the mud. No. You did the right thing, you protected your sister from possibly more hurt. You can't take on any guilt from this."

His arms tightened around me and he searched my eyes for a moment before closing his and swallowing hard. I laid my head back on his chest and closed my eyes too. I was so tired and my body was beginning to ache. My head throbbed and I didn't know how I was going to make it through the rest of the day. It was still early, most people weren't even out of bed yet and here I was needing to crawl into it.

The comfort of having Will's strong arms around me and his

pervading scent of sandalwood lulled me and I gave up the fight to stay awake. I slipped into sleep with a sigh and let my body relax against his.

I AWOKE TO THE SOFT SOUNDS OF A GENTLE SNORE AND THE BARELY contained giggles of my two maids. I was warm and comfortable and I resented being woken, but something niggled in my brain that caused me to resist falling back into blessed sleep. I opened my eyes to bright sunlight and realised that I was still in Will's lap and that he was the one snoring. Bridgette and Annette stood by the door to my bedroom with very wide grins and sparkles in their eyes.

I groaned. I couldn't go back to sleep, especially not while sitting in Will's lap.

I shifted, trying to extricate myself, but Will's arms tightened reflexively around me. I laid my head back down on his shoulder and took a deep breath of his wonderfully calming scent.

"Will," I said softly, "I need to get up."

"No," he mumbled and I chuckled quietly.

"Yes," I replied with a smile.

His arms tightened around me again and I felt him inhale before blowing it out. He placed a tender kiss on my head and then helped me to my feet.

I looked down at him, taking in his sleepy, mussed look. I hadn't thought of it beforehand, but Will must have travelled all night to be able to be here.

"You should go home and get some sleep," I said.

He smiled up at me, a goofy grin on his face. "I should probably let Georgie know I'm home."

I slapped his shoulder, "You didn't tell Georgie you were here?"

"I was a little preoccupied," he said, "I needed to see you."

"Thank you Will," I said earnestly, "Having you here has helped."

He stood and stretched and then dropped a chaste kiss on my cheek, "My pleasure, princess," he whispered in my ear.

I watched as he gathered his things together, wanting him to stay, wanting to spend the rest of the day wrapped in his arms, wanting to kiss him.

He slid his suit coat on and tucked his overcoat over his arm before picking up his briefcase. He reached out and cupped my cheek, a soft look in his eyes.

"Call me," he said, "After...everything. This afternoon or tonight, whenever, it doesn't matter what time it is."

"I will," I said.

He dipped his head and brushed his lips over mine. It wasn't a kiss, not really, but it was enough...for now. He left, waving over his shoulder as the door closed behind him.

"Your ladies in waiting will be here soon," Bridgette said, interrupting my wayward thoughts about Will, "With Alex and Meredith. Would you like to freshen up?"

I let them lead me into my dressing room where they had laid out several outfits for me to choose from. I had to face the full press corps and I needed to present a confident and stable front. I'm sure the rumours and speculation were running rife through the social media outlets. When they next saw me, I needed to be at my best.

I closed my eyes as Bridgette worked on my hair and Annette worked on my makeup. I chose the simple black dress and black Jimmy Choo pumps. This wasn't an occasion to be flashy, this was an occasion to show my serious side, to show Merveille that I could be relied upon.

I took my time dressing, not just pulling on clothes, but pulling on the royal persona. I was walking out there not as Alyssa, but as Queen Alyssabeth and they needed to recognise me as such. I refused to be a figurehead or a puppet and I wanted everybody to know that. Up until now, I had let the faceless 'they' determine my course, but today I was taking the reins. I was going to be the driving force behind my own future.

Dressed to impress, I walked with confidence back out into the sitting room. Alex and Meredith were waiting for me, as was my entourage. They all had very solemn looks on their faces and I slowed my steps. Benjamin was also waiting for me and I couldn't help the shiver of dread that crawled over my skin.

"What happened?" I asked immediately, "Is Jordan still in custody?"

"Yes, Your Grace," Benjamin answered formally, "But we've received reports that the major general is dead."

I sucked in a breath and held it. Jordan's father was alive when I was held captive in the cabin. Had he resisted arrest? Had someone else gotten to him?

"Tell me," I said.

"It looks like suicide," Benjamin said with a resigned sigh, "We will investigate further, but the early reports are that he died from a gunshot wound to the head. The weapon was recovered at the scene and at this early stage, there are no suspicious circumstances."

"Did he leave a note?" I asked.

"No," Benjamin replied, "But the disgrace that was about to befall his house was more than likely too much for him. He held his honour above all."

I snorted, "What honour?" I asked rhetorically, "The man had no honour. He would have been more concerned with losing face and reputation. Neither of those things constitute honour." I took a breath and shook my head. "Keep me apprised of the situation."

Benjamin nodded and I turned to the rest of the people gathered in my suite. "Anything else I need to know before I face the jackals?"

"The palace has responded to the photograph of you and Jordan that was leaked and the story about the elopement by saying it was a ploy to discredit your appeal for ascension," Jeanette said briskly.

"The news about the kidnapping has been leaked, probably by one of the police officers," Meredith said, "And they have a general idea that the House of Lords is involved in some sort of corruption scandal, but no details."

"Are there details for me to give?" I asked.

"I'll brief the press before you take the podium," Jeanette said, "We've stripped the story down to its bare bones to save on confusion or being distracted by tangents. Your brother had been investigating the House of Lords prior to his death. You discovered his investigation and were taken captive to try to hide the findings. Your security team recovered you unharmed and charges will be laid."

I nodded. No doubt I would get questions about Jordan and those photos, but if I stuck to the issues at hand, maybe I could avoid the messiness of being romantically involved with my brother's murderer.

I STOOD AT THE PODIUM AND LOOKED OUT OVER THE SEA OF FACES assembled before me. The palace had its own press briefing room, complete with family crest on the wall behind me and feeds to the major news networks. I was flanked by the nation's flag and the royal family flag and the podium in front of me was also branded with the family crest. There would be no doubt to anyone watching this where we were and who I was.

It was an oversight on my part that this was the first time I had been in this room, the first time I had addressed the palace press corps. My life had been played out on social media and in gossip magazines and to the serious journalists before me, it appeared that I had shunned them...and I needed to make amends. I needed these people on my side.

I smiled confidently at them and began to speak the prepared remarks. I had a speech writer, who knew? I had done so many things wrong up until now and I really needed to pull it together. Our nation was in crisis and in a power vacuum, someone always rises to the top. I wanted that someone to be me.

I had studied the effects of a power vacuum in developing and third world countries. Far too often when there wasn't a strong political force leading a nation, it was susceptible to militia rule or dictatorship. We weren't a third world country and we weren't prone to militia, but in the absence of power, chaos reigned. I needed to show the country that I could take control and steer us through this political crisis.

Jeanette had gone before me and had given them the basics of what had happened. I started to fill in the blanks, assuring them that I would step in and take control of the interim government. I may not yet have had my coronation, but for all intents and purposes, I was the highest ranking official in the country. The prime minister had been stood down pending an investigation, several of the lords and members of Parliament had been tainted by the discoveries of corruption and misdeeds that my brother had uncovered and the government was in disarray.

I had discussed the options with my core team and decided to seed some of that into my speech. I was putting the country on notice, change was coming. The detractors of my ascension were scattered and my claim on the crown strengthened. When I took power, the 'male only' mentality in government was going to change.

The barrage of questions volleyed at me when my address concluded surprised me. Not the amount, but the direction they were going. These journalists were not distracted by the gossip and rumours, they were intrigued by the potential shift of power and despite their disenchantment with the previous government and head of state, they seemed keen to explore the possibilities I presented.

It wasn't all good news, of course. There were still those that held on to the old ideals and traditions. We had never had a female in power and the questions were raised about the legality of it. What was written in our constitution regarding female heirs?

I silently thanked Priscilla and Dominique for drilling me on the finer points of our constitution. I was able to answer my critics with knowledge and facts. There was no law against a female head of state, there was no law against a female member of Parliament or a female member of the House of Lords. These things had been tradition more than anything else...because that was how it was always done, then that must be how it will always be done. I challenged that assumption and extended the invitation to all eligible women, if you want to be an MP or considered for the vacant positions in the House of Lords, then have at it.

By the end I was exhausted. I answered as many questions as I could but when I started repeating myself and questions became the same, only worded differently, Jeanette stepped in and shut it down promising more details at a later date. I smiled as I left the podium and then when I was out of sight of all the cameras, I sagged against the wall. My head hurt and my body ached. I wanted my bed and I wanted to sleep for a week.

But that was not to be.

The rest of my day was filled with meetings and briefings and I barely had time to eat. I finally sat down with some of my father's and brother's staff and advisors, who I was ashamed to say I had been avoiding. Some of them were nearing retirement, others wanted out and still others wanted to stay on. I granted each one their wish and handed the ones staying on over to Alex. If I was going to take control of the country, I would need a bigger staff than the one I had been using.

In all the chaos, Will managed to email me and his words of encouragement helped me get through the day. I hadn't even gotten around to explaining the photos of Jordan and me or the elopement rumours, but he took it all in his stride. We made plans to get together, but working out our schedules was challenging and it would be a couple of days before we could sit down together. In the meantime we had email and Meredith had sneaked me a very basic prepaid phone so that we could text and call. For now it would have to be enough.

The glaringly obvious absence from all the activity and the one I tried to ignore, was my mother. I knew she had been updated on the happenings; my kidnapping and the like, but she was yet to come and see me or offer any support. I knew she was opposed to me taking the reins, but I thought she would at the very least be concerned about my well-being.

I tried not to let it get me down and buried myself in work until I was finally able to fall into my bed later that night.

CHAPTER 24

T HE next few days and weeks were busy as I met with the remaining lords and members of Parliament. Due to the corruption surrounding my denial of ascension, the ruling was overturned and I no longer needed to plead my case. I would be the one to ascend to the crown and take up the mantel as head of state and I wouldn't even need a husband to do it.

Lady Isabella had been a tremendous help in that respect. She had scoured the constitution and discovered that what the lords had tried to do was, in fact, unconstitutional. There were provisions for female heirs, but they had been long buried. It also opened up the doors for female members of both the House of Commons and the House of Lords. Lady Isabella, herself, was currently petitioning for the House of Lords as the only heir to her father's duchy and his seat in the House.

A lot of women had come out of the woodwork after hearing my invitation to them, more than I thought there would be. Our Master-mind group was inundated with requests for help in establishing businesses and advice about education and training in various sectors. A very enterprising group of women had come up with a plan for a state of the art university that would be open to all women, and men, so that they no longer needed to travel to receive the education they needed.

My popularity in the polls soared and my confidence in my abilities grew. I may not be the charismatic leader like my brother, but I had my own strengths and I surrounded myself with good people. It wasn't all sunshine and roses and not everybody was open to the great sweeping changes I wanted. It may only take a small rudder to turn a ship, but it still took time to get it on a new course. I was willing to put in the time it required.

The days fell into a predictable rhythm. My mother eventually made an appearance, but she was cold and almost indifferent towards me. She was disappointed in me, but I couldn't allow her disapproval to sway me from my destiny. I would never have wished for this in a million years, but it was the hand I had been dealt and I needed to make the most of it.

Throughout it all, Will supported me. We didn't get to spend a lot of time together, but when we did it was the highlight of my day. It was good to have someone to bounce ideas off, someone who didn't have a stake in the government. He was always honest with me, calling me out when I was being a coward and backing me up when I needed to step out of my comfort zone. He helped to refine the ideas I had, stripping away the extraneous fluff and getting down to the nitty gritty which in turn helped me articulate it to the rest of my team.

As the day of my coronation approached, I knew that if I wanted Will as a permanent fixture in my life, I would need to make the first overtures. I didn't know how it could work with his business and his title, but I wanted to know that it could work. I wanted him to be alongside me, helping me, working with me. I wanted to know that at the end of a long hard day, I would be going home to him. I wanted to go to sleep with his warmth and sandalwood scent surrounding me and I wanted to wake up in his arms.

We'd had a rocky start, but his quiet manner and steadfast strength had grounded me and restored my feelings of safety. His kisses heated my blood and his intelligence and dry wit entertained me. I had fallen in love with him and I wanted him to know. I wanted to know if he loved me too.

It was a rare free afternoon and I had coerced Will into joining me for a horseback ride and a picnic lunch. I had picnicked with Jordan so many times and I wanted to replace those memories with new ones, so I packed the saddlebags with food that the chef had prepared for me and refused to take no for an answer from Will.

I rode Monty; he had become mine now and we had bonded over stolen gallops across the fields whenever I could extricate myself from my staff and the increasing demands of my life. Will rode his own horse, a big black brute called Gibraltar.

Jamie and Carlos followed in an ATV at a respectable distance. Since Jordan had been caught and sentenced, the increased security on my person had been scaled back. I only needed one person to accompany me through the palace and two when I was outside on the grounds.

Jordan's trial had been swift and he'd been tried with manslaughter (for my father's death), murder (for my brother's), kidnapping and attempted murder (for me) and various assault, bribery and corruption charges. The prosecutors had tried to have him charged with treason, but his defence team had argued that he thought what he was doing was for the best of the country, not the detriment. It was a lie, he had done it for his own selfish reasons, none of which had anything to do with Merveille, but the prosecutors let the matter drop.

He was being held in a high security prison and undergoing psychiatric assessment. I didn't have any concerns that he would be released any time soon and was content with the sentence that had been handed down. It didn't bring my father or brother back, but it did give me closure.

"You're quiet today," Will observed as we plodded along the bridle path. It was autumn, my favourite time of year and the weather was just beginning to turn cool. The sky was clear and blue and the breeze crisp, it was the perfect day.

"I'm contemplative," I replied with a grin.

"And what are you contemplating?" he asked, bringing Gibraltar to a stop and sliding from his back.

He took Monty's reins from me as I dismounted and hobbled the horses, allowing them to graze on what was left of the summer grass.

We unpacked the saddle bags, spreading a large blanket on the ground and then filling it with various containers from the chef's kitchen. I sat down and he joined me, sitting beside me so that we could hold hands.

"I'm contemplating the future," I said to him.

He studied my face, lifting a finger to brush a stray strand of hair out of my eyes.

"I hope you are contemplating me in your future," he spoke softly, tenderly.

"I am," I replied, "I just..." I let the sentence fade. How do you ask someone to walk away from their business and estate to be with you? Will had worked so long and hard to build up Pemberton Cheese and I was contemplating asking him to walk away from it.

"What is it Lys?" he asked, his face sombre, "Have I done something?"

"Oh, no, no," I assured him. I took a breath and took the plunge. "I'm in love with you Will," I said, "And I want you in my life, but..."

"But?"

"But what about Pemberton Cheese and your estate and Georgina? I want to marry you, I want you to help me rule Merveille, but how can I ask you to give up your life for me?"

He kissed me, his soft lips sliding across mine and I let my eyes flutter shut as I basked in his attention. He stroked his tongue across my bottom lip and I opened for him, allowing him in. His hand cupped the back of my head and my own hands came up to grip the front of his shirt. He deepened the kiss, plundering my mouth and causing a riot of sensations to cascade through me. I could kiss Will for hours.

"Yes," he said when he lifted his head.

"Yes?"

"I will marry you," he said with a smile. "Georgina is my heir, so the estate will go to her. The crown already has a substantial stake in Pemberton Cheese, so I'm not losing anything by signing my shares over to Georgie. I want to be with you Alyssabeth St. Benét, I want to spend the rest of my life with you. No amount of smelly cheese can come between us."

I tackled him then, launching myself against his chest causing him to fall backward and allowing me to land on top of him and I kissed him soundly as his arms tightened around me. His firm body beneath me felt good and I couldn't wait to delight in the pleasures of it. I had the rest of my life to enjoy them.

EPILOGUE

Alexandra

I closed my eyes and inhaled the spicy smell of the aftershave that had been haunting my dreams. Frédéric Bingham, Earl of Avonlea, had been invading my dreams and private thoughts for months now and whenever I smelled that scent, it had my heart racing and my skin prickling.

In the lead up to Alyssa's coronation, the earl had been spending more time in the palace. He was one of her most vocal supporters and she had added him to her advisory team. That meant that I had to spend a lot of time with him. His lazy, blue-eyed gaze had been driving me to distraction, as were the little incidental touches that were too frequent to be accidental but not obvious enough to be more than a tease.

But I couldn't afford any distractions today, especially not of the handsome, blue-eyed variety. It was coronation day and Merveille was about to crown their first ever female head of state. Everything had to be perfect and it was my job to ensure it was.

"Alex." His voice flowed over me like a caress and I steeled myself against the reaction it set off in me. I closed my eyes briefly, taking a deep breath and then turned to face him.

"Lord Bingham," I said, letting my eyes fall respectfully down.

"Come now, Alex," he said, "I think you can call me Freddie by now, in fact I believe you have been calling me Freddie already." His eyes sparkled with mischief and the lopsided tilt of his lips caused a full body tremor to go through me.

"Not today, Lord Bingham," I said, trying to keep my voice cool and professional, "Today you are the Earl of Avonlea and I am the queen's assistant."

He took a step closer to me, invading my personal space with his heat and his spicy aftershave.

"Oh, my dear Lady Alexandra," he murmured, his voice husky, "You are so much more than just the queen's assistant."

How could he flirt with me on today of all days? I had been warned by his sister, Meredith, that he was an incurable flirt and for some unexplained reason, I had become his *objet d'affection*. I didn't know what I had done to deserve the honour and I wasn't exactly disappointed with the attention, but it made doing my job really hard, especially when he took liberties like now. We were hours away from one of the most important events of our small country and he was flirting with me.

I took a step back, breathing in the air untainted by his scent and tried to clear my head.

"Not today," I reiterated, "Today I am nothing more than the queen's assistant and I am running late."

I sketched him a polite curtsey and continued on my way down the hall towards the queen's wing all the while trying to rid my traitorous mind of thoughts of the Earl of Avonlea. A feat easier said than done.

Frédéric

I WATCHED THE VERY WELL PUT TOGETHER LADY ALEXANDRA Fornette walk away and smiled. I loved getting her riled up, I loved flustering her. The way her cheeks pinked adorably when she caught me staring at her and the little intakes of breath when I brushed past her, making sure our bodies made contact were my obsession. Hell, she was my obsession.

I hadn't looked forward to returning to Merveille to take up the family seat in preparation for my father's retirement. I'd had a life and a lucrative career out in the real world which I'd had to give up to return to the fold and, to tell the truth, I'd been a little annoyed. But discovering Alex had taken the sting out of my return.

I had no intention of settling down anytime soon, but having a pleasant little interlude with Lady Alexandra was tempting. So far she had shown herself to be far too well-bred to fall into my arms, but I had plans to soften her up. Each time I saw her, I made sure to leave her a little off kilter and my plan seemed to be working. Besides, it was fun to watch her squirm.

One of these days I was going to corner her and taste those very tempting lips or maybe thread my fingers through her very carefully constructed chignon. She was always so well put together and my fingers itched to mess her up a little. I could only imagine how she would feel pressed up against me, all her soft, delicate curves moulding around my body.

But that day was not today. She was right to be on her best behaviour today. The coronation of the first female head of state in the history of Merveille was not something to be sneezed at and I had duties to attend to. I whistled as I continued on my way towards the queen's rooms, smiling to myself. Alex would be there and I would get another chance to ruffle her feathers.

She really had become a bit of an addiction for me and I looked forward to the moment I could savour her.

"Lord Bingham?"

I turned to see who was addressing me. It was one of the queen's household staff and they looked a bit out of sorts.

"Yes, what is it?" I asked haughtily.

"Um, there is a man here," the attendant said, "Demanding to see Lady Alexandra."

"Does he want an audience with the queen?" I asked, puzzled.

"Ah, no," he said, "I don't think it has anything to do with the queen," he replied, "The man is an American and he claims to be Lady Alexandra's fiancé." He said this last in a whisper, covering his mouth so that no one would overhear.

"Alex is engaged?" I blurted out and then shook my head. "Best take me to him. We can't afford any scandals today of all days."

I followed the attendant, all the while my head was spinning. Alex had never once mentioned being engaged, what the hell was going on?

A ROYAL ENTANGLEMENT, BOOK 2 OF THE YOUNG ROYALS SERIES is available now.

Keep reading for a sneak peek...

WOULD YOU LIKE TO READ WILL'S SIDE OF THE STORY?

Lord Darkly, a Young Royals novella is now available

SNEAK PEEK

A Royal Entanglement
by Emma Lea

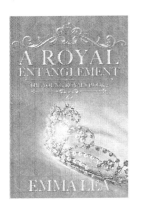

On the day of the new queen's coronation, a man from Lady Alexandra's past turns up unannounced in Merveille. Lord Frédéric intercepts him and discovers that Alex had left this man at the altar six months ago and now he was here to claim her.

The last thing Freddie wants is to get entangled with a woman. He liked to keep his options open, but now that he had returned to Merveille for good, his mother was trying her damnedest to get him married off and producing the next Bingham heir. When Alex asks for his help, he is only too eager to help her and maybe get his mother off his back in the process.

Alex hadn't told anyone the real reason she left everything she had worked so hard for in the States to return to Merveille and take up the position of Queen Alyssa's personal assistant. But now the main reason for her flight from the US has turned up on the palace's doorstep and she is backed into a corner. The only person that she can think of to help her is Freddie, but she worries that getting too close to him might just do more harm than good.

Available now! Keep reading for a sneak peek...

CHAPTER 1

Frédéric

I stood in the doorway and watched the American pace. He looked like hell. His suit, although expensive, was rumpled and his hair looked like he'd been running his hands through it constantly. He needed a shave and probably a few hours' sleep. A couple of fingers of brandy probably wouldn't go astray either.

This was the man Alexandra had been going to marry? I couldn't really imagine her with him, okay that was a lie, I could; I just didn't like the image. Alexandra had that straight laced, conservative look about her and I had no doubt that when she stood beside this man they would look like the perfect couple. But I had recognised something else in Alexandra that most people probably didn't see. There was a touch of wild in her.

I smiled at the thought of telling her that. She would deny it and she would get that cute little crease between her eyebrows that I itched to smooth away. She would deny it, protest that she was anything but wild, but I knew better. She may have hidden it deep, but it was there and I knew I could bring it out of her.

And I really wanted to bring it out of her.

But that little project would have to wait. The coronation was today and Alexandra was swamped with all of her responsibilities. The last thing she needed right now was that man in there turning up to claim his runaway bride.

And why the hell had it taken him six months to come and find her anyway? If the guy was so broken up about her leaving him at the altar, why hadn't he come sooner? Well, there was only one way to find out.

I stepped into the room and the man immediately stopped his pacing, turning to look at me with narrowed eyes.

"Who're you?" he asked with a sneer.

"Lord Frédéric Bingham, Earl of Avonlea and you are?" I stepped forward, not offering my hand and mustering all of the haughty, high handedness that I could channel from my parents and my upbringing in the royal court.

"Bradley Corsair," he replied, "Am I supposed to bow to you or something?"

I laughed, "No, of course not. I do have a few questions for you though," I said stepping closer, "Why don't you take a seat?"

"I'd rather speak to Alex," he said, still standing.

I smiled sympathetically at him, "I'm afraid that isn't going to be possible, especially not today."

Bradley sat heavily on the antique settee. He wasn't a big man, but he was solid and he seemed to take reasonable care of himself, his jet lag notwithstanding.

"How was it that you managed to get onto the palace grounds?" I asked knowing that both Von Bartham and Benjamin would have a fit knowing that he had gotten past security.

"I followed a crowd of press in," he replied without thinking.

"They didn't check your identification?" I asked, annoyed that after the recent troubles with security in the palace that it had been so relatively easy.

He shrugged, "There was a bit of a crush and I kept to the middle of the pack."

I nodded. "Do you know what is happening today?" I asked.

"Uh," he looked around the room to get some kind of clue as to why a crush of press would be entering the palace grounds en mass. "Not really, no," he replied, "I really just needed to find Alex."

I studied the man before me. He did look rather distraught, but not exactly heartbroken. There was something else that was making him edgy, nervous and I really didn't think it had anything to do with Alexandra.

"Do you know what Lady Alexandra does here in the palace?" I asked.

"Um, some sort of secretary? That's what she was back home, anyway."

I had to hold back the snort of disgust that threatened to escape. Alexandra was so much more than a secretary, even before she had become the queen's personal assistant.

"Her role here is a little bit more than that," I replied, picking at imaginary lint on my pants. Alexandra was probably in panic mode right now wondering where I was, but I needed to get this matter put to bed before this buffoon started stomping through the castle and making demands. "Which is why you won't be able to see her today. I'm sure we can find you some comfortable accommodation and set up a meeting in the next couple of days."

"No," he replied standing, a wild look in his eyes, "I need to see her today, now."

"I'm afraid that's simply not possible," I replied calmly, staying seated and not reacting to his spike of anxiety.

"Why the hell not?" His voice had risen and he had resumed his pacing.

"Returning to my earlier question Mr. Corsair, do you have any idea what today is?"

"I told you already," he said turning to me, "I have no idea what today is."

"And you have no idea what Lady Alexandra does here in the palace?"

"No, I do not."

I stood with a sigh and an apologetic look on my face, "Today is the coronation of our new queen," I said, "And the reason you cannot see

Lady Alexandra is because she is the queen's personal assistant and will be a little too busy today to deal with you."

He sat with a thud back onto the settee and I winced with the impact on such a delicate piece of furniture.

"I suggest you take me up on my offer of accommodation and a meeting at a later date."

He looked up at me, "There is no accommodation," he said, "I've checked."

I just smiled, "Leave it to me," I said, summoning one of the hovering palace staff.

"Find Dayne and ask him to organise somewhere for Mr. Corsair to stay." Dayne was my own personal assistant and the man was a whiz at getting things done, "And maybe notify Benjamin to have someone escort Mr. Corsair to his lodgings." I hated to do it to the queen's personal security team leader, but he needed to be apprised of the situation. I turned back to Bradley Corsair.

"Now, if you will excuse me," I said making a show of looking down at my watch, "I have somewhere I need to be. Dayne will be here any moment to get you settled and I will contact you tomorrow about setting up an appointment to meet with Lady Alexandra."

I didn't wait for his nod before I left the room. I was already late and Alexandra would be in a fit, but that was nothing to what she would be when she found out about her visitor.

Alexandra

I froze as I felt the heat of him on my back. I knew who it was, how could I not? I had been obsessing over the man for the last six months despite trying to deny it. He had gotten under my skin from the very first meeting and, try as I might, there was no way for me to shake him. And he seemed to know it.

"We need to talk," he whispered in my ear and I only just controlled the full body shiver that threatened to rattle through me. His warm breath on my ear, his scent, his body so close to mine that if I leant back, just a little, I would be pressing up against his firm chest.

I cleared my throat, trying to get my vocal cords to work.

"I'm a little busy right now," I managed to squeak out.

"Tonight," he said, "As soon as you can get away."

"I hardly think it is appropriate..." I trailed off, my mind wandering to places that they shouldn't especially when I was in the middle of a coronation.

"You're going to want to talk to me," he whispered, leaning closer, his hand brushing my shoulder lightly, his lips skimming the shell of my ear.

I closed my eyes against the onslaught of sensation and swallowed hard. The things this man did to me without even touching me. I took a deep breath...bad move. My nose was now full of him, the smell of him overwhelming me.

"Meet me in the Rose Room," he said, "It's important."

I opened my eyes as he stepped away and noticed a change in the demeanour of the security personnel in the room. It was subtle, but there was definitely a change and it was enough to put me on high alert.

There had been threats against the queen, there were always threats, but in the lead up to the coronation, they had increased in both number and ferocity. She had been kidnapped a few months earlier by someone that no one had suspected capable of such a crime and since then security had been overhauled and stepped up, although to most people it didn't look it. Most people assumed that now the immediate threat had passed, security had returned to normal, when in fact it had just gone more covert. There were extra security around the castle, they just weren't the visible type.

I turned to talk to Freddie, to ask what was going on, but he had moved away and was conferring with his sister, Meredith, on the other side of the room. She was also part of the queen's security detail, but her role had changed somewhat over the last few weeks, not unlike everything else. She now served as The queen's second assistant as well as being part of her security.

The two women had been together a long time and Meredith knew the queen better than anyone else, so it was a good match, even if it did leave me feeling a little bit like the third wheel at times. Not that they hadn't tried to make me feel welcome and included; both Meredith and Alyssa (Queen Alyssa) had fully embraced me into their clique, along with the four other women that made up the queen's ladies in waiting. But there was a special bond between Queen Alyssa and Meredith that couldn't be replicated.

Freddie chose that moment to make eye contact with me and he gave me one of his secret smiles. One that had my pulse rate skyrocketing and my skin flushing. And he knew it too. His eyes widened as he catalogued my response and his grin got wider.

He was incorrigible.

Not that I would have him any other way. I might not openly admit to being flattered by Freddie's attention, but I couldn't lie to myself. Not that it mattered. Freddie flirted with anyone in a skirt and the fact that I hadn't fallen at his feet like most other single women (and some married ones too) only seemed to egg him on. He liked the chase, he liked the thrill of cornering me and getting me flustered. I knew that as soon as I started to respond positively to any of his advances, he would lose interest.

So while outwardly it looked to everyone else that I really wasn't swayed by his charm, inwardly I relished every little bit of it. It may never go anywhere, but it did make me feel good. And if playing hard to get meant that I remained in his sights, well then, that wasn't such a bad thing.

Freddie winked at me and I turned away so he wouldn't see the smile on my face or the flush that crept into my cheeks. Meredith had warned me that Freddie was an irrepressible flirt, but it was one of the things I really liked about him. He'd charmed me from the moment we met and even though I knew I needed to keep myself from falling for him, it was flattering all the same. Freddie was a good-looking guy and I liked spending time with him.

And he was a good distraction...and I needed that. I needed something to keep me from thinking about the reasons I had come to Merveille in the first place. The offer from the palace had come at a time when I had needed an escape and I had jumped at it. Now I was waiting for the other shoe to drop because I knew there would be consequences for my actions. It was just a matter of time before they caught up with me.

A Royal Entanglement, the second book in The Young Royals series, is available now.

Want to be the first to know when the next Young Royals book is available?

Sign up on the website (www.emmaleaauthor.com) to get an alert email.

ACKNOWLEDGMENTS

This book was a very different one for me to write. Merveille is a completely made up place, pulled completely from my romantic dreams of places I wish I could visit. I have always loved stories about princesses and their fairytale castles and it was like a little fantasy to write one myself.

With each book I write, I try to push myself further and I could only do this with the support of my husband, sons and friends. My husband is such a big encouragement to me and I love being able to discuss plot points with him and ask his opinion when I write myself into a corner. My sons, although they rib me about writing romance, love that I am following my dream and I hope that I am teaching them by example. And of course no one could do this without friends to bounce ideas off and debate the finer points of male body types. Thanks to Kathryn, as always, for her faithful beta reading and spell checking and to my ARC group.

Of course, thank you to you, my readers, without you this would all be for nothing.

And thank you to Brooke for your work on this revised edition!

ABOUT THE AUTHOR

Emma Lea is a part-time barista, artist, cook, mother and wife. She lives on the beautiful Sunshine Coast in Queensland, Australia with her wonderful husband, two beautiful sons, her dog and cat (both of which are female because, hey, we needed to balance all that testosterone!)

She is a ferocious reader with eclectic tastes and has always wanted to write, but never had the opportunity due to one reason or another (excuses, really) until finally taking the bullet between her teeth in 2014 and just making herself do it.

She loves to write stories with heart and a message and believes in strong female characters who do not necessarily have to be aggressive to show their strength.

If you enjoyed reading this book, please share the love by leaving a review and telling your friends!

To connect with Emma Lea
www.emmaleaauthor.com

THANKS

Thank you for reviewing this book and recommending it to your
friends and family.
Honest reviews are important for authors and I appreciate the time
you have taken to share your thoughts.

Would you like to receive an Advanced Review Copy (ARC) of my next
book? If so, please contact me via my website
(www.emmaleaauthor.com) or my Facebook
(www.facebook.com/emmaleaauthor) page

OTHER BOOKS BY EMMA LEA

This is Emma Lea's complete book library at time of publication, but more books are coming out all the time. Find out every time Emma releases something by going to the website (www.emmaleaauthor.com) and signing up for her New Release Alerts.

SWEET ROMANCES

These are romantic tales without the bedroom scenes and the swearing, but that doesn't mean they're boring!

The Young Royals

A Royal Engagement

Lord Darkly

A Royal Entanglement

A Royal Entrapment

A Royal Expectation

A Royal Elopement

Bookish Book Club Novellas

Meeting Prince Charming

Broken Arrow Trilogy

Broken

Cursed

Eternal

SWEET & SEXY ROMANCES

In my Sweet & Sexy Romances I turn up the heat with a little bit of sexy. No swearing, or very minimal swearing, and brief, tasteful and not too graphic bedroom scenes.

Love, Money & Shoes Series

Walk of Shame

Strictly Business

Skin Deep

In The Money

All At Sea

Love, Money & Shoes Novellas

The Five Year Plan

Summer Fling

Standalone Novels

Amnesia

HOT & SEXY ROMANCES

Hot & Spicy Romances turn the heat way up. They contain swearing and sexy scenes and the characters get hot under the collar.

Recommended for 18+ readers

TGIF Series

Girl Friday

Black Friday

Good Friday

Twelve Days

Twelve Days of Christmas - Her Side of the Story

Twelve Days of Christmas - His Side of the Story